THE THIEF ROMERO

By A. F. Melendez

ISBN: 0615925693
ISBN 13: 9780615925691
Library of Congress Control Number: 2014903492
57841984, Philadelphia, PA

For my mother who has supported me throughout all of my troubles.

Special thanks to Lauren Zapata for all your invaluable insight and help, as well as the positive encouragement of my story.

THE THIEF ROMERO

1

Armored truck, Neo-Nazi and Chainsaw.

On the cold October morning, Romero wandered by the road turning his head in both directions and saw the armored truck approaching down this lonesome expanse of street.

This road was dead center between two stalled construction projects that had halted because of a union strike. This road now barren of the clamor of machinery from the site on the right and the left made this strip of blacktop the perfect place for an armored truck to be knocked off.

The truck barreled on by. Romero gave it a short glance and walked slowly to his car parked further up the road. His car meaning his car for this job. He had as a front for his ill-got gains, a piece of a car dealership, and Romero would pop in and drive out with one of the cars when he had a job. He would switch the license plate under the dealership owner's watchful but knowing eyes and he would have his car. Romero had pieces of a few businesses around the city. They served him well when he was both working, and relaxing at home in peaceful semi-retirement.

Romero was in search for a new *job*. His booker, Morris, set it up by getting him in touch with the crew. Romero took the five hour drive from Philadelphia to hear further of the job, meeting in King's dining room with the map laid out across the table and the men around looking at it, and with all involved present discussing details. Brad Geiger had been there. Geiger was a Neo-Nazi and loose in the head at times, but he was the man for assorted explosives. Joe Deltoro was a New Yorker and strong enough to handle one of the machine guns. Bill Cohn who was equally strong and able to handle one of the Thompson machine guns. Romero's role was to be second in command; he had gotten enough respect in the world where his general presence was called for just to make sure there were no structural problems with the plans. Romero would carry a gun and wear a mask and yell and do all the typical stuff. The crew would do the heavier work, like, assaulting the truck and wrangling the hostages. Romero would drive the getaway car and help unload the dough.

Romero drove back to King's house and waited for the others to return from collecting supplies.

He lingered by the dinner table and studied the map some more. The plan was crude but considering it was an armored truck it would have to be. Armored trucks are not easy to rip off. The trucks are rigged up with all kinds of set ups to deter a crew from making off with the currency. There also could be an alarm and a tracking device.

When it came to hitting an armored truck it had to be shock and awe.

Romero did not exactly need money. He had been bored and felt the general pall of aggravation, and he didn't have much of a social life back at home to distract himself from his gainful unemployment. No one would call him a social outcast. He was just low key. Romero was not all about spending money and making sure everyone got a gander of his new Armani or Rolex or the blonde on his arm. Despite his common lack of gregariousness, he dealt with his routine back in the city with some comfort. He thought himself the lizard sitting on the flat rock watching time pass before the next juicy job came buzzing along. Considerable time had passed between jobs. Romero was becoming tired of the same old schedule day in and day out and therefore he jumped at the chance to work again. He needed the excitement and a chance out of the sedentary life wasn't something he was willing to let pass him by.

Romero's mind felt sharp and clear, and he repeatedly looked out the window for the guys to show up.

Five men; one armored truck and how much would that net? Christ, he hoped enough. Complications arose when there was not enough of a take, such as back stabbings and killings. The best time for someone to try something would be when the bags are opened and the money was being counted.

King came in and was carrying two large duffel bags, and Romero wordlessly took one and followed King to the table where he placed his duffel on top of the map. He unzipped exposing several firearms and ammunition inside.

"Lot of guns," King said.

"How much?" Romero wondered.

"Two Thompsons and two clips each fully loaded and at least one sawed-off also loaded." King inhaled. "Ten hand guns. Revolvers not automatics as you requested, and all fully loaded."

Geiger came in after hanging by the doorway listening, and he carried a large paper bag with a plastic one inside of it and he set it on the middle of the table gently, his face tense and when he had it down he smiled sickly at it and asked, "How come Romero, you don't like automatics?"

"I like them," Romero said, "Just can't afford to have them jamb in the middle of taking down a score." He tilted his head looking at the Nazi. "Right?"

Not necessarily true. Romero didn't want to say he had owed an arms dealer a favor and took a couple of revolvers off his hands to pay it off.

"You the pro, you the pro," Geiger smiled, blue eyes cold as icebergs. "I got them boom shit." He laughed touching the paper bag. "It goes off it'll knock the fucking truck on its ass. And when it does, why I'll slap this bad boy onto the back and boom that door right open." Geiger then cackled.

They heard a car pull up and doors slamming and then Deltoro and Cohn came in and wordlessly began pulling the various guns out.

"How's the scene?" Romero asked both of them.

Deltoro said, "The truck came back up from its run. They took out several metal boxes that looked like it had some bulk. If the pattern holds then, tomorrow will be a lighter load. The day after?" Deltoro lit a cigarette. "There

4

should be enough cake to go around for this fucked birthday party."

Geiger clapped his hands and did a dance, his feet patting the floor. "Who wants to go out and get laid!?"

They went over it again and again. When Romero saw the tension build and boredom of the monotonous planning of the job setting in, he decided that the best course was for the group to decompress and relax and have some fun. He knew that over preparedness was sometimes more potentially dangerous than under preparedness.

Deltoro and King went to a bar in town to watch a game and drink. Geiger knew where the hookers were at and tried goading Cohn to go with him. When Cohn refused, waving him off, Geiger called him while laughing, 'a lousy limp dick kyke' and then jumped across to him and patted him roughly on the back to let him know that his anti-Semitism, while genuine, was currently in the background to the camaraderie of the job.

Romero and Cohn watched Geiger leave with some alleviation of his absence and Cohn gave Romero a look of exasperation and said, "I'm not even Jewish."

The two of them did their own thing. Cohn watched the TV while Romero went outside to the backyard. Romero brought one of the duffel bags out with him where he chose a revolver and stuck it in his jacket pocket. When it did not fit he tried another, until one did. It was a chrome snub nosed S&W 642 Air weight with a shroud over the hammer to stop it from snagging when being pulled from—say it with me—a jacket pocket.

He had not been in any townships in a while, and the crickets and cicadas were almost unnervingly loud.

Romero hated bugs. The thought of thousands, hell millions of them under his feet and in the branches above, nearly made him go back inside. He pulled the gun out again and aimed at the tree trunk up ahead. Then he settled on not chancing on directing attention to the house where armed criminals were hiding out. Although, he didn't think the one pop of the gun would attract too much inquiry. If police came on by, Romero could calmly answer the door holding the tea pot he saw in the sink. He could say, *'No officer, I did hear a loud pop but it was way over there,'* and he would point in any direction. What would they do in a nice area like this? Barge in pulling weapons? Still just because he felt bored, he thought, it was no reason to take even the smallest risks.

Romero said he was going back to the motel and Cohn nodded a goodnight to him from the couch. Romero felt more freedom as he was walking to his car. He needed to decompress from the tension the other men gave off. Geiger just gave off weird energy.

King was going on loudly huffing air like he was oxygen deprived and Romero knew that was his nerves. Cohn was almost like Romero; he seemed calm and said little but his eyes were always jumping around in his head. He could not stop his analyzing of the job. He was like a computer. Romero considered over-thinking terrific, of course, but being aware of it was enough. Deltoro was loud and a drinker and too much a gregarious fellow. He had already crowded Romero, trying to swap war stories with him, and Romero's anxiety would climb drastically. He would have to shift around on his feet and come up with a way to extricate himself from Deltoro's runaway monologues.

He turned on the television and flipped through the channels. Nothing could keep his attention for more than five minutes. He turned off the TV, having given up on it and lifted the phone on the bedside table. He thought briefly that he would call Morris but then he stopped realizing he had nothing new to say. Of course, he considered he could just call and say he had accepted the job, but he had never done that before and did not see any reason to start now. Romero would only call when it was crucial.

Call anyway? Romero thought. No forget it.

He went out to the car with the gun in his pocket and drove around. He wanted to be in a city, seeing the lights, and action. He already felt tired already of the blandness of the town and looked for a place where he could drink, maybe have dinner with a crowd more familiar to him than the corn shucking type he saw roaming around. It was almost desolate, and the people that Romero saw were not so nice on the eyes. Romero felt uncomfortable seeing the look of town's people with their slow manners, shuffling around in his face. He lived in the city and was accustomed to people being in a rush even when it was obvious they had no place they had to go. Most of the people of this township were virtually old, and some seemed to look as if they were farm hands.

Romero surmised that maybe he just missed being home. He considered this to be his final job, as he did not need the money. Romero was not rich, but his fronts generated a satisfactory amount of profit which allowed him to live in luxury if he so pleased.

He found a bar and restaurant where burly men played pool far off beyond an arched doorway, and flat screen televisions hung on the walls. Romero saw all this and began to feel better. This place could be any bar back home.

He went up to the hostess, and before she could greet him, her eyes widened and she said, moving her hands up to her cheeks, "Oh my god! Romero, is that you?" She looked familiar. She had curly black hair and an unkempt librarian look. He couldn't recall if she had looked the same before, but she looked exhausted. Then it came to him.

Sarah Medlow was with him his freshmen year in high school. She looked almost the same then as she did now, aside from a more weary appearance, and while they were not friends they were friendly enough when they drifted into each other's orbit back then.

"Do you talk more now?" she asked and laughed letting him know she was joking.

"More? Yes," he said, and she showed him to a table where he sat by the window where he could see his car directly under a street lamp, illuminated. Almost making him want to barge outside to move it before he stifled the feeling.

"Listen," Sarah said, "I got a half hour left why don't we catch up then? We'll sit at the bar. If you're not in a rush?" Her old awkwardness returned and was noticeable by her waving hands and face. It was a real moment of surrealism for him. He said sure as he planned on sticking around anyway and she said that was great and left. A pretty waitress asked him for his order, and he ordered the sirloin steak, mashed potatoes, and a glass of water. He watched her leave and he surveyed the place closely. He felt in his pocket for the gun and made himself push it deeper inside.

Romero thought about his first meeting with Morris in the can, but his reverie got cut short by his food arriving, and he ate hungrily. He kept looking out the window wishing he moved the damn thing but he breathed deeply, calming himself. Romero wondered if there were buses and cabs out here in the sticks, and then thought it possible.

Romero went to the bar, and Sarah was there. He told her everything except his criminal history and why he dropped out of high school.

"So I've been investing and joining many business ventures. I seem to be doing okay...You?"

Sara didn't exactly have things go her way. "Obviously," she turned her palms to the ceiling, "I'm a hostess, and I'm going to be 34." She laughed dryly and drank her shot down and took another.

"Well what did you do?" Romero asked.

"Oh, I was an art teacher."

"That sounds pretty good."

"It was until I got laid off." She took another shot and again with the hands toward the ceiling, mock face of terror, "Now here I am."

"Times are tough," Romero said. "I want to keep working, but it's harder." This armored truck job was the first significant break he had in a while. It was perfect.

A lone armored truck going up a lonely long stretch of road with emptiness around for miles because of a union strike. Some shock and awe with a dash of speed and it could work. He didn't tell her this. He said, "So now I just don't invest as much. I do fine with the places I do own and will have to live off of them. I can. I'd like to live grander but..." He shrugged.

She was single, and she didn't have kids. She didn't want to get married or have kids either, but she didn't seem too convincing. "I think I may have too high expectations," she said. "Of what? I don't know. They are really high though." She was now gripping a rocks glass of bourbon. "Then when life turned out so-so I couldn't handle it." She looked at him beseechingly. "Isn't life kind of so-so? I wish I had an adventure. Do you know what I mean? Maybe a little danger too. No, no danger," she settled. "Some *spontaneity.*"

"I get bored sometimes," he said. "But when I get back into investing the risks are never worth it. It used to be but, you can't gamble when you're bored. I have to fill the void with something else." He looked into his drink and continued. "I've been lucky so far. I was real unlucky at one point, and it cost me six years. I don't want to relive that experience."

It was never about the money for him, he had enough to justify his lifestyle and spending habits. He loved the adrenaline that would rush through his entire body and make him feel more alive and confident. That is why even though Romero spent six years in the joint, he still dared to play the game yet again.

"Six years?" She squinted her eyes seeking clarification.

"Oh..." he tried thinking fast and sighed and just said, "I just mean I've had some failed deals. I mean really epically bad deals, and I've just recouped my losses."

She held up her rocks glass. She said, *"To filling the void."*

He raised his drink so it touched hers. *"To filling the void."*

She asked him: "How's the city? It's been awhile since I've been back, years."

"It's a good sports town still. The nightlife, well, the downtown scene in general is thriving more than ever.

It's become a place where there's always somewhere to go downtown within walking distance."

"I would love to move back."

"Why don't you?"

"I don't know." She looked dreamily at the ceiling, the light made orbs in her eyes. "But I need to find another job there, and I don't know if I'm that secure yet financially. Well, actually I do know."

"Parents?"

"My mother," she nodded and drank. "Not," she stood up and punched the wooden barstool, "a very supportive woman. Love her. Not supportive." Sarah slammed her fists down on the bar and asked the bartender for another drink, her bracelet colored beads shaking and making a rattling noise. "So if I do move back I'll have to move back in with her until I find work." She groaned and ran her hands through her hair and Romero suddenly knew how her hair became such a mess. He wondered how many times she had such episodes. She looked at him, sat back down and apologized saying, "Sorry to make a scene."

"No. It's fine. Really." It was too. He liked talking to her.

"You remember the fat kid Kearns, uh, Ritchie?" she snapped her fingers.

"Redhead?"

"Yeah," she nodded enthusiastically, "he's a cop now. Real thin. I mean rail thin."

"He was so timid," Romero remembered.

"I dated him briefly," she blurted and laughed.

Romero followed her outside where they shook hands. She weaved a little and Romero wondered if he should make some move. He didn't particularly feel like it, and all he asked was if he could drive her home. Sarah said she had driven worse off, and they shook hands again promising to catch up.

Catch up with what? he thought.

The next morning they ate quietly at the now clear table and had their coffee and gathered their things for the last day of planning. Geiger would be driven by King who would drop him off at the predetermined spot on the side of the road. There the truck would hug the grass strip that ran alongside the road due to a nasty pothole created by Geiger himself. Buried in a ditch would be the total amount of explosives that would topple the truck on its side. Geiger would rise out of another hole, pre-dug, covered by a camouflage tarp, and he then would run, slapping the next bomb on the rear door held in place by an adhesive. King would be ahead of the truck as it neared the ditch and he would double back when the truck went over. It would be Romero, Deltoro and Cohn following King and Geiger. Romero would be acting as wheel man while Deltoro and Cohn cow the guards with the heavily intimidating machine guns as Geiger and King would begin unloading them, tying them up and throwing them to the ground. They would unload their score from the back and get the hell out of dodge where they would meet at the house, divide the kitty, and Romero would drive back to the city feeling the usual elation and humming of juice in him when he took down a score.

If nothing went wrong.

Romero sat in the backseat with Deltoro driving and Cohn shot gun, and they watched the unloading of the truck at a safe distance. They were beside a fast food joint on top of a hill that overlooked the spot with one way traffic between them and the bank.

"Today's a heavy load," Cohn mused.

"Shit. Does this mean tomorrow's load will be lighter? Because if it is," Deltoro said, "we're fucked. We're fucked, and I don't want to be here longer than I have been.

This town is grating."

"Nothing to do here," Cohn added.

"Shit to do!" Deltoro slapped a palm on the steering wheel.

The truck loaded with three guards took off back into traffic. The three of the heist men trailed until once again they were on the barren strip of road, where they encountered few vehicles going in either direction, which was typical. They just observed this road once more with the truck far ahead of them somewhere.

Romero stood at the phone outside his room and gave his booker, Morris, a call. "What's going on?" Morris spoke softly as he usually did.

"It's doable," he told Morris. "We're moving tomorrow."

"How's the town?"

"Don't get why people would want to live anywhere but the city," Romero told Morris, "King is used to it, hell wanted to be living here, but the others? They'll be glad to get out of town. I'm with them."

"City boy," Morris replied dryly. "Enough of a kitty for all of you?"

"The load tomorrow is usually heavy. Although there has been a complication."

"Tell me."

"Today's load is usually light, but today it was heavy. So we wonder if it should be chanced that tomorrow the pattern won't be broken just because of today's load."

Romero only heard silence on the other end and was about to speak when Morris moaned in thought. Romero could imagine the skinny old man in the coke bottle glasses tapping a long finger against his lips.

"Don't chance it," Morris told him. "Never chance it. You got to stay in that shit-

kicker town longer, then do it. The kitty is worth it. The kitty is always worth it."

"Another fucking week!?" Deltoro whined, pacing back and forth hands over his eyes, "I'm going to lose my shit, Romero!"

"He's right," King said. "We want the mother lode."

"Unless," Cohn said. "Unless we slightly deviate from the original plan."

Deltoro said, "Meaning?"

Cohn leaned on the table on both hands looking out under his brows at them. "We watch tomorrow. See if the load is heavy or not and if it is the observation car should be waiting and following behind. So that would be myself, Romero and you, Deltoro. Not from the original spot as planned so time is a factor. We're going to have to play catch up."

Geiger said, "Isn't there a reason we didn't want to do that in the first place?"

"Yes because we watch over by that fast food place," Cohn commented. "The trip from the street, down to make the turn into traffic to follow would be at least ten minutes because where we are is up on a hill where the best vantage point is. The truck circles around the bank where it's hidden from view. The freeway? It leads *into* the city... the *opposite* way we're going. Ten minutes is about what it would take to get there."

"Exactly ten," Deltoro nodded, "We timed the route as we didn't want to play catch up all the way to the strip where we'd take the truck." He sighed looking down at the table. "Which is what it looks like we'll have to do." Then looking exasperated he moaned, "Unless we wait another week."

Geiger clapped his hands. "Let's vote!"

So they voted. It was Geiger, Cohn and Deltoro with a GO, and King with an unsure NO and Romero shrugged. He said, "I can get us there in time. So I say, go."

Geiger trolled for more women, and the rest of the men went to a bar. They drank at a booth saying nothing, each of them occasionally chewing on peanuts. It was Romero's suggestion that they split up. Some of the customers of the establishment, as well as employees shot the four of them looks of suspicion. The last thing they needed before a score, but more trouble was coming when they arrived at the house. It was Geiger screeching tires and nearly running them over on the driveway up to the garage. The men parted at the halting car, the tires smoking and headlights strafing them. Geiger jumped out, and he was bloody.

It was a black hooker. She had an afro and her eyes were open. Her throat slashed.

Her skirt bunched up around her waist and panties on inside out. They were blue.

"Cut the light," Cohn said.

Geiger turned off the lights. They huddled looking into the cabin at the dead woman lying sprawled in the back.

"Geiger what is this shit!?" King spat. "You bring this here!?"

"Bitch was crazy," Geiger said shaking his head. "Nigger cunt tried to rob me... I took the knife from her and gave her a lesson."

"Bullshit," Cohn hissed.

"Park this in the garage," Romero said. "Geiger, King, Deltoro, make the car spotless. Use bleach if you have it. Don't wipe the blood, you have to blot it. Come on Cohn. We'll take her." He pointed at the woman.

"We're going to dump the body?" Cohn asked sounding disapproving.

"No," Romero told him, "We're going to destroy it."

They wrapped her in heavy duty trash bags using electrical tape to seal it up airtight. They put her in the trunk, where dead bodies in their profession tend to go, and they just drove looking for inspiration. This inspiration came when Cohn spotted from the passenger seat a fire burning behind a brick building and a chain-link fence with razor wire above. They did a circuit of the building.

A western theme restaurant as it turned out.

Romero and Cohn left the woman in the trunk and prowled across the grass field to the fence. Cohn knew what it was, "It's an incinerator," he whispered. "Looks plenty old, but that fire is enough." He patted Romero's arm, "Looks like we're in luck."

Romero drove into the empty lot as the restaurant was closed for the night.

"Right there," Cohn said shooting a finger beyond the windshield where a small path cut to the back where the incinerator burned. They parked directly in front of the path and Cohn jumped out of the car while Romero popped the trunk. He followed Cohn, carrying the body over his shoulder.

Cohn pulled the steel door of the incinerator wider. The sounds of crackling debris in the flames were detectable as was the low roar of the fire. Romero pushed the corpse in where it landed with a muffled thud. Smoke wafted out in a thin tendril, and Cohn slid the door back, and they jogged to the car.

At the house, it was all cleaned up, the blood especially, and towels and rags used to do it were gone. King griped about how Geiger should buy him a new set of towels. He began calling him a miserable son of a bitch and a hypocrite for messing with black tail.

"Where is he?" Romero asked.

Deltoro pointed in the house. "Watching the TV like nothing happened, the sick fuck."

"Cohn," Romero turned to him, "you worked with him before: Is this common?"

Cohn popped his shoulders. "I don't know of him doing anything like this before, but I do know that he doesn't have a healthy view of the ladies. Once we were on a job knocking off this department store and he tried to get me to cover for him while he took one of the female hostages into an office." He scratched his chin and sneered with disgust. "I didn't have to ask to know what he wanted to do. He wanted to *rape* her."

"And?" King pressed.

"I told him I don't cotton to that, and if he tried it he was out on his ass, and he'd have no crew to work with," Cohn stuck a cigarette in his mouth and spoke through it. "When I told him it was like I wrenched a favorite toy away from him. Or like pulling a sirloin steak out of a wild dog's mouth." He lit the smoke. "Nasty," he said inhaling.

"Alright King, we'll just get back to our motels and get some sleep," Romero said. "Back here tomorrow and we'll make it happen."

King added, "Unless Geiger goes slash happy again."

It was a heavy load. Deltoro and Cohn exchanged enthusiastic words while Romero drove them, just a hair, above the speed limit toward the strip of road. He was trying to make the time to get there or leave King and Geiger in the lurch with no back up.

Make the time before the bulls got to the radio and summoned assistance from the other bulls. It all hedged on timing.

When he got to the road, he checked again for law. He increased pressure on the gas pedal while in the back Deltoro and Cohn put on their ski masks and gloves. They gripped the Thompsons on their laps and once in awhile flicked a look at one another.

Romero saw what might be the truck up ahead. The bright blue sky and the sun was coming through obstructing his view. He sat up and was nearly pressing his nose to the windshield, and although he could not see the truck clearly, there came a muffled blast that confirmed its identity.

"Christ!" Deltoro shouted.

"Shit!" said Cohn. "Hit it Romero!"

"Hit it man!" Deltoro called.

"Shit!" Romero roughly whacked the wheel. "We're close! It's cool! Don't panic!"

"Just keep hitting the gas!" Deltoro said.

Finally after what felt like several minutes they stopped screeching rubber at the toppled armored truck. Geiger up to the back door and as swiftly as he appeared he sprinted back and then slid on his shoes and waved wildly for them to go back.

Go back? Romero tried processing, confused all of a sudden.

"The bomb!!!" Geiger hoarsely shouted.

Romero hit the reverse and went a few feet before the car swerved. Romero remembered to right the wheel and the deafening roar came and the windshield shattered.

The front end rose and dropped and all he heard was ringing followed by far off muffled voices calling behind him.

Romero had braked too close. It was because he was late. Because of the random pattern interruption of the damned bulls inside the truck, it almost got him blown up.

That and fucking Geiger for being fucking Geiger.

He was in a fog, and he knew it was a concussion. He felt like he was not part of the scene he was watching. He was watching Deltoro and Cohn pull the bulls out of the back of the truck while holding their fearsome machine guns. King was backing up the car. The trunk popped open followed by King coming into view. He waved Geiger to the car and the Nazi-asshole-rapist-piece-of-shit began climbing out the truck. Two steel boxes under each arm. He deposited them in King's trunk and Romero abruptly remembered his part in the score and on legs like stilts he climbed out, remembered to stoop back in and pop the trunk which nearly made him pass out, and joined Geiger —the sick fuck—in emptying this rolling vault.

The bulls, or guards, were hogtied by the side of the road, and their expressions stopped being fearful and became just enraged. Their firearms confiscated and tossed away overhand.

"You can't drive that into town!" King shouted into Romero's right ear then shot a look at the guards and took his arm, moving him quickly a few yards. "There's an auto dump up ahead here!" he pointed off the side of the road at some spot unseen. "Keep going straight on the road along with us until you see a beaten track! Keep going and park in that dump and we'll come back! Okay!?" He shot another look at the guards who did not seem to hear and why should they? They caught the worst of the blast.

Geiger tossed the guards into the back of the truck and jumped in beside King in their getaway car. Cohn and Deltoro were in the back along with them, leaving Romero with the perilous trip up the road to another route.

Romero nearly took out a VW bus and saw the fright in the teen girl's eyes. He wondered how he could find any path—but there it was! He got onto it just in time. When he turned off the road, he saw the flashing of lights behind him. He kept driving and soon he saw the tall grass ahead of him. Then he was driving with high grass and iron gates around him.

The cars were old, rusted. Rats went this way and that way and ignorant cats showing it in their direction and thinness went the other. Romero parked in a tin rickety garage that looked like a boathouse. He groggily climbed out and rested against the vehicle that was, like him, beaten to shit. In an undetermined interval of time, he went around to the trunk and unloaded the cash and searched somewhere he could hide it. It came to him that if any place is good enough for a heist crew to meet at then here was the place and the cops might know it. He would move the money but leave the car, and if he was lucky when the worst happened, and they did come they could search the car, find it empty and abandoned, and assume they took off with the load after the meet up.

He found a crumbling interior of a Ford pickup in the high grass. He examined, and found that it would have to do and began loading the inside of it up. The exertion made him dizzy and he made himself stop and rest. He listened to his heart going from a heavy thud to a gentle one, and now he heard something else in the constant ringing in his ears.

It was a car and the unmistakable squawk of a police radio.

Romero hunkered down as far back in the thick grass as he possibly could. He searched through the bars of the iron fence watching the police car cruise slowly into the yard. Two bulls inside. If he were lucky, the cops would do a lazy circle around the place and head out, giving a coast is clear to superiors and leaving him, and their money, alone. The police car vanished behind the tin garage and passed by him and back out the fence.

Romero waited five minutes monitored by his watch and ran to the Ford shell. He emptied it carrying the boxes further into the high grass where he fell several times fighting through the green. He took out his folding knife and cut a clear spot in several areas. Time seemed to crawl, and when he finished, he was sweating and huffed air, and brought the boxes into the clearing he had made. He began covering them with loose high grass.

Romero went back to the spot in the grass beside the fence and pulled for his gun but could not find it. He carefully retraced his steps to the car. He found it on the floor by the brake pedal and he made off back to his spot where he collapsed to wait. He breathed and waited. He felt the sweat roll on down his forehead, and down his cheeks, and a breeze kicked up suddenly cooling him. He became tired and found that he was laying back. He could not form a clear thought, and even though he knew it was a terrible idea with a concussion, he shut his eyes.

Romero popped his eyes open, and he became scared. He did not have a bad dream exactly. It was more as if he had become aware in the blackness of sleep of some presence that was dangerous. He almost did not want to open his eyes, on account of what he might face. When he did the sky was black and pinpoints of stars littered the heavens. He heard the grass sway in the breeze. It was cold.

He pulled the gun free and checked the cylinder finding it loaded with the comforting brass. He stepped out and walked toward the garage.

Two policemen with flashlights were pointing their lights into his car. One was aiming the beam into the back and the other at the driver's seat who then stooped down searchingly.

It seemed they were both alone, and he knew he had to make a move.

Romero stuck the gun in his waistband and crawled through the grass slowly moving like some gator. A calmness and inner stillness, the waiting in anticipation for the strike had him.

The cop at the front of the car rose, and he was holding between two fingertips a cigarette. He said, "We have evidence, Ritchie."

"Oh yeah?" said the redheaded cop rummaging through the backseat.

Romero rose just behind the cop holding the cigarette. He stuck the gun under the officer's chin and pulled the trigger. His partner's eyes went wide, and he tried reaching for his gun. He was not quick enough.

Both of their bodies went into the trunk of his getaway car.

The boxes of money were there, and Romero was not about to stay any longer.

He'd have to take the money with him. He'd have to take a chance on the road.

He tasted copper suddenly. He stuck two fingers in, and bloodied they came out.

The explosion probably made him bite his tongue or cheek or it was possible it came from inside his nose and leaked down into his mouth, the explosion rupturing a vessel in his nose perhaps and whatever the source he was sore now and was certain he would be more so tomorrow.

He loaded the score in the backseat and buckled himself up. He hit the lights and the car eased out whining some. He got to the road, and there were lights still out in the distance. He drove the speed limit to King's.

He parked and searched around, and got out walking across the street to the row of houses. He tried all the doors of the parked cars and came up gold with a vintage station wagon. He abandoned the car making sure to wipe it thoroughly. The cash with him in his new ride and he took off for King's place.

King's car was not in sight. Romero figured he stowed it in town, or chanced it keeping it in his garage. Romero knocked and rang the doorbell. No one answered.

Romero went around back between the house and the garage and found Cohn sitting with one leg up on the porch railing with a beer beside him on the table. He was in a deck chair.

"Christ," Romero said with relief, "get me a cold one too, huh?"

Cohn said nothing and didn't move. He wasn't asleep either.

He came around and faced Cohn finding a screwdriver jammed into an eye socket. Cohn's mouth was open. A trail of dried blood was down under the wounded eye as if he wept the stuff.

Romero felt the bottle and it was still cold. He took his gun out and went in the door to the kitchen. The metal boxes of their score littered the floor, all of them empty.

He found Deltoro and King in the living room both dead on the floor. Both of them shot in the head, twice each. Romero could tell they had been killed while they were standing.

He figured from a look of the scene that Geiger had taken them by surprise. He wondered further of what could have happened. Did he get into a fight with Cohn? Perhaps some sharp words had been exchanged. Perhaps about Geiger being a piece of shit rapist?

Geiger then lost it stabbing Cohn in the eye, killing him? Maybe by accident? Heat of the moment? Perchance Geiger decided if they let him live he would be finished either way so why not kill them? He could make up for all the money he would forfeit no longer connected to a crew.

Whatever the answer, Romero knew Geiger was currently a wealthy man.

Romero stuffed the money away at his motel room and walked across the parking lot past his new car and crossed another parking lot where a diner was conveniently located. There was also a well maintained phone booth of all things.

Romero dropped the coins and feeling edgy he cracked the door to shut off the interior light. Lest he be seen from the street and by Geiger. He had changed motels and was now in what looked to be an urban setting some distance from haunts he frequented while out in the sticks. Still he was anxious and tired and he peered into the diner and became hungry.

Morris was outraged. He said, "Take what you got on you and drive back. Forget them. Their dead and you got your cut. Hell, you got more than your cut."

"It is plenty," he said.

"How much is it?"

"Half a million and eighty-three bucks."

Morris whistled. "To hell with Geiger, unless he gets his ass busted. Then what?"

"Rat," Romero said flatly.

"He knows your last name and what you look like. Does he know where you live? Think carefully."

"I don't believe so," Romero mused. "Still this guy is trouble, and if I can I want to take the chance of tying this thing up. If I can, I want to seal this off."

"Half a million dollars," Morris said dreamily. "Hell of a score. That the biggest you've ever landed," he said.

"Absolutely," Romero agreed. "Before my biggest score landed me a hundred grand and change."

"So you can hang it up?"

"Maybe."

"Until you get bored?"

"I'll find a hobby," Romero told him, "I'm not going into the can. No chance."

"So you find this Nazi and clip him, come home and I'll launder your dough as always and maybe you can move out of that basement and into an actual apartment somewhere."

"Get married, have kids," Romero chimed, holding his growling stomach.

Morris, sounding incredibly deflated by the turn of events, recommended he switch motels and Romero told him he had. "You have money now. Stay in one of those luxury suites, would you?"

"The motel's fine," Romero said.

"Hey a suite is safer than waiting on some ground floor unit for a bullet to come crashing through the window as you pass by, right?"

"Sure—maybe—we'll see."

"Keep in touch."

He hung up and went into the diner and took a seat far away from the window and ordered bacon and eggs and a glass of OJ. He put a plan together. Geiger was brash and not that smart. He was probably scrambling about where to go and what to do, and if he were out celebrating, Romero knew black tail might be involved. It was because Geiger was a braggart Romero knew where to look.

Romero drove to the bar on 12th and North and put a hand in his pocket on the gun. He went around back with the loud music washing out from an open door. It was some type of country tune. He rushed past finding himself in an alley where a man was drinking and swaying and further ahead a black woman in too short-shorts was smoking.

Romero leaned beside her and turned his free hand showing her the rolled money in his palm and the black girl put on a sour smile and threw away the smoke and motioned for him to follow her. He did, and they came to a dumpster where she turned toward him, asking him what he wanted. Before he could answer she began naming sexual favors along with prices.

"I'm looking for a rough looking guy named *Geiger*." Romero watched her.

"Am I getting paid or am I getting paid?" she rolled her eyes some and jutted a leg out with attitude.

"Here," Romero handed her the money. "That's five hundred. I'll give you five hundred more if you can help me find him. But he can't know," Romero held his finger toward her to accentuate the point.

"I know who you talking about," she said stuffing the bills away between her breasts. "Mothafucka took off with Clara, and we ain't seen her, and we losing our minds looking for that girl."

A deep voice called, "Hey!" and Romero watched a mountain of a black man come walking up flanked by two other women, hookers for sure, one white the other black. This man had a sizable looking bald head and eyes that were as dead as if they were a charcoal drawing of eyes. "Asking questions, white man?" he asked.

"Clara," Romero asked, "is one of your girls right?"

"That's right," he nodded never breaking from his cold gaze. "She's been missing. Went out with some white dude. Some real racist cracker trash too.

Motherfucker owes me money and my girl."

"Clara's dead," Romero told him. "Sorry. You should know."

The big man wrinkled his brows and gave Romero's alley companion a look and said, shooing her off with a hand, "Go make some money! The fuck you standing around for?! Suck a dick!" He made to hit her, and she took off. The big man with an index finger rigid held it by Romero's nose leaning toward him. "You telling me that cracker killed one of my girls? Is that what you telling me, son?" The big man's flesh seemed to fight to contain his rage inside him. "Why are you telling me this man? You want something?"

Romero gripped the gun handle making himself keep it in his pocket. He said to the glowering mountain of fury, "If I had to bet I'd say he's with one of your girls. You find out where he is, and I'll kill him for you. And pay you the money you're owed."

The big man stood back and spread his arms and said as if excepting a challenge, "I got my girls in flop houses around this town. I lift a phone they damn well answer and tell me whatever I want to know." He jerked his head to the side. His dark mood lifting and he even smiled, though his eyes never changed. "Come on son!" he motioned. "Come on! Let's handle this!"

His name was Emmett Grandview, and he ran women and drugs. He treated his women with a tolerant respect but never failed sharply to crack the whip when they malingered failing in bringing in their earnings to him. Romero sat on the leather couch in the back of the bar where it turned out Grandview, or Big G to his friends, operated out of. It was the headquarters for his criminal empire.

Big G smoked a cigar and over the course of two hours he made calls. He would dial and listen and ask one of his girls where they were at and then they would tell him obediently. He queried if they were or had been accompanied by a white man and he gave them Geiger's description. It took two hours of making calls, but of also recalling numbers that hadn't been answered and all the while, Romero sat on the couch. At the hour mark, he saw a marijuana cigarette in the ashtray on the long wood coffee table and gestured for Big G who watched him make the motion of lighting up and smoking it. Big G nodded and Romero lit it up using the lighter on the table. He felt his anxiousness recede with the smoke lifting to the ceiling and becoming nothing.

He heard, but wasn't paying any attention as Big G came around the desk.

Romero was startled and dropped the reefer in the ashtray and looked up to see Big G holding a piece of paper by the side of his face.

"He just showed up," Big G said.

"Great." Romero recognized the address. It wasn't too out of the general area he and the crew had travelled while planning the job.

"My girl knows what's going down, so she ain't going to go crazy."

"Great." Romero stood and put the paper in his pocket inside his jacket. "I'll be back when it's done." He walked to the door and was aware of Big G trailing behind him.

He felt the big man's suspicion. Sure enough as he got past the doorway a large ebony hand gripped his shoulder and Romero turned facing the flat eyes again.

"My money, *son*," Big G growled lowly. "You won't make it out this town if I don't say so. You here?"

Romero only smiled and nodded. The hand let him go and he went out to settle his score.

❖

The flop house was above a pool hall. Romero crept up the stairway, which was dark, and he had the gun up ahead of him pointed to the ceiling. The room he looked for was the last door down the corridor.

At the door, Romero could hear the commotion beyond it. Geiger was calling the woman beyond a *black bitch* and loud sounds of flesh smacking against each other sounded followed by the woman grunting in convincing sounding pleasure. Romero gripped the knob and turned and was none surprised when the door was unlocked. A courtesy from this hooker who knew of his impending arrival.

Geiger flew off from his doggy position behind the woman. Stark naked he jumped off the bed and predictably reached out for the gun on the dresser. Another revolver—naturally.

Romero aimed in a low crouch and fired over the bed. He missed and Geiger threw himself bodily to a far wall, his eyes rolling up white. Romero rising up felt a stinging at his neck. He collapsed to the floor with his vision darkening. It was in a dimmed murky perspective that he saw his gun spin as it hit the wood floor and twirl off under the bed. The last thing he saw was the spontaneous appearance of a large foot in brown leather dress shoes stepping from behind him and blocking his view of his gun.

Romero woke and was shivering. Water was dripping off of him. He found himself without a shirt. He shook his head trying to clear it. He realized he couldn't move. His arms were fastened behind him, and his feet were bare, and the only consolation was that he had pants on.

Footsteps were behind Romero and he threw his head back sending tendrils of light pain to his head. It was Big G, and he was wearing white overalls. Romero looked down and saw that Big's shoes were wrapped in plastic. Clear plastic. Romero then recognized the shoes. So it had been him. He trailed him and now here he was for god knew what reason. Romero blinked at the still solid giant of the man and he looked over at his companion sitting beside him who, like him, was shirtless, shoeless and wet. Geiger was sniffling and his chest was showing every ragged intake of breath. A thin cord of blood had run from the side of his forehead to his belly button.

"Sorry son," Big G said to Romero. "I took you out with this here." He held up what Romero recognized as a tranquilizer gun.

"It's fine," Romero croaked, his mouth feeling filled with cotton and his eyeballs felt dry.

"I was thinking," Big G walked and stood in front of them. "I was thinking on what the hell was going on. And I seem to remember something." He pinched the air by an ear while looking down to the floor in analysis of some sort. "The town was buzzing about this armored truck job early today." He nodded focusing on Romero. "Yeah. So here you and this cat show up, and I'm saying to myself now, what is going on here? This fool," Big G reached his lengthy arm grabbing Geiger's neck and twisted Geiger's head to face Romero, "is burning some serious money. That's what my girls told me. Sure enough," Big G threw away Geiger who rocked back and forth in the seat on the verge of falling over, "what do I find? A brick of bills bound in paper bands. Gee," Big G mused, "I wonder where they came from?"

Geiger croaked, "I'll get that money back you nigger monkey, you don't get to rob me!" and he spat toward the big man's shoes.

"Okay," Big G said and went behind Geiger's chair and tilted it back. He then dragged it along across the room where Romero could see an opaque plastic screen hanging. The big man dragged a scowling Geiger behind it and their forms became a milky translucent blur.

"You sure about that?" Big G asked the form that was Geiger.

"Suck my Aryan cock, nigger," Geiger said and laughed.

Romero futilely tried slipping his hands out of his bonds, but they were too tight.

Romero then hit upon the solution introduced by Big G himself. The chair he was on was movable and he tried standing. He found he could although with some difficulty. When he did finally get his wobbly legs steady he smiled and turned for an exit. Unfortunately, he saw two black men with serious fixed expressions on their faces standing silently on each side of the exit.

Obediently he turned around and set the chair back down behind him and sat.

Romero heard a cough of some motor and looked through the cloudy membrane.

He could see Geiger squirming on the chair, and here came Big G holding high over his head, with its shape unmistakable, a chainsaw.

"Cocksucking nigger! You're dead you—" Geiger was interrupted as the said nigger brought the chainsaw down on the crown of his head, and blood spattered the screen. The chain-link took hold, and more blood came. Romero stood again and turned toward the door and sat the chair down, watching the never changing faces of the guards, as that Nazi fuck, who was responsible for this whole mess met his end.

Romero was awash in relief when Big G untied him and said he could go. Romero looked over the big man's shoulder, as much as was possible, and he saw that most of the screen was crimson. Dripping sounds were audible as the gore came down the plastic. Also, covered in blood was the overall Big G was wearing as well as the face mask looping his neck suddenly.

"I got the money, man," he said. "I was just delivering some justice for the bitches on the prowl who work for me. You see?" He titled his big head.

"Compensated plenty too, huh?" Romero said standing on shaky knees.

"Three hundred grand," he grinned. "Let's get out of here," he placed a hand on Romero's shoulder. "I ain't about ripping you off for your cheese. I respect that shit, you know? I knew a cat upstate who used to pop safes and banks and shit. You may know this man. His name is *Morris?*"

About one year after Morris got out he got sent back for a parole violation. Cops had found in his car an unregistered gun and off Morris went for two years; out in one for good behavior. When Morris went back inside, Big G was a few days in.

"That cat knew shit, man," Big G cackled. "A lot of shit. Taught me how to clean my money." The big man opened his arms, and Romero knew he was talking of the building. "I have a piece of that bar. I own that pool hall and this butcher's shop. All my cash come in here and is squeaky clean and righteous for the man—yes sir!" More cackling from him. "When I put it all together that you and him hit that truck," he threw a thumb back at the gore, "I told myself to call Morris and ask him if he got his ends mixed in it, and I did, and we cleared the air. He said you were his pet, and I could keep that dead piece of shit back there's cut."

Romero drove with him back to the bar where Big G gave him use of his office phone and Romero called Morris updating him. Morris told him about Grandview keeping the stolen three hundred thousand Geiger had ripped off saying Big G wanted it for damages and to be honest, Romero told himself, he didn't care. He was just glad Geiger was gone.

He said goodbye to Big G and then drove to King's house and went around the block. When certain that no cops were around he parked at the back and went and found a still dead Cohn lounging on the chair. Only difference in appearance was the presence of flies on him, droning loudly, and that his propped up leg was pulled some back toward him from rigor mortis.

Romero dragged him into the house and put him beside Deltoro and King. Then he went around opening all the windows, upstairs and downstairs. He grabbed a newspaper and some magazines and other assorted papers and piled them around the bodies. He went into the garage and found a hose and he was off into the street. He siphoned gas out of a car a block away filling a used laundry detergent bottle. The bottle he found while rummaging for more refuse paper in the trash. At the house, he poured the gas on the bodies, dug into Cohn's pocket and found his lighter and dropped it. He watched the flames spread, and he made a fast stride out the backdoor.

He sat in his latest stolen car at the end of the block, another ancient vehicle, a car he targeted for hot wiring as newer models were too tough. He lamented the change of times where thieving was becoming considerably harder, and he saw the black smoke rising more thickly above the treetops in the pale early morning sky, and he drove off.

He slept and woke in the evening, deciding he could have a drink before he left.

He took the car to the upstairs restaurant and bar. He finally saw the name of the place which was *Shooter Bill's* and parked ahead of the streetlight making sure this time he was around when Sarah got off.

Romero tried looking for her, but she'd already left, and he drank awhile feeling lonesome. It used to be that drinking lifted every foul mood he was in, but it had yet to happen this time around and he had reached his limit in drinks where he knew any further he would be doubled over the next day. He paid leaving a healthy tip, and on his way he saw the news on the TV overhead. The cops bodies had been found. He broke into a light sweat moving faster toward the stairs and exit.

He was back on the road. The road was dark and largely abandoned. Just himself racing up with a gun and half a million dollars, the biggest score he had ever netted. Although it had put him well over the top, Romero only played with the weak thread of quitting the life. After this abysmal job, he certainly had critical thinking to do. He did have more than enough money at the moment, so there was that.

Take your time. After all, he thought. You're still young. And there's plenty of miles left on this dark road.

2

The card Score.

It was Monday, and Romero was waiting for his first client to arrive for their breakfast meeting. He took a table by the floor to ceiling window and watched the people out in the blaring sun parading on their standard normal lives of office work which was an abstraction to him.

Romero sat up when he saw the slim fellow with an accountant look about him come in. Dave Nelson was his name, and Romero hoped this job would prove promising.

"Hi. Romero, right?" Nelson sat across from him and put out his hand, which Romero shook.

"Can we order?" Romero asked. "I'm famished."

"Yes, sure," he nodded.

"What?" Romero asked, looking the client up and down.

"Nothing—just—you order. I'm not hungry." His client paled some.

"Fine," Romero responded, signaled a cute waitress and said, "Well now I'll take some bacon and eggs sunny side up and a tall glass of water with smaller glass of OJ. Thank you."

"No coffee?" she asked, smiling down on him.

"No coffee, thank you," Romero said, returning his own smile.

The waitresses turned heading off with the order.

"So what seems to be the issue here?" Romero asked Nelson. "Why don't you tell me exactly what it is I can do for you, Nelson."

Nelson said, "An ex-girlfriend has something I want back. Her name is Angie Summers. She is holding, in her safe, my prized collection of classic baseball cards. They are in mint condition and very rare. They are in her apartment and right now as we sit here she is looking for a buyer." Nelson's eyes became wide and he looked out at Romero with hope, wringing his hands and Romero thought he suddenly looked a lot older than when he walked in.

"I can take care of this, Nelson," Romero said. "Now give me her address and phone number. A picture if you have one. I want to know who to look out for when I hit the place."

"You can get them back for me?" Nelson, hope in his eyes.

"I'm an asset recovery specialist. I can recover anything of yours in someone else's possession." Romero waved his hand in a flourish. "It's what I do."

"Asset recovery specialist?" Nelson laughed. "Is that what you call yourself?"

Romero shrugged lazily tilting his head. His eyes hooded, and he gave a faint smile. "It's a lot better than thief or professional hoister. Asset recovery is better because it's not the truth but not a lie either."

"Huh," Nelson bobbed his head, nervously tapped his fingers on the table.

"Well I can't tell people I'm a thief now can I?" Romero gestured pointing the top of his pen at Nelson. "Now give me the info."

Romero wrote it all down on a notebook he pulled from his coat and listened closely to Nelson giving him the information: Address so he knew where to go, phone number so he could make sure the pad was empty by duplicitous calling, and picture, obviously so he could know who to look out for while going through the place.

Nelson told him his ex kept a green safe somewhere in her apartment and that he knew it was there but had never seen it. His ex, Angie, had it throughout their relationship and all the sudden it was gone. Nelson knew in his gut that the cards were in there. Wherever *there* was.

"Why did you two break up?" Romero asked, "She sleep with somebody else?"

"Other issues," Nelson waved further inquiries off.

Nelson knew the baseball cards had to be valuable because a pal of his from New Jersey had flipped out when he heard about the Mickey Mantle card he possessed. This friend said it had to be valuable, and convinced him that even if it weren't he shouldn't let his bitch of an ex-girlfriend deprive him of his boyhood collection. A gift his father had passed down to him. So no way he should let her pull that shit. He should man up and, in fact, there was a guy he knew who specialized in such matters, and would straighten it all out.

This friend had been the catalyst that had brought him his first client in asset recovery. In the underworld, such things happen in that manner. A guy knew a guy who knew of a guy and now go see this guy, and he'll give you a number, and he'll take care of it. In this case, Nelson was a recommendation from his booker Morris who was a known safe cracker who did time upstate. Romero had learned to be a better criminal from Morris, and while Morris kicked his feet up in semi-retirement he now ran clients over to Romero. It was Morris's idea, *thief for hire.* Morris with his criminal feelers out, would recommend his talents for hire all across the country. There were associates of his, glad to help and arrange clients to call for his and Morris's highly skilled assistance.

Asset recovery. When jobs weren't coming for scores around the country, this is what Romero would do. And maybe keep doing if he decided on retiring.

Romero didn't need the money. He was doing good. His last job was an armored truck and things had gone sideways. The crew got killed, and while it was plenty hairy,

Romero did walk away with half a million dollars. The money naturally laundered but boredom drew him to this notion of freelancing his talents. Romero admittedly thought it was insane, and for a while it looked as if everyone else on the grapevine thought so too, until Morris called saying an old associate of his had recommended Romero's services to a fell a named Nelson.

Romero took all the information down and stuffed the pad way.

Nelson pulled a picture from his wallet, looked sourly at it, and handed it over.

She was a golden blonde, her hair straight and seemed to glow in the sun. She sat smiling up toward the camera from behind the wheel of a car, whose door was neon blue. Her face was finely boned, and she seemed sharp somehow, intelligent.

"That's from when I bought her a new car," Nelson informed. "That was three months ago, I think."

"Okay." Romero shoved it in his pocket maybe too roughly for Nelson who winced. "Good."

The drinks arrived, and Romero again smiled up to the waitress, and in turn, she also smiled back down at him.

"I need those cards back," Nelson said. "I mean they're quite valuable to me.—A true treasure."

"You agree to the price?" Romero squinted at the man.

"Yes. I settled that with your man Morris," Nelson said anxiously.

"I'll have to mess up the place to make it look like a random robbery." Romero looked over his shoulders for eavesdroppers, and when he confirmed no one was listening he added, "I'll also have to steal some stuff other than the cards to throw her and the police off the track."

Nelson frowned, then, "Do what you must. I just want you to find that safe and get those cards back."

"Okay," Romero said, "Tell me though. How did you hear about Morris? You seem like a square guy and all. I don't see you associating with criminal types."

"I know, well," Nelson nodded, jittery. "I heard of him through Phillip Freemont.

It was when I was gambling in Atlantic City, and I told him the story. He recommended your associate. I called Morris and here we are."

Phillip Freemont was a fellow heister usually based, as Nelson said, in Atlantic City and Romero hadn't heard from him in a few years, and Freemont was, he considered, probably still shaken up about getting shot at on his last job. Apparently it was a card game, and one of the players was connected and pulled a piece and clipped him in the shoulder.

"Okay," Romero softly said, putting a hand on Nelson's shoulder. He squeezed. "I'll get your precious cards back. You agree to the fixed price correct?"

"Yes?" Nelson nodded. "10,000."

The food arrived. Romero waved Nelson off as his steaming plate was lowered in front of him. He told Nelson he would call when he did the job, or on the chance, he needed some other information. He went about eating and ignoring Nelson's presence expecting him to leave.

"One last thing," Nelson said.

"What?" Romero asked, shoveling food into his mouth.

"You should also be on the lookout for Paul." Nelson made a nervous fuss with his hands. "Should have told you about him, I'm sorry. Paul Lewis."

Romero put his fork down and sat back. "Paul who?"

"Okay." Nelson sighed, "Paul is her boyfriend. He—I'm certain knows all about the cards and is probably the one trying to get her to sell them because she didn't care an iota about them until she began screwing that loser."

"Will do then, Nelson." Romero chewed and once again began ignoring Nelson, waiting for his exit.

Dave Nelson dropped some money on the table and offered his hand and Romero shook it reluctantly. As Nelson turned to leave Romero said suddenly, uncertain if his typical cold manner being the best way to go with this client, "Sure you don't want to eat?"

"No. I'm buying your breakfast. Again…thank you," Nelson said.

"Sure thing, Nelson. Thanks a lot."

He watched Nelson leave. His head was down all the way out the door.

Romero climbed into the VW Beetle that was his standard ride in the city, and he drove into a neighborhood of row houses. He cut off into an alley between his building at the end of the street and the next neighborhood and walked to his door. It was a heavy green door with multiple locks. He used several keys to open. He entered his badly lit home, shutting the door behind him, and he walked down the flight of steps.

When down below he flicked the powerful overhead lights on.

His basement abode sat under the row house resided by a couple named Donaldson. He obviously had no windows at least not the standard type. The ones he had were frosted; thick that you could sometimes see warbled feet passing on the street above and these windows he covered with a small curtain set. He also had four cement pillars that stood solidly along the room and a cubicle that was supposed to be his bathroom. He had a shower and chipped toilet. A sink also, of course. His bed sat against the far wall, center. On either side were nightstands, and there was a large trunk filled with his clothes and other belongings.

He sat on a chair in front of his gunmetal desk then wheeled it over with his feet to his chest. He opened it and began picking out clothes for later. Romero tossed the clothes aside deciding on going in what he was wearing. He went through a phase of trying to look like a maintenance man while doing a B&E. But it felt downright silly and a real old school over-the-top crook type of thing to do. Best thing to wear honestly if you're going to knock over some small safe in some broad's apartment is standard street clothes, because the last thing you want is someone going, 'Oh yeah! I did see some guy,

Mr. Officer. He was wearing all black and carrying a toolbox and a duffel bag and, yeah he also was wearing a black knit cap, sir.'

He grabbed a beer from the fridge and lay back on his bed. After a few more minutes, he paced the floor thinking the job through and called Morris. They caught up on what each of them had been doing in between jobs and after the small talk was over Morris got to the point. "What kind of safe?" he asked.

Consulting his notes, Romero said, "Some small standard green box with dial and handle. Should be able to get through it easily. The client said the problem though is finding it. I might have to toss the place."

"A little apartment in the city? You'll find it. And if not you're as dumb as that client of ours. Want a drill?"

He thought it over and then decided if he needed a drill for the sad tin box she had hidden away in the pad of hers. "No thanks," he said.

"How small a safe?" Morris inquired, "Cause if you find it, you can run off with it."

"It's not so much the safe that's the job," Romero told him. "He can't look like he was responsible. I'm going to make it look like a typical burglary and trash the place."

"You going to tail the woman?"

"Yup."

"Where?"

"You never heard of it," Romero teased, then he told him.

"*Low Side Hang*," Morris said reverently. "Yeah, yeah I know of that place.

Though I don't see an old codger like me hanging there soon. So you're going to follow her to make sure she's at work and then shoot on over and knock the safe off?"

"As good as any plan," he said.

"And what does this client of ours want?"

"Baseball cards."

Morris snickered quietly over the phone. "Christ," he said.

"Client says they're very valuable."

"Well I love baseball and used to have a collection myself. Then ogling something day in and day out lost its appeal, and I went right to robbery. So this lady friend won't return the poor boy's cards?"

"Yup."

"Bitch should die," Morris said flatly. "They're like vampires you know?"

"Sure," was all Romero said knowing it was all shit talk. Morris was in reality a softie.

"Freemont recommended me," Romero told him.

"Freemont? Yeah. I remember that bum," Morris said. "Got shot by a wise guy, right?"

"That's him."

"Wonder why he wants to do you this favor?" Morris mused.

He got off the phone with Morris on the suggestion that they would do lunch soon, and he wondered on what to wear. He put the TV on for background noise and didn't really get into any of the programs or advertisements and then would turn off the TV at night-fall, and he would head out to case the girlfriend of his client where he would then do a reconnaissance of her place.

When television lost its appeal, and he had a little more time, Romero called an old school chum. When she didn't answer he checked the time figuring she was out at one of her experimental social events. She had taken up knitting. It had been a book club before that, but she didn't care for the attitude there.

"What kind of attitude?" Romero had asked over the phone.

"It was *Crime and Punishment* we were reading," she said. "They got judgmental with me when I wanted Rasky—that's what I called him—to not get caught or turn himself in."

Romero was glad to hear her say that.

Her name was Sarah Medlow, and he had a sort of reunion with her during his last job. They had caught up with each other and even though in school they weren't friends they had spent some time talking about this and that person. Romero had discussed with Sarah the smallest detail of what he remembered about his one semester there and they had kept in touch just keeping each other updated on as much of their life as they possibly could. For Romero, this was hard because most of his life was involved in criminal circles and so Sarah only knew of him as a business owner living in Philadelphia. They didn't know why they kept calling each other across state lines, but they did. Maybe it was because, as Romero figured, they were both loners. Romero hadn't had a girlfriend in a while and Morris was a friend but not the kind you saw every day. Morris was plenty happy living his old codger life and manning his phone at his house in a charming neighborhood and then afterword he would walk to the corner bar where his every day friends were waiting. Morris had said some of his friends were retired ex-cops. They would talk the hours away and drink and eat there, and Morris was plenty happy with it. As far as Romero knew the old man had never been married nor had any kids.

He didn't want to say it, but the idea of him ending like that scared the shit out of him.

There was Big G, Emmet Grandview, a pimp and drug dealer who now resided in Philadelphia. Romero had also met him on that nightmare of a last job. He had watched Big G wielding a chainsaw and delivering his own form of justice to a neo-Nazi who had raped and killed one of his girls. Big G kept the three hundred grand this Neo-Nazi named Geiger stole, and he packed up himself and moved to Philadelphia where he did mostly the same, except with more of an image of respectability. Big G drove a Lexus and wore elegant suits now. His smile is now more convincing, and he managed to find a way to hide the savagery in it. And even though Romero hung with Big G at one of his clubs in the city occasionally they weren't exactly tight. Big G was too blood hungry for Romero who saw him as pulling with his own gravity a tremendous amount of violence.

Romero, on the other hand, lived peacefully after jobs and was, in the words of an old girlfriend, incredibly boring.

Romero tried Sarah again and nothing. He tried her cell but hung up before it rang not wanting to interrupt whatever group she was trying to fit in. He just saw her in his mind awkwardly trying to either shut her phone or answer it while people in said group watched her resentfully because she had broken the vibe of whatever they were absorbed in together.

Knitting group? Yeah, he remembered. He then checked the time and saw he had to go out anyway.

Romero stepped into the lit neon blue foyer of *Low Side Hang* and ahead beyond the glass double doors lay more of the same lighting, and he pushed passed the doors and found the bar up ahead, thankfully lit properly. Off to the left was a section where round tables were grouped, and these tables with their white linen were now blue with the lighting. At their center was a candle holder that glowed lighted smiling faces in discussion. A woman clapped her hands, laughing and nodding, at something someone said at her table.

Romero sat up on a stool and immediately a slender woman dressed in black, and her hair no longer the gold but flaxen color, arrived in front of him from behind the bar. "What would you like?" Angie Summers asked.

"Whatever's on tap," he replied.

Angie returned with a glass and set it down in front of him, and he watched her depart to another stool beside the register where she sat crossing her legs, and looked out toward the tabled area. She just seemed to be watching and waiting.

Romero sipped at his beer.

The bar was occupied by two other people. One a guy with long hair scribbling into a book, and a black woman drinking red wine and playing with her phone.

Romero thought on it carefully. It was 8:30 on a school night. The place wasn't likely to start getting any busier, so he took another sip of beer and said, "Excuse me."

Angie didn't seem to hear as she began playing with a lock of her hair absently as she continued looking off. "Excuse me!" he called louder, and then Angie turned her head seeing him with a far off expression on her face. She seemed to remember where she was and jumped off her stool and began walking over.

"Sorry," she said. "How can I help you?"

"Well I'm looking for Paul who works here. Do you know a Paul?"

Angie nodded, "Yes. He's my boyfriend. He's not here tonight. It's slow so…"

"I understand." Romero nodded understanding now that she met him on the job.

"How do you know Paul?" she asked.

"Honestly," he said searchingly, "I don't…I don't exactly remember. You see I was stone faced drunk."

"Oh," she nodded.

"Yeah I was drunk, and Paul, he helped me out."

"You just wanted to *thank him*," she leaned her head back just getting it. "I understand. Okay."

"I'll guess I'll stop in some other time to offer my thanks."

Angie leaned toward him on the bar, her arms crossed, "You can come back Friday. It's *super* busy, and he'll definitely be here."

"So he works nights like you?"

"Yeah," she said, "It's the best time to bartend. There's a lot of business."

"Well," Romero stood up and went through his wallet. "Here," he threw a twenty down. "Keep the change. And ask him if he remembers, will you?"

"Yeah. Okay." Angie scooped up the twenty.

He drove.

He sat out in his beetle with the interior lights off and watched Angie Summers apartment from the street. His gear loaded up and waiting.

The lights were on in one room, which he guessed, was the living room. Romero wondered if he could get inside. Maybe even knock and see who answered. He sat and thought of his options in the tranquil and dark interior of his car. This was also what he liked about this job and he couldn't help but think of how much fun he was having.

It was ridiculous. He was sitting back in the night just watching. Just watching his target's place. Even though he had a laugh it was essential. Sometimes you came up with something that was imperative when casing a place. Other times it was as straightforward as it seems, but you always had to case the place beforehand. For example, he now knew the building had no security cameras or alarm systems.

There was something oddly terrific about sitting off in his car. Just waiting for whatever came next. He couldn't understand the compulsion to work some lousy soul crushing standard job in the city where he would just sit in some office all day; or do what his father did working in the freezers cutting meat day in and day out, earning peanuts for the many hours of strenuous labor.

As he sat behind the wheel, he looked for *the whatever* that would come and make his job breaking into her pad a challenge. *This whatever* came in the form of a shadow moving across the window shades. Romero sat up. Nelson didn't live with Angie anymore, so that ruled him out. It was Paul of course. He was off tonight lounging around his girl's place.

Not tonight.

He started up the bug and took off giving himself another night before he hit the place.

Sarah said, about her quilting group, "I was surprised by the number of men there."

"Really?"

"And we all met at this lady's bookstore, sitting at this long table—"

"Just knitting?"

"Just knitting—"

"And there was a lot of men?"

"Well, not a lot, I should say," she laughed, "Just more than I expected—and some young too—and they didn't seem gay and I know that's a stereotype."

Romero lay on his back on the bed, phone to ear and writing pad on his stomach, which he would toss a look at, occasionally. On the pad was Nelson's info scribbled down from their meeting. Romero said, "I had this hell of a day chasing down this lead."

Through a mouthful of something she said, "I thought you said you were hanging it up."

"What are you eating? Cookies?"

"Yeah," she coughed and laughed. "Sorry."

"No it's fine it was just unexpected. Anyhow, um, but this lead looks promising."

"Promising?" she skeptically wondered.

"Well I'm watching carefully now," he told her. "I won't do anything just yet.

And, anyway, what I'm doing now is low risk compared to what I used to do."

"Meaning? What?"

"Well if I lose anything it won't be much at all."

She hummed enigmatically, and he wondered if his investor con backfired. Had he expected her to know so little about investing that he had exposed his fraudulent self?

Sarah then told him, "I have a bad feeling about this, Alex."

It pleased him to have a conversation with someone for a change who he was on a first name basis with. Typical encounters with associates was to call each other by a last name or even some alias. Even Morris didn't call him Alex except after that last soured job involving the armored truck. He patted him on the shoulder after Romero gave him his payment for setting up the job, and the old man pinched his cheek and laughed offering him a beer, which Romero took, recounting the job more fully and Morris told him that he was sorry the job went to such shit and had used his name in the interval.

How odd it sounded coming from his lips.

"You have a bad feeling?" he repeated.

"I'm not psychic, but I listen to my gut. And my gut did not like hearing about this lead you've been following."

"You're sure it's not the cookies?" he said.

"You're bored," she countered. "We talked about how we should try filling some of that void in our lives, remember?"

"Yes," he said, "You're right, and you've been doing that with your book club and now the knitting circle and hopefully one of them will take. As for me, I can't see myself in a book club, I read, but I can't see myself having some in depth discussion about the moral ambiguity you felt when reading *Crime and Punishment*." He sighed. "Nor can I see myself knitting either. I'm sure a man can knit as good as a woman, and I'm not bulking at the activity as a man, seeing as I'm hardly a sports fan, and I go blank when some standard Joe tries to engage me in baseball talk when I'm trying to enjoy my beer in a bar. It's just as a man there aren't many options when you're not social. Women are expected to be timid in interacting, but not men so there's no apparatus really for us."

He thought for a moment. "Not that I'm timid either. I can carry myself confidently I just don't connect with other people well. I always feel like people see me as some alien disguising himself as a person and doing a lousy job of it. Also, I'm not exactly miserable. I have enough money, although I'm not insanely wealthy, but I'm comfortable. I'd say I date pretty infrequently and though none of the relationships went anywhere I've never been heartbroken. I'm no stud, and yet I manage to meet women I find attractive, and I can charm them, even though I don't feel authentic when I'm doing it. Sorry Sarah," he suddenly said. "Didn't expect to go on."

"Are you kidding!? This is great! Keep going!" she chortled encouragingly.

"I'll say this though," he grinned.

"What?"

"I felt pretty authentic letting it out. Opening the dam like that. I didn't expect to say so much about myself."

"Feel pretty good?"

"Christ I feel like a weight has lifted."

Before they said goodnight, and ended the call, she repeated her unpleasant feeling about his current gig.

"It's nothing," he tried convincing her.

"Just promise me you'll listen to your gut. Okay?"

"I can do that," he told her. "I'll take a moment to listen to it. See how it reads the situation."

"I'm being serious, are you being serious?" He could see her finger pointing at him across the phone lines.

"Yes. I'm being deathly serious."

After he hung up, he looked down at his gut. It wasn't much of one as he managed to stay in some reasonably decent shape. He saw less gut and more of the pad just lying there, and he lifted it once again, and read through it. All he felt was the ridiculousness of the job and yet the excitement that built inside him when he considered how much fun he'd been having.

Jesus, Romero thought to himself, *Why did I say all of that?*

Romero woke up and rolled over to shut his alarm off. He sat on the bed and smoothed his tie as he often slept in his clothes. He yawned, tasting paste in his mouth, and he stood slowly and shuffled to the bathroom where he brushed, and urinated while groaning loudly.

He went outside and locked up. He crossed over to his beetle to case out Angie Summer's place, and make damn sure no one was there, so he can get to the safe. He was mildly irritated that this woman would be so bitter as to keep something that didn't belong to her in the first place.

He got to her pad and waited, not five minutes, before she appeared and he followed her to North St. where the university was located. He pulled up next to the park a little off campus and he wandered to a tree-lined street, heavily shaded by the leaves. It was hot out. The sun was glaring overhead. Romero loosened the collar of his wrinkled shirt as he ambled on.

He followed her from a safe enough distance and then she began climbing the steps up to a building. He waited for a few cars to pass, and then he crossed over following a brick wall until he came to a column which he casually stepped behind and leaned against.

Romero watched peeking around the column as Angie sat on the top step. She was engaged in some conversation smiling and nodding in perpetual agreement with the petite brunette sitting beside her, and then he observed them, after a few minutes, getting up and climbing the rest of the way where Angie pulled one of the blue steel doors open, and they vanished passed it.

He waited there for almost two hours when the blue doors opened and groups of women and some men, somewhat effeminate, came climbing down the steps. Angie was talking to the petite brunette again this time more seriously, and he gave them wide berth as they continued farther away from North St.

He figured he could have knocked off the safe in the space of time, but he wanted to know her routine pat, so he wouldn't make any mistakes. Romero wasn't about to do anymore jail time and even though he had some fun playing the spy now, he wasn't about to take any unnecessary risks, or stop from being the critical professional he thought of himself as.

And yet he wasn't being professional. Was he? He considered this as he followed them, and if they caught sight of him then they would have seen the scowl that popped onto the blank canvas of a face where feeling and thoughts were usually an improbability to read. Most people thought he looked tired or bored. He didn't like what he was thinking, but he did. He was taking a risk. He was prolonging this. And it was because it was fun!

Some professional, he scolded himself.

Angie and the petite brunette stopped into a cafe not a few blocks down. He took a position behind a waist high brick divide, and as he casually could, he watched them both through the glass as they sat at a table with their drinks. Their conversation seemed a lively one as both of them would laugh out loud and tilt their heads back.

Eventually, he watched as Angie went back toward North St. and the petite brunette the other way. He waited out the distance and then took off across the street and tailed. She got into her small neon blue car and took off, but he didn't need to follow her in his car. He knew she was going to work the 11 AM shift today when the bar opened.

She would also later man the bar at 10 PM to 2 AM.

A hell of a work schedule, he said to himself.

He didn't want to wait anymore. He would do now what he should have done while she was in the class that extended period instead of playing James Bond and wasting his client's time.

Romero pulled to the curb outside of Angie's apartment, and he casually walked with duffel bag over his shoulder. He discreetly scanned around for any possible eyewitnesses. He buzzed her pad. After waiting and buzzing for one minute, he went around back and climbed up to a dumpster, the duffel hefty over his shoulder. He jumped some feet to the fire escape. He tried the fire emergency door. It opened easily. He stepped into the hall brazen.

If Paul were there? He was either dead or deaf. Considering that he most likely wasn't deaf, or a corpse he would assume, quite accurately, that he was out.

Romero climbed the steps and tried to be as quiet as humanly possible. When he reached the fourth floor, he stood like a statue, waiting outside the door listening. He knocked and when he was certain it wasn't currently occupied he picked the lock with his kit. He worked it open and slipped in, closing it right behind him.

It was a small place and painted white, and beyond an archway, there was an even smaller kitchen where a smaller Formica table sat. He bypassed the kitchen and immediately crossed into the narrow hall to the door beyond.

The bedroom was a cubby hole where most of the space seemed to be occupied mostly by the bed at its center. He went to the dresser drawer setting aside his duffel.

He then carefully opened the drawers where he sifted through underwear. Like in most drawers there's the occasionally misplaced piece of clothing. The miscellaneous odd and end, but nothing else of interest. He tried fixing it so that it looked undisturbed before closing it.

He prowled the closet on his knees, and he found no safe but a strongbox. He searched and searched, and the only thing present, was this box. Romero considered that she could have decided to move the contents and place them elsewhere, noticing that the safe was not only unnecessary, but impractical. It must have taken up space in this little bedroom—and hell, this freakishly tiny apartment. The strongbox was one of those fireproof ones. Romero examined the lock, pulled his picks out and began to work the tines in. He tried each one of them until he found the one that offered a satisfying clicking sound from the lock. He popped the box's lid up, showing a bunch of envelopes, where instead of baseball cards, were a bunch of pictures; family, friends, lovers? He searched further and even more thoroughly but alas, no cards.

He stood thinking by the window and then turned, leaning against the wall. With two fingers, he yanked the shades down and peered down into the street. The coast was clear. He didn't see her car, so he let the blinds go. He squinted down at her bed, which had been haphazardly made. He knelt beside it and dug his hands under, feeling around for anything. He gripped something and pulled it out and was greeted with a pink vibrator, which he dropped to the mattress with not even a flicker of amusement or incredulity. He put it back and went to the sink in the bathroom where he washed his hands. Back in the bedroom, he gave the place a thorough search, knocking on the walls for any hollow spots that he deemed suspicious and he checked under the bed and dug around for any hidden spaces in the closet and came up with zilch.

He called Nelson who was working and obviously preoccupied as Nelson asked Romero to hold for a few moments and finally returned with a series of questions, asking what Romero found. Suddenly a car's tires squealed outside and on guard, Romero just said they should meet. Nelson numbly agreed and Romero hung up on him. He went again to the window to peek down at the street. It was still clear, so he let himself give the apartment a grid search. Romero examined the surface of the walls. The blue panty that was on the floor. There was a cigarette butt in an ashtray on the nightstand. Eventually back in the bedroom, he lifted the occasional odd and end on the dresser. He read some of the labels on her assorted eye shadow containers and blush assortments. After checking the time, Romero went to the window and watched the street for her car.

He stepped out of the room, closing the bedroom door behind him. He caught himself and returned for his duffel and then proceeded to walk into the living room where Romero then pressed his ear against the door to the hall listening for any sounds.

One noise greeted him. It was the creaking of a door on its hinges and footsteps walking along outside. Romero heard a muttering, a female voice griping bitterly about something and the only word discernible as the voice along with the footsteps got close to the door was, *'Harlot.'* This older woman outside then seemed to have dropped something on the floor, the other side of Angie's apartment door. He listened closely as the feet wandered off patting back further up the hall. He listened to the creak of the door hinge again and finally the sound of the door all together slamming shut and a bolt being thrown in a lock.

Shutting the door behind him, Romero cast wary glances down the hall and then downward to find a small pile of envelopes. Obviously the woman was angry she had received some of Angie's mail.

He realized he would find nothing. Eventually he shook his head at his client.

Nelson had made some mistake and he would have to tell him of that.

In the car, he took a drive around the block and sniffed in aggravation and headed off.

He would deliver the grim news to Nelson unless of course, he came up with a startling clue as to where the safe was. Otherwise, Romero could check out hobby shops for some other something to fill his days and nights of semi-retirement.

Romero waited for Nelson who appeared out of his office building's lobby.

Nelson wandered, stopped squinting in the bright sun in front of him and then behind him. Romero honked the horn and Nelson saw him, waved awkwardly, before running and joining Romero sitting beside him in the passenger seat of his VW Beetle.

"Want to get something to eat?" Romero asked.

Nelson was too nervous to eat, he said. "You couldn't find the safe?" Nelson blurted out, confused and disappointed after Romero recounted his circuit of her place.

"There was a strong box, but that was all." He put up a hand to stop him before he started. "I checked. And there was nothing in the box, except pictures."

"Well, I know it's in her apartment," Nelson said trying, seemingly, to convince himself.

"Doesn't seem to be," Romero with a finger tapping the wheel while enjoying his favorite sport, people watching.

Nelson looked at him with confidence, and replied, "They are there. I know it. So what do we do?"

"Do what?" Romero now baffled and wanting to leave. "Spy on her twenty-four hours? Set up a camera to watch her and make sure she isn't socking them away in some bat cave like Bruce Wayne?"

Nelson, the ballsy prick, said, "Why not?" with a look of cold calculation that made Romero feel momentarily back in his old life of dealing with heist men. All of the sudden, Romero put his palm on his stomach and felt some unease.

"I have money," Nelson proclaimed.

"I didn't say you didn't. Well, you're the boss."

So, Romero and Nelson continued discussing what was to be done. They finally came to an agreement that Romero would be paid to keep watch on her until she revealed where in the home she kept the cards. Nelson knew they were there but hopefully with a camera rig, any nook or cranny would be found to be the location.

"Probably not there," Romero said as Nelson put a hand on the door handle to leave. "She must have sold them already. The place is too small. No safe. I'm telling you they're gone."

"She didn't sell them," Nelson said, stern and colder than before. "I'll pay what you want. Just watch her." Outside he turned back to Romero, "And if they're not? I'll pay you to watch that asshole Paul." Then Nelson shut the door firmly.

He watched Nelson walk back to the building with swagger and now Romero's gut bubbled with intensity as if his intuition was trying to speak to him.

He called Morris. They spoke while Romero untangled the fiber optic camera's long cord. He had purchased it an hour ago.

"Where'd you get it?" Morris asked him, munching on chips of some sort.

"This place that sells shit to private investigators and husbands worrying about their cheating wives and wives worrying about their husbands."

"Give me a name pal, I want to check this place out."

"Dickhead security," Romero dryly said.

"Dickhead?—Oh, you're being an asshole. I don't understand why even take this job?" Morris complained, "Pull the plug and fuck it, we'll wait until something else comes along."

"I took this job because I'm bored," Romero said. "I kind of like the challenge this has turned into. Not to mention he's offering more money if I stay on and find the cards."

Romero twisted the head of the cable with the fisheye lens this way and that way and watched in the monitor as the room twirled with it. The images were sent via a transmitter and he became suddenly aware that now he was spending his own money for what would probably be a one of a kind type job. Then admiring the set up of this device he realized he couldn't be sorry about buying this cool gadget and who knows, it could be a godsend later on.

"You there?" Morris sang.

"Yeah. Just testing the gizmo."

"So you bought that thing to work this one gig?" Morris coming up late in his observation.

"It's no different than any other job I get contracted to do. You have to knock someplace off, you need to bankroll it first. For guns and explosives and all other kinds of stuff. It's the same here."

"Alright," Morris conceded. "Listen. There's a job in Houston in three weeks."

"Oh?"

"Yeah, it's coming from Baker and that black asshole, Father Garrison. They want to know if you want in?"

"Baker? What is it?"

"Something about a distributer of illicit substances having a counting room for his ill got gains. The three of you and the figures run from about half to one million."

"I'm going to pass," Romero said surprising himself. "I'm sticking with this relaxing and not taking risks anymore. I'll do this boneheaded job, and probably not do anymore after. Had some fun but I got to find cleaner, less destructive ways, to have some fulfillment."

A short pause and Morris said, "Christ! You done Mr. Enlightenment?"

He had rigged the fiber optic cable along her bedroom doorway, it blended with the dark wood. The wire was thin, rendering it to be almost invisible, aside from the protrusion at the top which was the lens. This lens had to be positioned properly for the bedroom to be front and center. The battery that was attached was harder to hide, but Romero managed to snake it behind her dresser and whether or not she saw a thin cord, only two feet of it visible was something he would have to leave to chance.

In a week, if Angie didn't reveal where the secret nook and safe were kept whatever cleverly hidden panel, than he would position the fish-eye camera, elsewhere.

He wandered downtown and ate lunch and stopped by a bar and had two beers and meditated on the counting room job he had dismissed and wished he didn't feel lousy for doing so. Father Garrison and Baker *were* a good team.

His first run with a crew had ended with arrests and their going away to other prisons. It wasn't their first offense by a long shot, and he hadn't seen them since. If they were still in the life, *"doing jobs"*, then he never encountered them, although he couldn't see why not; more likely they were still inside serving their longer sentences.

Houston, Texas? Christ, he thought.

Romero got back to his car and took the long way home. When he arrived it was then that some feeling, some instinct, came to him though it wasn't his gut. He went to his trunk and knelt down; popped it open and dug around pulling out a burlap bag that was buried at the very bottom. He carried its considerable weight to the gunmetal desk and worked loose the thread string sealing it shut and pulled the mouth open to reveal guns gleaming black and silver and chrome. Revolvers and pistols. He fussed over which one to take and fought to understand why he felt he needed one in the first place.

However, after deciding to trust his instincts, he settled on the 1911 Springfield with a seven-round capacity. He checked the clip, found it was empty. He stuck his hand at the bottom of the bag feeling along and found the boxes of ammunition.

He stuck the gun in the small of his back and stood momentarily in thought. He titled his head and then he nodded at the small satisfaction of having the gun. It occurred to him that the odd nature of this job had put him on edge. He would obey his inner guidance system and carry the heat.

Romero swung by for the van and the keys were waiting for him behind a rear tire. The manager of the garage he had a stake in chewed on a Twizzler, pretending he didn't see him do this. He would also pretend he didn't know why the van mysteriously appeared parked outside the lot come morning.

Outside her place, Romero drank beer in the back of the van stuffing the discarded bottles into an empty milk crate he had earlier used to prop a foot on as he kept watching. Kept waiting.

He struck gold around 2: 15 AM while he lay in the back of the white and paneled van. He felt more than pleasant from the drinks, and although he was enjoying looking at the monitor, all bright in the darkened interior, it was difficult with his eyelids feeling like heavy iron gates calling to be lowered. The small monitor was rigged with its own VHS recorder/player. The tape was inside unmoving as he didn't need it at the moment.

Might be if she spontaneously began unlocking the safe and he needed various viewings to jot the combination down. If he got his hands on that safe. If there is one.

Finally, Angie and Paul appeared in the bedroom, and Romero propped up on an elbow. The images broadcasted via transmitter back to the monitor. He took note of Paul Lewis and found him not that far off looking from Nelson. He was another blonde guy with a blandness to him.

They were disrobing. He sat back. He was finding it hard to keep his eyes open.

He made himself stand a moment before hunkering down on his ass. The pressure to close his eyes was too strong.

They began having sex and Romero watched, his mind on the counting room score that would be going down without him. He wouldn't do it he told himself. He considered that maybe, he had an addiction. He wasn't going to take a chance with his freedom anymore on some thrill.

I have money, he thought. I have investments that I let grow for me. I live comfortably. I will always be able to pay my bills. I'm not exceedingly wealthy, I don't need to be. I don't need flashy things. Romero wondered if he were a hoarder. He thought that would be something pleasant to talk to Sarah about. Maybe the reason he wanted to keep investing was because he couldn't have enough money.

Christ, and they were still having sex.

He walked, hunching himself passed the heavy curtain that separated the back cabin to the driver's seat. Outside past the windshield it was still plenty dark and no one seemed about and up ahead there was traffic going north and south.

Romero returned to the monitor and Angie and Peter were now standing facing each other and they were mostly dressed. Paul was about to put on his shirt and Angie was hiking up her jeans and in a bra.

Romero watched them now via their reflection in the mirror over her dresser. He had a better view of them as they stood in some dialogue with each other about whatever these two seemingly uninteresting people talked about.

Something seemed to alarm Angie and Peter on the monitor as he studied their reflection. Their heads whipped around toward the bedroom door which was still closed.

Peter shot Angie a look and slowly began to lower his shirt back over his stomach, fuzzy patch of hair, blond, adorning it. He then cautiously treaded to the door where he cracked it open.

Peter gave Angie a look, his face was pale, and his jaw slack. Silently he told her something that had Angie racing around the bed to the phone on her nightstand.

Romero suddenly thought, Nelson if you ruin this— but he didn't get to finish his thought.

Bullet holes peppered the door and Peter was riddled with wounds that had him dancing back and back, blood whipped on the bed as slugs ravaged the door and Peter— poor Peter behind it. He fell on his back. His shirt was blood soaked and his eyes emptily staring toward Romero, center on the monitor. Angie, her mouth open, in complete silent horror could only gaze shocked and still at the corpse who lay on her bed a blood ruined mess. In the monitor, the reflection showed the bullet ravaged door slowly swing open.

Romero could tell now that this dark blue ski masked man wasn't Nelson. The man was squat and muscular looking, but it could have been the teamster jacket he was wearing and the baggy black dress pants. He held an Uzi fixed with a sausage looking sound suppressor and he inched his way into the room.

The killer stopped when he saw Peter, dead, bloodied Peter, on the bed. His head swiveled to Angie, her hands waving lazy jazz hands in defense. He cut her down too with a few rounds that trailed up from her waist to her neck the walls turning crimson. A scene as in an abattoir. Blood dripped in tendrils down the wall. She slid down. Her head rolling coming to a rest against the bed post. This squat killer gave both bodies a look over and with a hand he scratched himself over the ski mask. He seemed to be perplexed.

He kept scratching himself. Romero could see the pinkie ring he was wearing.

Romero watched through the reflection in the blood dotted mirror past the perforated doorway. It was open enough to allow him to see this unexpected guest whiz by the bathroom and then to the kitchen where he swerved around the table and stopped in the living room where he dropped to a knee and roughly tossed aside the Persian carpet and Romero saw the glint of a knife as he popped the floor boards up; one then two and three. This killer hefted out the green safe, and Romero mentally kicked himself for underestimating Angie's ingenuity. He watched as the killer replaced the boards and carpet and took off.

Romero needed his camera equipment back, he knew it, and so he pulled his gun and checked the chamber for a round which was ready. He again passed through the curtain and climbed on the driver's seat where he gave the street a scan before climbing out the van. He gently shut the door and circled around, the gun held low against his thigh.

He peered into the lit foyer from behind the glass pane. He was greeted by a clear coast, he tried the handle and pulled, the door opening easily. He knelt and inspected the lock. It was damaged somehow and kneeling further on both knees, he fingered the broken remnants of the locking bar. He knew from his own experience that it had been zapped with what probably was a can of suppressed air.

On holding it upside down you could easily turn a can of suppressed air for keyboard dust and debris removal into an efficient freeze and smash tool for locks. What this asshole must have done was sprayed between the lock and the doorway. Then with a chisel and one good, hard whap, shatter the bar allowing him access into the foyer.

Romero carefully with his gun arm extended way ahead of him began to climb the stairs. Sounds from the street were audible. As Romero climbed, the source was revealed.

It was the fire escape door. It was propped open with a fire ax of all things, that lay on the ground keeping the door open. He crept over and sucked in air and swung the gun and himself out the doorway. The roof next door, tarred and barren, the top branches of a tree a block away and the night lights and the sky was all he could see. Below him, stairs lowered and empty.

The shooter was gone.

On the fourth floor now he caught sight of the open door next to Angie's. A pair of feet poked out. Bare feet. Old feet, toes toward the ceiling. He silently wandered closer keeping his ears sharp. He wondered if he had ducked into the old woman's apartment and for all he knew the bastard was still in there. His escape was ready and waiting.

Romero couldn't see it. He got to the doorway and sucked air once again and twirled in gun up almost tripping over the old prune's wrinkled feet.

The interior was empty and silent. A quiet picture flickered on the television set.

The green word, MUTE, on the lower left of the screen. Below him, the old woman lay, butterfly wings of blood around her, her chest punched with holes. A scattering of brass discarded shells lay by her on each side and some well into the apartment along the wall.

Speculating, he supposed that this squat, teamster jacketed killer, must have leaned into the doorway firing into her. The shells must have hit the door and bounced off and over the gun into the apartment.

Romero continued on to Angie's where he toed the door open bringing his gun up. He bolted in and swept the gun over the room finding no one. With his heel, he eased the door closed behind him and jogged toward and passed the kitchen. In the darkened, narrow corridor, he pushed into the bedroom through the perforated door.

He listened for sirens, when nothing greeted his ears he moved.

He got his camera and fumbled with the battery pack and transmitter housing wedged behind the dresser—with his fingerprints on them—and he rolled it up over his shoulder.

He looked at Angie lying by the wall, ravaged by rounds, and her eyes were open.

She was staring out at him, her face seemed to question.

He had his own questions.

A brief conversation between other tenants on the floor below stopped him. He eyed the open fire exit and made his escape that way. He shoved his gun into his pocket and keeping the strictest eye out, he walked casually to the van. As far as he could tell, he made it without a single eye on him and climbed behind the wheel, slowly pulling out.

Romero considered it a healthy sign that he was three blocks away when the blaring sirens and flashing lights of squad cars passed him on his way home.

He drove the speed limit.

He parked the van outside the auto lot fence, left the recording equipment inside, and slipped the keys back where he had found them and jogged north. All the while, he considered how much of a problem Nelson could be when the police ask him about his dead ex. How much pressure could he take from them? Five or maybe six blocks ahead lay the elevated platform where he could catch the L train. From there he would have to walk three blocks to his place.

Romero pulled out his cell and stopped on the dark sidewalk under a streetlamp.

He changed his mind and instead continued further on until at the end of the block he came to a solitary pay phone. He had no change and wandered across the street to a gas station and broke a one for quarters, and back at the phone he called Nelson's number.

Nelson groggily answered, "Yes?"

"It's me! We have to meet now!" Romero urgently pressed.

"Uh, oh, okay. Fine. Where?"

Nelson pulled his car slowly into the abandoned parking lot behind the shut down *Shoe Depot.* It was a private place blocked off from the street and the building shielded them plenty. There was also a high chain-link fence with green life overgrowing behind it blocking off view from the homes that lined the street beyond.

Romero jogged over, and when Nelson parked he popped in sitting shotgun.

"Well?" Nelson asked. "What's the emergency?"

Romero observed Nelson, scrutinizing him. "You tell anybody that you hired me?"

Nelson looked befuddled. He frowned, shook his head and said, "No. What's going on?—Why see me so late? You found the safe, or you didn't. So what's the problem here?" Nelson, his face too pale even in the dark interior. Romero could see the blood leaving it and he knew.

"Listen to me closely, Nelson. You got something you got to tell me, huh? You hire anybody else out? Tell me Nelson."

Nelson, his eyes like saucers, breathed heavily and he made himself close his eyes. He took three deep breaths followed by three deep inhales. Romero allowed patience and just watched his tensely coiled client. Nelson managed eye contact and took some tone of challenge in his voice. He said, "Yes. Yes I did."

"Okay." Romero sighed, "Why?"

"The guy who recommended your services?"

"Yeah? Freemont. What about him?"

"It was his idea," Nelson still and suddenly exhausted looking, his torso hunching in his seat. "He called me up and said he wanted to meet, so I said yes. He played it like he wanted to be buddy-buddy, but I knew he wanted to gear up to something."

Romero nodded at Nelson then made a motion for him to keep going.

Nelson continued: "He said it was the perfect set up. He said it would be better if when you hit the place, he came in and killed everybody. That he would get the cards out of there and make it look like the robbers turned on each other." Nelson, his eyes bulging as if realizing his intent by consenting to the plan. He swallowed and went on saying, "It was supposed to throw suspicion off of me."

"How'd he know I would get the cards? I didn't even know where they were. He did. And how did he know?"

"He already found them after you first went in. He told me everything. About you going up the fire escape. When you came down later, he went in the same way you did."

Nelson tried not to smile. "Said he found the safe the moment he felt the floor underneath him coming into the living room. Said he could have gotten the cards then, but Paul started coming in. So he hid waiting for him to go in the back, then he went out the door.

He would have killed Paul and taken out the safe, but he said he wanted you there."

"What else?" Romero probed. "He didn't think I found the cards?"

"He followed you." Nelson shrugged wearily. "He knew you didn't find the cards the moment he saw us talking in your car. Saw how upset I was."

"What else?"

"He called earlier and said you had gotten a van. He checked through the windshield where it was parked outside her place. Said you weren't there."

"Assuming I found out where the safe was. That I was knocking it off," Romero finished. "I was in the van. In the back. Behind the curtain watching the monitor.

Remember? I was going to spy on her and see where she hid the safe? But you had to rush, now this idiot Freemont is going down for murder. He'll take you down with him and then my name is going to get caught up in this."

Nelson began to shake uncontrollably, he sniffled, and a sob escaped him. He bit on a knuckle and shut his eyes to block the tears.

"How much you paying him?" Romero asked. "Double?" Still Nelson just sobbed.

"Where's he staying? He's here in the city correct?" Romero asked feeling empty all of a sudden. Feeling robotic. Feeling nothing but the cold clarity.

"He's staying at the Stratford Hotel." Nelson wiped his eyes with the back of his hands, lips quivering.

"Room?"

"Number 311."

"Alone?"

"Yes. I mean, I guess."

"Thanks. Now listen here..." Romero made to whisper into Nelson's ear turning fully toward him, his mouth working; then with startling speed he rabbit punched Nelson in the throat making the other man's eyes bulge, and Nelson leaned his head croaking toward the steering wheel. Romero slid behind him putting one arm on his chest and with the other he brought his hand up cupping Nelson's chin and with one swift, hard twist, he broke Nelson's neck, a low crunch sound filling the interior of the car.

Romero sat back and exhaled loudly. He checked around him and found they were still alone—well actually he was still alone now and he supposed he wasn't getting paid for the whole damn exercise.

He began the process of moving dead Nelson from the front seat to the back. He had taken off Nelson's coat and draped it over him just stopping it under his nose. If for whatever reason the police were to pull him over or pass an interested look into the interior, the only thing they would see in the back is a sleeping companion, probably drunk.

Nelson poor old Nelson, Romero thought. But Nelson wouldn't be alone. There was another body that had to drop and maybe he would vanish two of them in the same deep hole in the earth somewhere.

It was easy to get access to the construction area of the new addition that was being built.

There was one guard booth manned by a large black woman whose head was always fixed on an angle talking into a phone. Romero took two tours driving around the place.

He slowed down twice examining the farthest section of the aquarium's new additions site being built and he parked Nelson's car and waited. A few minutes passed, he took another tour, slowed once more, and parked, more assured.

The construction was taking place under a blue tarp that would billow in the wind.

He had spotted no additional security and no cameras either. Soon this area was to be filled with water and sharks of a variety he couldn't say. They would swim in artificial reefs.

There was a shovel and he began digging into the ground. A labor he found incredibly difficult as the surface was already littered with small stones he had seen in other shark environs. He stopped and scanned the area for some cleaner place.

A mound of dirt further off was free of stones; packed against the wood boards. A digging machine sat unoccupied beside it, and Romero rubbed his chin at the possibility of firing it up. Then he nixed it to avoid noise and searched the area and began again digging beside the compacted area. When an oblong hole was ready he retraced his steps to the car and spied the female guard with her head out chatting it up with a police officer, all smiles, who was sitting in his cruiser. Both of them laughing and conversing on as the sky had begun to turn a brighter blue as morning raced ever closer threatening any cover he had left.

Romero hauled him to the site over his shoulders. He sprinted alongside the wood boards that shielded the construction site from the road and the view of the booth. He didn't stop beating feet until he got back to the hole. He collapsed beside Nelson with his broken neck, and he breathed, his lungs on fire, his shirt sweat soaked. He rose to his knees and shot a look frantically around the enclosed area. He grabbed the shovel, using it as a crutch, to steady himself on his feet, and he resumed trying to cover up the body.

When he was done, the sky was becoming uncomfortably bright. Romero had added another, although not too noticeable mound, to the clumped, dug up earth, pushed beside the wood paneling that surrounded the site. Then it was on his way back to Nelson's ride that he heard a loud barking laugh. He took a position behind the portable toilet next to the dumpster catching four men in hard hats with lunch pails. They were large and muscular walking together toward where he was. Romero waited a moment to hear any sign his presence was noticed in the site. He wondered about footprints then nixed that thought, doubting any prints would be noticeable on the stone ridden ground.

Minutes passed, only to reveal more men heading to the site. He heard the familiar sound of barking laughter. Romero pushed off the putrid portable John and fast walked to retrieve the dead Nelson's car.

He gained entrance to the Stratford Hotel as a customer. He took a room on the second floor and grabbed the key offered by the man behind the desk. Romero then sauntered to the bank of elevators, cautiously glancing around him.

Romero had showered and dressed accordingly and made a significant effort to pack all the essentials for a stay at the hotel and he had also taken his duffel just in case.

Before he left, he had dug deep into the trunk again.

He arrived to his room and put his stuff on the bed, looked at the phone and wished he could call Sarah. Be that some other person once more lost in the talk. Then he thought about calling Morris, but it was not smart to have that kind of discussion on the hotel phone—not even on his cell. Romero felt lonely suddenly. He wanted this over with. He wondered on any feelings about killing Nelson but, he didn't honestly have any.

He was a problem. He had to seal Nelson off and so he did. Just like he was going to do with Geiger back in that town before Big G took him out for him and just like he did with those meddlesome cops.

Romero got ready and stepped out to tour the corridors keeping another lookout for the seemingly ever present cameras these days.

He didn't see any.

He found room 311. Romero knocked lightly and low-ered the duffel beside him.

He heard a shuffling inside the room. Nothing hap-pened for a long while and then another shuffle. There was silence, so Romero knocked a little louder and feet could be heard pacing with energy to the door. Romero put his hand on the suppressor, tried tightening it but it wouldn't screw further on. Freemont was then on the other side of the door. The man asked who it was in that grating Jersey accent of his. His presence darkened the peephole and Romero swiftly pressed the barrel of the little automatic against it and the gun coughed once expelling a brass car-tridge and Freemont's body thudded down to the floor on the other side.

Romero got the door open in record time, damaging it some. It was a quick break in using Freon and a chisel and hammer he had in the duffel. Hopefully he would be gone before the staff noticed. Romero glanced down at Freemont's body and then shut the door. He held his gun up on one hand and swept the place until he found what he looked for on the floor beside the unkempt bed.

It was the green safe, all about the size of a microwave standing on stubby little legs with its door heavily dam-aged and wide open. The baseball cards littering the floor shredded into several pieces. Freemont, Romero consid-ered, had apparently found that the cards were utterly worthless and had torn them up in a rage. Freemont was always stuck for cash, and this act of fatal stupidity didn't surprise Romero. Nelson's ignorance of the cards value did. Then Romero wondered if Nelson did know. Romero then considered on Angie possibly suspecting along with Paul? For Nelson, the only value was what? Romero continued thinking. Sentimental? Sure it's possible to pay a lot of money to get something of sentimental value back, but Nelson confused a lot of people. The cards are shit. Paper. Old paper and not valuable at all except to him, and Romero kind of dug that and now he felt sorry about snapping the poor bastard's neck.

Christ! What a mess this is, Romero thought. He also thought that he wasn't sorry about capping Freemont. Then he took it into account though that maybe Nelson did know the dollar value of his cards, that they were worth nothing. Maybe the bitter fact that she kept them from him was enough. What if it were all actually about Angie and her boy-toy getting iced? That could have been the real motive the entire time. That Nelson was lying and he truly engineered Freemont going to Angie's with that gun. That Freemont's plan was actually Nelson's.

I don't know that, Romero told himself. I can't ask him now. He stooped down and lifted one of the cards. Mickey Mantle, in fact. Some fabrication of a classic card perhaps. Romero pulled the pink stick of gum out of its torn body. It was hard, whatever taste left was faint. He now decided to put this behind him and so he tossed the place and robbed Freemont of the ten thousand in his wallet and pockets. Romero knew he carried a lot of cash on him. Freemont was a showoff. It was in his nature buying expensive things around others.

Ten grand, and five quarters, and two pennies. At least he got something for his trouble. Right amount too.

"Christ," Morris said across from him on the couch. "They the only two you whacked in this mess?"

"Yeah," Romero nodded.

Morris looked like he ate something sour and leaned back. "Well I guess you did what you had to do," he said. "Freemont? Fucking asshole."

"I was expecting the police to get to me at the hotel, like an in depth interview.

But all I got was a detective asking me if I was sure I didn't hear, or see anything suspicious."

"You're here, so you must have done well." Morris sipped his coffee.

"Yeah well, and this." Romero pushed the Metro newspaper over to the old man who cleared his throat and read the front page. Morris's mouth moved while he read and then he laughed. He looked at Romero and back at the article and laughed once more. "Christ! Jesus! I forgot about that! That son of a bitch Freemont got capped by a connected man in Jersey, right? Yeah!" he laughed some more, coughed and began to read admiringly the front page banner. **Atlantic City thief murdered in mob retribution?**

Romero said honestly, "You know I forgot about that, too. They finally got him for robbing that card game.—Or so the papers say."

"You broke the man's neck?" Morris said a few moments later.

"I took some Karate," said Romero, "I didn't want a belt or anything, you know?

A black belt. I just took courses in some defensive moves and offensive moves. I rabbit punched Nelson so I could incapacitate him, and get hands on him. Then I did as my instructor told me, and I managed to break his neck pretty cleanly."

Morris took a second and said, "I didn't think they taught that sort of thing."

"They don't. Or maybe they do because, like I said, I was only there for some moves I thought would be useful. It all came to cracking a joke to the instructor afterward. He wasn't really suspicious or anything. We got to bullshitting; he let it slip how to do it. I'm still pretty surprised that I got the job done. The whole process felt lightening quick."

"The job in Houston?" Morris queried. "You in?"

"No."

"Sure?"

"I took a job somewhere else," Romero said.

"You mean another asset recovery bit?"

"No," Romero's head shook. "No, it's another score. A onetime heister you'd know yourself called me direct. He was in the city, and we met. We went and had lunch.

It's supposed to be in New York...The job."

"Who?" Morris flummoxed.

"Jim Muller."

Morris tilted his head so swiftly he could have been a canary in a past life. "He's the fellow who shot himself in the foot and spent the job on the floor."

"No," Romero smirked. "No Muller's the one who got caught dumping the getaway car by a state trooper."

"And he kept his mouth shut, yes, I remember," Morris said. "He's a stand up fellow. Tell him to call me why don't you? Probably thinks I'm dead."

Morris pushed his coke bottle glasses down his nose, watched Romero pull out a magazine from his jacket pocket and read off the front briefly before stuffing it away again. "You up to something now? Where are you going and what kind of magazine are you hiding?"

Romero smiled sheepishly. "It's for painting. There's an art supply store I want to visit before I get home."

"You? Painting?" Morris waved an invisible brush.

Romero smiled. "I think I might have talent."

"And before you go and prove how much talent you have, why don't you explain why all the sudden you're off to New York when all you've been doing is babbling about quitting?"

"Two million dollars." Romero paced to the door.

"Split between how many of you?" Morris had the pad and pen ready.

"Nobody else," Romero spoke guardedly, "It's a solo job."

Morris bore at him with his eyes and then brusquely shot a finger at him and demanded, "Sit down, now!"

"What do you have now?" Sarah asked him from the speaker.

"It looks sort of like a pelican."

"Mine looks like a bald eagle," she sighed. He heard her slam the piece of charcoal pen.

"Try again," he urged her firmly.

"O*kay*," she pretended to gripe.

"Well I do think I have some faint resemblance of a pelican," he told her.

They were talking over the speaker phone, and he found this type of back and forth amusing.

"Well I got the head right at least!" she laughed over the line.

"What if I told you I stopped an hour ago and was watching TV the whole time?"

"I would probably never call or pick up the phone again," she laughed.

"Well my bird can't fly, but I have noticed a steady improvement," and Romero set the etching aside. "We might even be able to paint one in someday."

"Keep trying," she encouraged. Sounds of charcoal scratching the paper. "Because it's exactly like you said. I've noticed it. There's a steady improvement."

3

The thief and the Russian.

Romero listened to Muller as they had their lunch. Muller had gone on about being back inside after the failed job he had participated in. He had gone on about the lousy food, and his hand shook, Romero noticed. It shook as Muller went on and on about how soul crushing it was to be back in stir. He went on about how difficult it was being the one of the few white inmates and Romero patted his shoulder when the food came and told him, as if reminding Muller that he was out, that he was lucky and still had a lot of life left.

"So this job?" Romero pushed. "What it is? Tell me how I'm the guy to do it."

"It's in New York," Muller told him.

Muller was a thickly built little man with a neatly trimmed mustache who's hair, which was once combed carefully years when Romero first saw him, was now a mess, just downright unruly. Romero recalled the smirk Muller used to have while running the wet comb through his hair and how much a stickler the man was with his clothes.

"New York, New York?" Romero said. "What's going on up there?"

"Red Mafia," Muller told him. "They control a place on Brighton Beach called the *Kitty Sonata Bar*," he scanned the crowd of the place for any eavesdroppers. "I happen to know that one of the red boys keeps at least two million in the safe at the back of the place."

"That much?"

"Until the bulk of it is packed and shipped home to be laundered where the godfathers get their piece."

"So you want to hit the place and split the dough?" Romero said, bodily he thrummed with the possibilities of that amount of a score.

"I want you to hit the place and keep the dough," Muller told him. "The only thing I want is that son a bitch Golovin to be hurting." His name was Simon Golovin. The red mobster who kept the money, and control of the *Kitty Sonata Bar*.

"Simon Golovin?" Romero queried, skeptical.

"I hate that mope," Muller was whispering fiercely. "I got married last year. She was a dancer at the Kitty Sonata Bar—"

"It's a strip club?"

"It's not supposed to be," Muller told him, "It's allowed dancing and lap dances and sometimes things would happen in the VIP area, but my wife Lana, she's a secretary now, has this Russian scum stalking her and leaving lewd threats." Muller's face was becoming tight. "Even after she quits." Muller's expression was fearful and enraged. "I can't whack the guy. But I figure if I could cause him some serious trouble, you know—"

"They'll do it for you," Romero finished giving the place another sweep of the eyes. Romero wishing he would stop meeting to discuss illicit matters in public places. "I owe you one. All of us guys on that score do." Romero speculated some, and with a resigned look, he shot Muller a brief thumbs up. "Alright."

"Alright," Muller hissed enthused. "Alright. Thank you, thank you, thank you."

Romero wandered around the art museum and pondered the proposition.

Everything told him that Muller was stand up. He didn't feel he was being tricked and walking into a betrayal in anyway. After all, Muller had taken some years for him and the crew on that fateful job years ago. If anybody could be trusted, he didn't see why it couldn't be him.

Romero saw it this way. He owed Muller for what he did for him. Never mind the other guys but him specifically. As he listened to the echoes of his shoes around him in the corridor of the museum, Muller's wife was being stalked and harassed by some hood from one of the bloodiest criminal organizations in the world. Romero knew the extent of the Red Mafia's violence. Their record spoke for itself as they ran the pipeline that was sought after by other criminal enterprises. This pipeline was the envy of the underworld.

The Red Mafia protected it, as well as other assets, with just as much brutality as one would expect.

Do I want to chance myself falling into their crosshairs? Romero pondered energetically with his steps increasing in speed up the corridor ahead of him, art unseen.

Two million dollars, he ruminated dreamily and slowed his pace. *Christ.*

"Lets palaver," he told Muller when let into the man's hotel room.

"Great!" Muller pumped Romero's fist. "Come in." Then he sprinted on over to the desk by the wall and pulled from a leather carrier bag a folder which he gently eased out and handed over to Romero.

The folder was filled with pictures of the *Kitty Sonata Bar*. The shots were at night with the bar's blazing neon green lights. There were also shots in the daytime that were of the same locations around the building. Everything from the front door taken from across the street. One taken of the rear door from the alley, and the dumpster and cars parked at the back of the building, where employees kept their vehicles. There was even a picture taken of the bathroom. Also, there was a piece of ripped paper bag reading:

Alarm code. There were digits scrawled underneath in black marker.

"Thanks," Romero said. "Maybe I'll use this." He hefted it and put it on the bed.

"So it looks good?" Muller asked.

"Yes. I owe you and I think it's worth the risk and I trust the info."

"Great," he clapped. "So when do you head on out? You're going in by yourself? You don't have anyone else to...you know? Go along? Moral support?"

"No. No, it's alright Muller. Since when do any of us in this line of work need moral support?"

"When you're right, you're right. But if you do..."

"I know. Thanks."

Romero told him to go home, he would drive out himself for the job. Romero packed the duffel in the trunk of one of the Mazda's on the lot and drove out back to his place to pack leaving his VW Beetle behind the fence in the Mazda's spot. He would naturally pick it up later when switching vehicles.

Later on the road he blinked at where he was going and why. It had suddenly dawned on him, why he was on the road. Or at least what he'd said to put him on the road. A favor? Romero blinked some more. Really? A favor? Risk everything and get my stupid ass shot off? Bombed or god knows what else just to do some guy I hardly know a favor? And yeah there was the 2 million dollars, but still. Haven't I gone through this before? he thought. How many risks for more money I don't need before the shit hits the fan? Before I'm either in traction, dead or in the can again?–*But 2 million dollars!*

Romero parked outside the motel, walked out and around the building where the dumpster was. He had with him the folder Muller gave him, and he wiped it thoroughly with a wet piece of toilet paper of any prints, and he chucked it inside.

Romero removed a cold piece from his suitcase. It was a Colt Commander with a seven round capacity clip inside and he had a spare magazine stuffed inside his suitcase.

He took his time organizing his tools from the duffel on the bed. He made an inventory.

When done he cleared the bed, sat down on it, relaxed for a few minutes then called Sarah.

When the phone picked up, his words got caught in his throat when a male voice came on the line. Romero hung up after being asked repeatedly if he were there, and he dialed again on the off chance he'd made a mistake.

He hadn't. It was a man and he hung up and paced around trying to figure out why he cared about Sarah's sex life. He wasn't in love with her. He didn't even actually have a clear view of her when he'd met her on the armored truck job. He recalled that her hair was unkempt and how it must have been like that because of the incessant running of her hand through her hair and pulling in stress, the woman was wound up, real anxious.

In love with her? He wasn't even sure he could have those feelings for anyone.

Hell with this, he scolded himself, Get on with the job. When the day's over we can have 2 million dollars in our possession, laundered, and we can truly take our lazy slacking off to a new level with trips to the Hamptons or see Europe. Yeah, you do want to see Scotland and Ireland. Didn't you have the fantasy while in the can about roaming these countries and staying for extended periods of time in their hotels and eating at their lavish eateries and drinking at their finest pubs? Didn't you pour over the travel books while in prison feeling the hunger of it inside, that knot in your chest? Of course you did.

Romero was now determined to pull the heist off, Red Mafia be damned.

Romero entered the *Kitty Sonata Bar* like everyone else, he went through the front door and checked out the three shapely women in thong bikinis as they gyrated to the pulsing beat from the speakers. They did their pole work and whipped their hair. There was a blonde center and the two flanking her were brunettes. They were men crowded around in seats and a few sat at tables. There was a lonesome man or two at the bar and Romero could tell from something in their features that these men off by themselves were friends of Golovin. They had some certain unidentifiable feature that just called out to him as Russian. They were hard looking. Not men to be crossed in the least.

There was a window in the men's room that was large enough for him to get through and he caught the sensor rigged to it. He wasn't surprised of course. Outside he caught the security cameras pointing outward and expected more of them out back.

Romero considered trying to find somewhere to hide out until closing. He would be armed with his supplies and break into Golovin's safe.

Romero told himself not to hold his own breath.

Should I be doing this alone? He circled the thought in his head. Sure. I have the alarm codes so that's no problem, and I can handle the load...Right. Alone is the way.

Romero ordered a beer and he paid and roamed around trying to look as inconspicuous as he was able. Trying to look like any other Joe who's checking out the ladies. Romero caught sensors at various other points, spotting the keypad when he arrived in front by the main entrance. He knew breaking in through that door wouldn't be smart. He needed to get in through the restroom and be fast getting to that keypad and disengage the alarm. And thank god for the alarm code because Romero could do most heists. He could knock off an armored truck, but god help him if he could tackle some cheapo alarm system. Romero would admit he wasn't a technology savvy guy. It was becoming the brave new world out there and heisting was harder than ever. The world's next greatest thief would have to be able to operate DOS and Windows. Until then, men who just used force and weapons, their hands and feet, would have to keep running and dodging all of the mines in the field possible.

Later, he returned making his way to the bathroom. Once inside he saw two men washing their hands in the sink. They could have been Italian Mafiosi as they wore running suits opened to show tee shirts and gold chains, but once more there was the feature of Russian in their faces. He couldn't understand what it was, but they were Red Mafia. He walked by them stepping into an empty stall, and sat down watching the two gangsters below the door. He observed their feet and then they exchanged some words in their native tongue, and walked out letting the music wash in before the door closed, sending it back to the low thud he felt in his chest.

Later he had another beer and ran over the plan. He took his beer and sat where he could see Golovin's office and when the door finally opened, he wasn't sure what he saw.

It could have been a green filing cabinet or his safe. Romero didn't think Muller made that dumb of a mistake and so Romero rose and adjusted as casually as he could for a better view of the office.

A leggy beauty gyrated over him and was making eye contact with him. Romero felt rude every time he shot a glance toward Golovin's office. He tried his best to seem shy about her attention. This woman sparkled, the light around her and the others flanking her, was beet red, it faded and brightened. Spotlights overhead stayed on showing the faces of the men surrounding the stage. They were all of the same stock it seemed and only upon turning around he saw some Manhattanites sitting at a table. They looked like executives, or maybe lawyers, and they were laughing and drinking, their eyes glowing in the lights. They were real Harvard types. Romero saw entitlement on their faces, and he blushed with anger, and envy. Then he remembered who he was, what he had done, and all that green he might have his hands on if all went well.

Golovin's office door opened once more. A strongly built man came out wearing a sweater that could have been blue or black. He had curly hair and a strong face that didn't look mean but strong and capable of violence. The eyes glittered in dark slits. He looked like an Easter Island statue. That was what his face looked like, Romero finally realized.

He watched the office door. It was open partially. He stood and wandered circling the table area. Finally, he had the perfect vantage point.

It was a green Mosler safe with a standard silver handle and black faced dial with white numbers. It was six feet tall at least and Romero stopped himself from smiling.

Romero watched the dancers leave one after another and then other employees. Two cars sat behind the back of the building, both of them with their own spectral glow because of the green neon above.

The rear door opened once more, and one of the running suit men were there, and he walked with a spring in his step, tossing the car keys up and down in his hand as he went. Romero watched him as he climbed into the car and pulled out. When he left Romero then waited for whoever came out last.

Several minutes passed, and nobody came out. Romero had a panicked thought that Golovin slept over. Finally, the rear door swung open and Golovin himself emerged.

He watched the Russian climb into his car. The gangster then sat for a full five minutes.

Each minute chaffing Romero and then gratefully Romero watched Golovin pull out and drive off the lot and into the street.

Romero circled around and was behind a wood fence that separated the neighboring bistro from the strip club. He ran alongside it. Beyond the fence, the security cameras loomed. He found safe middle ground behind the fence and lifted himself up to peak over. It was pointed toward the parking lot, predictable enough, and he saw one plainly above the back door. The only other camera was fixed to shoot the mouth of the alley that would lead to the restroom window. Romero huffed over the fence and landed quietly on his feet, raced, and he put his duffel against the wall. He easily popped open the restroom window as he had disabled the lock permanently after the two running suits left him alone. He then eased himself roughly down and as soon as his feet hit the floor, he made a dash out the men's room. Out on the floor he fought the pen light out of his pocket and used it to a cut a clear path in the thick dark and skidded to a stop in front of the keypad where the countdown was now to 3. Romero typed from memory and as he pushed ENTER the digit then changed to 1 and he held his breath.

No blare of sound came, and the readout told him there wouldn't be either.

Could this be the easiest 2 million dollars I'll make? Romero mused. He pondered further that it just might be, and he had this thought buzzing in his head as the adrenaline flowed through his system, and he began picking Golovin's office lock which gave after a tense twenty minutes of mounting frustration at the difficulty of the damned thing.

Romero was a heister. Guns, explosives, teargas and the stark will. But he was no cat burglar, not any decent one he would admit, it was the guns and yelling that made him his small fortune.

Once inside the office, Romero stuck penlight in his mouth and unzipped the duffel and began pulling out the magnetized power drill and his liquid nitrogen gun and canister which looked like nothing more than a black steel super soaker with some bulk to it. Next he pulled free a headlight headband which housed a halogen bulb that was incredibly bright. Romero turned this on and stuffed the penlight into his back pocket. He searched for an outlet and plugged the power drill, and if, on the off chance, there were none available, then the battery would do, though it made it more cumbersome to carry.

But he was careful, and all bases had to be covered, every emergency possible studiously considered.

Romero drew a small penny sized dot where the locking mechanism was located with a black marker, and he stuffed the earplugs in. He made sure to lock the door from the inside and push the chair against it, leaning it back, wedging it under the doorknob just in case. Also, just in case, he put the gun beside him on the floor making sure the safety was off, and he went to work.

Romero flicked on the magnet and then came a thrumming feeling with a minute sound of a buzzing and then a 'Thunk!' sound as the magnet stuck to the safe. Next came a whir of the drill bit which then became a wail as it began to burrow into the safe's green face obliterating the black dot Romero drew.

Every so often he would stop and listen. He would rise and pull one of the plugs out and press his ear to the door, but no sound came except those typical at a quarter to four in the morning in the city that never sleeps.

Some bars in New York were being forced to close early around 2 AM, and the *Kitty Sonata Bar* didn't seem to be the exception. Driving around he could see the developments. It was obvious that this force would eventually, from the local pressure groups put demands for perceived needed changes. Some bar owners would even blame it on hipsters who were pouring into the gentrified areas, and bars where swank and excessiveness was the norm were now being forced to become classier for the new clientele in their midst. It was a business move, but a move some bar and club owners felt was an impediment on their operations. Say, for example, an organized crime faction trying to run drugs and girls out of their establishment at all hours if possible.

He had the hole. It revealed the brass locking mechanism inside and he went about lifting the nitrogen gun. Romero aimed at the brass inside the perfectly round hole the size of a door knob and he pulled the trigger letting a white blast of liquid nitrogen layer over the mechanism. The spray was hissing loudly, he stopped the stream, and watched some as the cold mist was pouring out of the opening. He hoped he hadn't over done it. When the mist cleared he saw the brass color was gone replaced by grey brittleness.

A hard whack with the hammer and chisel and the locking mechanism gave it up falling into pieces and Romero pulled the door open. There were two suitcases one on one shelf and one below on the other and both heavy standing vertically. He opened one and was greeted by green. Lots of green and the next case was the same story. Romero shut them and cleaned up.

Could it be this easy? he wondered. Then: Hell it was kind of fun actually.

Romero was at a tunnel and he slowed at the light leading into its mouth looking for the street sign. He had suddenly become lost and needed to get his bearings, and when he recalled he needed to take a left from the tunnel he clicked his tongue; smiled waiting for the light to change.

The bullet starred the windshield ahead of him, and Romero instinctively hit the gas. He barreled through the tunnel leading them, whoever they were, away from his motel room. Romero raced like the wind with his head down, eyes barely seeing over the steering wheel. He made himself sit up, and looked into the rearview mirror. He saw Golovin's stone face bobbing up and down behind him in his car, right on him and right as Romero realized why he looked so large, he felt the impact of the car from behind him. Another gunshot and the radio console blew up next to him. Romero nearly swiped cars passing on the lane beside him then corrected, and waited for his opportunity.

He wanted to U turn. Another gunshot and the entire right side of the windshield disintegrated and Romero's right eye burned, and he could no longer see out of it. He was no longer touching the wheel, his eye hurt and then he felt the impact of Golovin's car, and Romero found himself spiraling around out of control, it made him forget trying anything. Romero rolled into a ball.

The crash was deafening.

Romero heard sirens, and he fell out of the driver's seat and with one eye he saw that the car had its front end crushed, but he knew it could move and he climbed back to the wheel as some man and a woman behind him shouted at him not to do that and he reversed and took off. In which direction he wasn't sure.

He tried not to look, but blood was pouring from his right eye, and he knew he had lost it. It was gone. Blind in one eye. Romero punched the dash and made himself drive the speed limit as the radiator hissed and whined sickly. He made himself pull the car over and watch behind him. Cars were slow in appearing. The sky was brightening as the morning approached. He wanted to get to the motel, but he didn't want Golovin or his men to be on him as soon as he climbed out the car.

Bitterly, he decided the son of a bitch wasn't coming, and he put the gun aside on the passenger seat and took off the next few miles to the motel.

Golovin, he blazed vehemently. At least I know where I can find you! He parked across from the motel, and he went into the trunk for his stuff.

The suitcases were gone.

So this was it, Romero swayed sickly out in the street with the air cooling the accumulating sweat on his skin and his bloodied face and gone eye tickling. He froze a second and lifted a hand carefully to the damaged eye, and he pressed feeling the eyeball seemingly still present. It moved side to side as it would have usually; there was a pain that made him hiss air loudly, and he groaned. Forgetting the money, he went back to his room.

He went into the bathroom and made himself look at the mess the right half of his face had become, but as he washed he found it was more dried blood from a single wound than anything and he found the source above the eye, not the eye itself. Hanging was skin flap. He eased it up where he felt another incredible pain. It revealed his eyelid, which was closed with blood crusted on the side. Romero gently pulled the lid up, and with relief, he saw his iris and more importantly he saw out of the eye itself. Romero dropped the lid, it fell back dead, and he wondered on it and knew he needed to get to a hospital. He raised the lid again a few more times and eventually within a few minutes time the pain had lessened. He moved the eye to the left and to the right and aside from a tear of blood seeping minutely out the irritated membrane, he could blink it subtly. All in all, it seemed to be getting some strength back of some sort.

Romero drove some blocks to a pharmacy and got a first aid kit and some eye drops. Back at the motel he cleaned and dressed the wound as much as he was able knowing he needed stitches. He cleaned out his eye with the eye drops. He packed and left to get back for home bringing with him unwelcome news for Muller who wanted revenge.

He was surprised at how little he cared about it when all was done. He was glad to have his eye and if he lost two million he could live with it.

He couldn't stop thinking about Muller. About Golovin and his menacing attack as if expecting the robbery. He couldn't believe that Muller would set him up either, because, he had proven he was a stand up guy. Nothing deceitful came off the man.

Romero liked to think he could read when he's being deceived by someone. Hell, he read a serious of books about body language as an interest; they had worked for him before. All in all Muller was authentic. Wasn't he?

So what happened? he wondered. What happened and what do the Red Mafia know of you if they know anything at all?

He told the doctor supplied to him by Big G that he had been in a car accident, and he knew some glass had gone in his eye. The doctor, an elderly black man with white hair and mustache, stitched him up and rinsed his eye. He said to use eye drops and told him to keep the membrane by the socket clean or there would be an infection, and he *would* lose the eye. Romero paid the under the table doctor 2, 000 dollars. Exhausted, he went home where he slept for a few hours before making himself awaken to get in contact with Muller.

As the phone rang on the other end a thought came, and he hung up. He saw no reason not to be sure, be cautious, he nodded to himself putting the idea together in his mind. He made the reservation over the phone and got room 111 which he purchased under an alias: Alex Merlino. He used one of many a bogus Visa cards in his supply.

He then called Muller's cell telling him what room, that the door would be unlocked but to knock *Shave and a Haircut* so he would know it was him.

"Shave and a haircut?" Muller whined.

"Regent Motel. Remember."

"Regent. Right."

He called Big G telling him about his problem and could he help and that he would explain everything later. Big G chuckled and told him to spit what he had to spit.

Romero spat leaving the big man on the other end of the phone in surprised silence.

"Red Mafia, huh? Shit. Gunmen, too?" More of his chuckling and he said, "Sure.

I'll seal you off, baby. Got nothin' to worry about no more, son."

He waited across the street inside a doorway and a familiar car turned into the driveway of the Regent Motel. This car parked, and three men came out. Golovin was one while two of them were the running suits. They went for the door; he could see by their hands that they were readying to reach for guns.

So now he knew. Romero steadily with anticipation followed the men as they stopped outside room 111. The two running suits flanked either side of the door while Golovin was hunkering down below the peephole. Then Golovin raised a fist and knocked *Shave and a Haircut.* Nothing. Now Golovin knowing the door was unlocked slowly turned the knob and jumped back kicking it the rest of the way open. The two running suits stormed in with the block head Russian behind them closing the door.

Romero waited and heard nothing. He wasn't expecting to unless one of the Russians got a shot off. If Big G's men were as talented as he said, then their silenced 22.'s, would disable the Russians, and it would be over. Guns in general, that carry a heavier caliber can't be effectively silenced. A 38. will always be loud even with a suppressor. A 22., on the other hand, is small caliber enough to make the much famed low coughing noise seen in most movies. Romero's only indication it would be over is when the signal came.

It did. Room 111 opened a crack. A tall and skinny, do-rag wearing black man, looked around at the empty lot. He began waving a white hand towel, probably the bathroom's, out the room before ceasing and shutting the door.

Muller answered the door to his room and blanched when he saw Romero.

Muller said, "So I told Golovin I knew a guy who could break in. Then when you did he could be in the clear, we would be able to split the profits." Muller laughed bitterly. "Well not split, but I was going to get a cut. Just 100, 000. But to me Romero?

That was a perfect number." Muller massaged his face and then stopped, slapped his knees and stood to wander by the window. Romero's Beretta 25. following him around the room.

Am I going to leave another body in a hotel room? he thought.

"Red Mafia would kill him and me if they thought we took the money." Muller stared out the window. "One more week and it would be gone packed up for oversees laundering along with the other suitcases with their dirty money."

Silence.

Romero said finally, "You were pissed about us making off while you did time in the can?"

Muller nodded and frowned. "Actually... no, I just made myself believe I was to make this betrayal easier. The stone cold fact is, Romero, is that I needed the money."

"And the girl?"

"There is no girl," Muller confessed further. "I made that up to get some sympathy points and thought maybe a damsel in distress would put the story over the top. This..." He raised his finger showing the wedding band. "This isn't even mine."

"You need the money because you owe the Red Mafia?"

"No. Italians actually. Of course, it's from gambling. I owe 76, 256 dollars." He laughed. "That's what I need."

Romero sighed letting his mind run things over.

"So Golovin is dead? Really?" Muller asked with his face twisted, mouth grimacing.

"Him and the two running suits," Romero told him and scratched his gun hand. "I have my own associates that handled them for me."

"And you're sure they're dead?"

"Muller," he said, "I'm as sure as I'm standing here. And what I want to know is does the Red Mafia know my name?"

"No," Muller said, and seemed in thought some before he gave another shake of the head. "No. At the end of the month, or the first of the next month, yes. I think Golovin was greedy enough to wait and see if another suitcase was coming. He wouldn't report the robbery to them and mention your name yet. He would want be sure they'd give it to him as he had a strong track record with their dough. He would wait until he saw the money gone. Give you some cover to run before his people scrambled. Then he'd get you and take the money while they hunted a ghost. Now," Muller sighed. "What happens to me?"

"You're the only one who knows apparently about my connection with the robbery." Romero leveled the gun at Muller's stomach. There was a silencer attached and Beretta 25. was the right caliber. Still Romero didn't pull the trigger.

A stretch of time passed. Romero lowered the gun and said, "You're leaving.

Pack up."

Later, as Muller drove them toward the airport, Romero told him to pull over.

Muller did on Market St. where cars and trucks hissed, roared around them in the bright sunlight. "What happened to the suitcases? The money?" Romero probed.

"In New York still," Muller stated. "I'd imagine."

"You sure?"

"Don't see why he'd keep it with him," Muller told him.

"Where does he live?"

Muller sucked in his cheeks and looked beaten down at his lap. "Shit," he moaned.

"Yeah," Romero told him. "I'll be taking that. Now where?"

Muller gave him the address and Romero was surprised that it was in the general area within walking distance of the bar. Muller said it was a loft.

"Okay," Romero said and pulled the Beretta back out. "Drive. Drive us somewhere where we can be alone, okay?"

Muller held up his hands. "Don't do this."

"I'm not going to shoot you," Romero laughed. "I don't want anyone to see me put you in the trunk. You and I are going to New York."

Muller looked as if he would vomit.

Romero got in through the fire door at the back of the building. He froze and smashed the lock and handed the tools to Muller. Muller resentfully stuffed them away in the duffel, zipping them up as he acted as Romero's assistant.

Romero was confronted with a large steel sliding door for an entrance, and he found the bar running into the housing for the locking mechanism. Romero dug in the bag while Muller held it open for him. He took out what looked like a roll of toothpaste, and he squeezed some grey powdery paste onto the lock mechanism's housing which looked like a steel shoebox planted vertically by the door.

"What is that?" Muller droned.

"A little thermite."

The heat cut through emitting a wild burst of sparks that had them down the hall watching closely as it burned through violently. Romero opened the case in the wall for the fire extinguisher; he waited until the sparks died and pulled the pin. Then with the door slid open, Romero waved Muller in who looked as if he were sleepwalking.

The space was a bachelor's dream pad. A large flat screen television set and sound system. A video game console with some games stacked up on a shelf that took up an entire wall. A large floor to ceiling window offered a view of the Brighton Beach area.

The walls were red brick and floors wood. There was also a bar and walk-in shower. You would think he was filthy rich already. The dead man was doing incredible.

The suitcases were on the King sized bed. Romero felt his heart leap.

They hustled the suitcases down the stairs, Romero holding one and Muller the duffel and other suitcase. The duffel causing Muller to weave some on his feet. They dropped the goods in the backseat; Romero said he had to go back in the trunk. Muller said nothing. He climbed in. He allowed Romero to hog-tie him, so he couldn't use the trunk's emergency unlocking device. A device most recent models of vehicles had.

Romero was no longer tired. Finding the money had him high and he even listened to the radio as he drove back. That is until he remembered what he had to do. So he shut off the radio and made a call on Muller's cell which he had confiscated. Romero called the car rental place using the operator and he made a purchase over the phone. He told the woman on the other end that he was coming to pick the vehicle up and could he leave the car at the rental place in Philadelphia, to which she said yes, that was acceptable.

Romero drove Muller's car around Brighton Beach and settled on the best place to ditch him. Romero parked inside an abandoned car lot. He went into the back and pulled his belongings out and carried one after another beside the chain fence and he crept to the trunk. He used the key and lifted.

Muller was watching him with eyes wide and face white. He didn't say anything but just stared. Romero told him to turn around so he could loosen the electrical tape that bound him up.

"Relax Muller," Romero said and patted the man's shoulder.

He helped him out, Muller trembling, knees were shaking with nervous fright.

Romero watched Muller watching him. Muller appeared in complete despair. "Come on," he said to the traumatized man. Romero lifted a suitcase and brought it over. He lifted it up to Muller who seemed baffled. "Take it." Romero shook the heavy case. "One for me.

One for you. Split down the middle."

Muller smiled. He frowned and then smiled some more. Some color was coming back to his face and he said, "You're serious?"

"I've murdered many, Muller. I'd rather lose half of two million than take another chance of capture that comes with a kill. I would if I had to, of course."

Muller took the suitcase.

Romero continued. "My friend who took care of Golovin and his boys made sure that their bodies disappeared. You see he never leaves a body lying around. That's his method. So Golovin is missing and so is the two million. Do you see?"

Muller grinned then held his stomach laughing. "The Russians will think he made off with it!" Another laughing fit from Muller. "Brilliant!"

Romero called a cab, when it arrived he put everything in the trunk and tossed Muller the key to the car. "Enjoy!" Romero called.

He watched Muller as the cab sped forward. Muller waved and began for the car with his one million with him.

He thought on his mercy and the dread of losing that other half of the money wasn't there anymore. Hell, Romero felt better.

I feel like a million bucks! Romero thought grinning.

Romero hung up the phone. It was over. Romero and Sarah and calls to one another. She had met a teacher—a history teacher—and she had grown a fondness for him that was quickly becoming something else. Romero said he understood; they promised to keep themselves updated on how they were doing. Sarah never said it, but what it came down to was the obvious inappropriateness of their phone calls especially as she was now seeing someone. Romero understood and wouldn't want a girlfriend doing the same. He hung up and sat on the couch for awhile. Eventually, he rose and wandered over to the pelican painting he had done a few months ago. He pulled it off the wall and in one swift motion with an anger that stunned him he broke it in half over his knee.

4

'Don't talk to bullets.'

It was the chilliest of winters in Philadelphia and Romero, who was in a pea coat, warmed himself watching the red Nissan park at the curb. He looked above briefly at the slate sky which would eventually drop snow to earth and then he waited. He waited for the woman who stepped out of the driver's seat. Her name was Diane McCall, and she was a trimly built woman with long curled dirty blonde hair. Romero nodded a greeting as she smiled brightly at him and waved fingers with one hand. He could tell right away that her personality was always the kind that was perky.

She stopped in front of him, and they shook hands. She asked him if he were ready; Romero said that he was, and she led the way into the building.

"I saw a loft in New York," he said, "and ever since then I looked for one that matched to my satisfaction. I really had some fixation on the place. I mean after I left I would look around my home and the feeling of cozy satisfaction I usually had was no longer there. For the first time, I felt that I lived in a basement. Then I came into some money; found myself suddenly on the shallow side of the rich pool but still I was in the pool and a friend of mine, Morris, told me it was time to stop depriving myself."

"I'd say he was right," she said.

She showed him around, it didn't take long. When he said he wanted the place she smiled assuring him he was wise. It was settled, he now had a new place overlooking a quiet street. The apartment was well off of the ground, and if he wanted to take the stairs he would have to climb five flight of steps. Diane told him there was a garage across the street if he felt comfortable parking there and he nodded saying he would think about it.

She was also nice enough to point out surrounding restaurants and bars, places ingeneral that she would go herself. While she was going on about a lounge nearby, he nodded politely listening. She dropped that she would be there with friends later tonight.

He considered if it were a flirtation. Then he mentally shrugged it off until she made another point of being there and telling him what time followed by asking him to stop on by and have a drink with her.

"Right," he said smiling, a fake uncomfortable smile.

At the basement apartment, he was packing when the phone rang. Romero picked it up. Since it was the landline, it could only mean Morris, who had something he was uncertain of discussing on Romero's cell phone. "Morris?"

"Yes son!" Morris boomed, "Listen, why don't you take a drive and come and see me?"

"Really?" Romero now peaked of interest.

"Yeah. Better come down here."

Morris, the old horse, led Romero to the kitchen counter where he sat across from him, each at a stool. Silence and then while tapping his digits on the tiled counter he said, raising a finger to the ceiling, "Friend of mine called. Okay?" Morris nodded to him gravely. "He said that a red fella is looking for some pro in Philadelphia who's a thief.

This friend said that this Russian is looking for somebody who robbed the Red Mafia of 2 million dollars."

Romero stood and paced some before stopping suddenly to rest on the stool. He said to Morris, "He have a name?"

"Ah!" Morris drummed the countertop. "No. No name. Now, the only name he knows is Muller's. Whether he handles him, or has handled him, will have to be a mystery for the foreseeable future."

"So right now their fishing?"

"Yes,"

"But what does it matter?" Romero told him. "If they don't know for sure than they'll come after me anyway just to be sure. I have a good network of crews out there, and I know a lot who won't talk. Still some might. Guys I worked with who are flashy and ultraviolent. Guys who are talkative and unstable. I've worked with some of these guys but not a lot. No, the men I've worked with won't ever meet a red fella or any other type of organized crime figure in their off time. They're not in the circles after a score.

They run business and keep themselves sealed off."

"They're like you," Morris pointed out. "They do their score and go home quietly. They don't flash around dough like an idiot, and they don't put an eye out in bar fights.

These guys are professional and like any professional after a score they become ghosts."

"That's right."

"Except you've done jobs with unstable elements who like the criminal lifestyle, and these men have to be dealt with in order to keep this certain red bastard out your ass."

He sniffed. "You follow me, Romero."

He said nothing to that and just brought a shoulder up.

"Do you know the names of these gentlemen?" Morris prodded, and his magical pad and pen appeared, Romero didn't see from where.

"I have their names," he said.

Morris jutted the eraser at Romero. "Well, tell me so we can clean up."

"I'm not doing that," Romero said. "And then what? Take the car out on a road trip murder rampage?"

"You want to make sure this guy or any other Russian doesn't put a foot on your doorstep, do you?"

Romero paced around the room, Morris's patient eyes following along. At some point, however, Morris sighed and began writing what names he could come up with for him and Romero went back to the stool and with a flourish Morris tore the paper off the pad and slid it across.

"Christ," Romero blinked, "Two names? Really?" he asked with a small measure of relief.

"The other two are in jail, Romero. Confirmed it this morning. Now these,"

Morris's fingernail tapped the sheet. "Put these two in the ground and rig it, so it looks like one of them stole the money. You said you had one of the suitcases the cash came in.

Do you still have it?"

"Yes," and he did. "So you want me to plant the suitcase to throw them off?"

"Oh!" Morris grimaced and pushed his glasses back up his nose, and he asked for the sheet back and jotted another name and passed it back. "Thanks for reminding me."

It was Muller's name.

"I let him live," Romero said. "Now you want me to cap him?"

"I don't want you to cap him, Romero, I want you to protect yourself. You should have thought through the whole thing. Muller is the only link that could give them a name. That and these two clowns who might make the mistake of running into a few questioning Russians and not having the goddamn courtesy to keep their mouth shut.

First rule about trust in this business, Romero. *Psychos* are only loyal to *themselves.*"

Morris ran a leathery hand over his bald pate. Cautiously he leaned forward. "Maybe I can ask Grandview to do it?"

"No," Romero firmly spoke. "I already owe him for getting rid of Golovin and his men. I have no problem with Big G; I find the guy entertaining but I'm not about to owe him any more than I do...What a quandary."

"It ain't easy, kid."

"Give me the list. Can you find out where the two clowns are?"

Romero packed to give himself something to do until the phone call came from Morris with the addresses of the next kills.

The body count is rising. He wondered if he could even kill Muller after sparing him that first time. Christ I can't even think of it. Muller was alright, but he got caught in a jam and he was desperate. He wasn't like Geiger who spilled blood just to do it. Muller wasn't a high roller violent jerk at all. Yeah he waved a gun around during a job, but that was all. Also, tried to have me whacked in exchange for a measly hundred grand. If, I were indebted to the Italians, as he was I probably would do the same. I mean for Christ's sake I'm a heister; a thief. I've murdered people. Two cops, broke a man's neck, shot the other in the head. Didn't enjoy it in any sick sexual way or feel better afterward, but I did it because I couldn't come up with any other way. And yeah! I'll be honest! Even though,

I didn't enjoy it, it wasn't as if I was riddled with guilt. I slept well that night. The night after too. I don't obsess over it. Every now and then I'll wonder if the bodies are still safely away from sight. Even if they're not how could it lead back to me? I spared Muller from a bullet because killing in this lifestyle I live is too risky. Every killing leads the cops closer to your door and I'm not about to believe I'm that remarkable that it won't happen to me.

Romero stopped packing as he became aware of having forgotten something.

Whatever it was it seemed incredibly important. He turned his thoughts to Morris and then Muller and could get no tug that this block of memory had anything to do with his current problem. No, instead it had something to do with his move. Then it hit him. It was Diane. If Romero didn't hurry with his shower and ironing, he would miss her tonight.

❖

Diane was walking from the bar holding a tropical con-
coction when she saw Romero, and they exchanged hel-
los and she led him to a table where a man and woman
sat together both of them with the yuppie look about
them, or maybe it was hipster, Romero wasn't sure. He
was distracted. Would Morris call? he wondered. That he
wouldn't be there and would he try his cell phone? Could
he whack two guys he used to work with even though they
were pieces of shit he ceased a professional relationship
with long ago?

At some point, Diane put her hand on his, and they
exchanged looks. Romero effectively tried to talk about
himself as a business owner. Romero felt the fraud doing
so and so he would turn the attention back by asking the
three about themselves. He'd read that it was an effective
technique to make people think you were a veritable con-
versationalist. All you did was just give them an excuse to
talk about themselves without making them look like jerks.
Romero thought this sound advice and used it often in situ-
ations like the one he was in currently.

The couple was married. He was Peter Donovan and
she was Lisa Donovan. He was a financial planner, and she
was a dog walker. Perfect. Peter with his black horn rimmed
glasses and scruff and Lisa with her short blonde bob with
a perky attractiveness that was bothersome for some reason. Romero was becoming distressingly bored wondering
when they would leave him and Diane to themselves.

A finger tapped Romero's shoulder. He turned to look
up at a man in black tee shirt. Romero saw the bar rag. "Are
you Romero?" the man asked hurriedly.

"Yes?"

"This man at the bar wanted me to give this to you." The bar man raised a suitcase. It was *the* suitcase. Or at least one of them.

Romero ignored it and stood looking toward the bar but the bar man said the man had left and paid him a twenty just to drop it off. Romero thanked the bar man who rushed off to serve waiting customers. The case felt empty. No, no it wasn't. Something was inside, not the one million.

Romero turned and smiled at Diane and the Donovan's. "I'm sorry. I'll be right back. I'll be in the restroom," he said and tried to walk casually.

He locked himself in the stall. He knew Muller was dead because Romero's suitcase was packed with clothes for the move and unless the man who brought this suitcase broke into his apartment and tossed the neatly folded clothes out and took it with him, but Romero didn't think that. He set the case on the toilet and for a moment wondered if there would be a bomb inside. It was too light for a bomb, and he sniffed the closed lips of the leather, nothing wafted out that was familiar. Romero put a hand on the zipper and ripped it open. Easily he lifted the lid with a finger as he leaned back.

Inside was a little velvet black case. It was the kind that contained pearls or some other high quality jewelry and could have been perfectly square except the edges were rounded. Romero opened it. His mouth became a grimace as he bore his sight down on the inside.

It was a hundred dollar bill soaked in blood. In black marker, the words written on it were **Death for thief!!!**

❖

"Death for thief!" Morris held the bill up. "Nice and theatrical."

"Right."

"So it's settled," Morris stirred his coffee. "Muller is dead, and probably it was of a brutal nature. Probably tortured the hell out of him for your name."

"And now there's a Russian gun out there waiting."

Morris shook his head looking down into the steaming whirlpool. "So it's settled. The Red Mafia know who you are, and they're coming for you."

"And how the hell do I fight against that?"

"You don't."

Later, Morris said, "Maybe you can convince this gunman you weren't involved.

If you can get the drop on him and tell him with a gun to his back and persuade him Muller lied somehow and for some reason. We could even rig the whole thing somehow, so the lie is acceptable."

"Sounds complicated."

"It is. Do you still have one of the suitcases from your cut, right?"

"I have two now," Romero said.

"So you have two then."

"So we need a plan to put into motion and getting said drop on the gunman could help?"

Morris nodded on his side of the countertop. "He has contact with his bosses. He can convince them you're not responsible. But we need leverage to make sure he does what we tell him."

"His life?"

"This Russian probably won't break if you wave a gun in his face. Maybe we can use some sort of reward."

"Like if I tell him I have my one million and does he want it?" Romero felt some hope in his chest.

"He says he'll take it and makes the call and instead of giving him the cash we kill him."

"Kill him," Romero continued, "and make it look like an accident."

"Some plan. But what if he wants to see the money before hand?"

"Cut up a phone book and I'll pack it in the case right. Add some money from my account, to give it some reality, and hope he only gives it a cursory glance."

"And if he wants to count it?" Morris went.

"So scrap that plan," Romero rose and paced once more. They thought in dead silence and Morris broke it with, "One of the assholes you were going to whack in order to protect yourself? What if you planted your suitcase in his place? What if we convince said Russian that this cat used your name in the robbery as cover?"

"How do we pull that off?"

"Ask the asshole."

"Huh?" Romero stared blankly.

"Let's see if this asshole knows what's going on. If he doesn't we use him because of his ignorance." Morris shrugged. "If he does know about your problem we move to the next asshole."

"And if asshole number 2 knows?"

"Sacrifice another heister. Sorry but it'll be you or him."

Morris called Asshole #1: Bob Derby. Morris and Derby exchanged polite chit-chat and Morris faked laughed at his jokes, finally he asked him if he knew about some Russian asking for Romero.

"You haven't heard anything about that?" Morris rubbed his chin. "Listen Derby,

Romero has this powder guy looking for him. I call him the Russian because Romero told me his name, but I forgot and all. I recall that it was a commie name. Do you think you could stop somewhere and cover for another brother?" Morris bobbed his head. "Romero's willing to drop you ten-G for the job. It's kind of special." Morris smiled.

"Great. Okay. Listen to this…"

The plan was to have Derby stop into town and retrieve Romero's suitcase from Morris and take it back with him to Jersey. He was to hold it for Romero until he needed it back. Unbeknownst to Derby the only thing inside would be flour wrapped to look like heroin. This, of course, to throw Derby off if he did peak inside. Derby would then go to Atlantic City for awhile, talk to some connected guys he knew, talk about some Russian looking for Romero about a job *he* actually did. That he, Bob Derby, had the suitcase to prove it. Morris told Derby that said Russian was making Romero's life miserable about his portion of what was in the suitcase. That he threatened to steal the case back, instead of letting the deal be brokered as was agreed upon in the first place by both parties. That the Russian was making threats against Romero's life. Morris told Derby that he wanted to create the illusion that it was Derby himself who was the idea man, and he only called himself Romero as an alias for when he burned the Russian of his cut. It was effortless because the Russian never met Romero in person but one of Big G's couriers. So it would be easy for the ruse to work out. He needed Derby to chat up some connected guys about how it was him, Bob Derby, who set up the suitcase deal and used

Romero's name to do so. That it was Bob Derby who used the alias Romero in order to throw off that, Russian son a bitch, who he knew would cheat him. The Russian, who was small time, would balk when he heard through his inquiries that Romero was just an alias, and the guy he was hunting was connected to a family, however, loosely affiliated, and the Russian would leave him alone.

Morris said, "Of course, the Russian won't be scared off, and he'll whack Derby."

"Might even start a Red Mafia vs. Italian mob war," Romero rubbed his chin.

"That would be nice," Morris stretched tiredly. "We just have to worry about word getting to the Russian. That and hope Derby is killed fast enough, so he doesn't spill the beans that would create further doubt in the Red Mobs mind."

"Until then?"

"Don't talk to bullets," Morris sniffed.

Diane began to dress, and Romero watched her from the bed. Diane's company filled the void plenty ever since his not-break-up with Sarah three months ago. It was so far a pleasant relationship. She even helped him unpack, and she wasn't too intrusive about things he had no interest in her knowing. Now she was off to work, and Romero would resume his day of wondering if the bullet out there would come or not. He would wait for the phone call that might never come and he would carry the gun on him everywhere he could to protect himself.

He was in the shower when Morris called. He dressed taking his time not wanting to excite himself too much by rushing to return the call. Morris hadn't left a message, and he made himself ponder that for a moment and then snapped himself to and made the call. "My boy!" Morris said, cheerily. "You read the paper!?"

"No. I don't like being kept up on that. Too stressful. All bad news and such,"

Romero took the phone to the window to spy down the street.

"Says in the paper that New Jersey mob connected Robert 'Bob' Derby who has an extensive criminal record from robbery, aggravated assault and suspected of murder of so and so was found shot twice in the head in his car. A meter maid found him slumped over the wheel, the killer apparently walked right up and fired into the side window, as it was shattered."

"Morris you're brilliant," Romero said with a genuine smile, real feeling inside.

"Well thank you my boy!" the old man sang.

"Are you enjoying your meal?" Diane asked him across the candlelit table. They were eating dinner at some trendy wood paneled interior setting and Romero picked at the food trying to feel comfortable in the good news from that morning. He kept wondering if the Russian was still out there. Maybe he wanted to come after Romero. To be sure. He knew time would tell. Derby was murdered not too long ago after the plan was put into motion.

It had been about three weeks and he wondered if he could wait that long?

"Dinner is fine," he told her. "Just distracted about work and such. Thinking about investing and I'm getting the itch to work again maybe."

"Well you don't really do much during the day. So that would be good."

"Yeah. Yeah I suppose. Or I'll do the gym thing. I'll get the membership and do that. It'll take some time off. Maybe I just need a hobby. For awhile I had one which was painting. It worked well, and the hours would fly."

"Why did you stop?"

"Then everything became about painting," he lied.

After sex, he watched her getting dressed and he asked her if she wanted to stay the night. She declined saying he didn't want her sleeping over anyway, so she'd just go home. Romero said she was being silly and to come back, and she shook her head before kissing him on the lips and heading out the door.

Three weeks and she still won't sleep over, he thought. For all I know, she has a husband. Maybe kids. At least a boyfriend. Then again it wouldn't make sense to introduce me to her friends if that were the case. Shit.

He saw something in the newspaper that made him buy it. Derby's murder was mentioned, but the predominant story was of FBI big shots who heard grumbles about a Red Mafia and Italian Mafia beef. Bloodshed was their primary concern, and there was some who speculated that the Italians desperately needed the ROC (Russian Organized Crime) pipeline and one murder of a crook who was only tenuously connected wasn't worth the trouble.

It took another week for him to breathe again. He was back at Morris's counter while the old man stirred another coffee, and they discussed their engineered events. "A man with Russian mob ties was found floating face down in the Hudson." Morris then sipped his coffee.

"It's him?" Romero queried.

"Found shot behind the ears twice. He had the tattoos that indicated that not only had he been in prison but that he was of fearsome character and that he had killed many."

"So he was the hit man?"

"I'd say the Russians consented to his murder in order to save the relationship."

Morris slurped more coffee and hissed because of the heat. He then bobbed his shoulders as if saying, 'That's it,' but then he commented, "Who would have thought an old bastard like me could con the Russian and Italian mob? With one phone call no less?"

Outside in their jackets the two men danced to warm themselves. They had stepped outside on the porch to watch the first flurries fall to earth. "Been awhile since snow," Morris told him. "Pretty's up the neighborhood. Makes it look clean. Makes it look like the distant past, when I was a young boy. Snow does take me back."

Quietly they observed the heavy flakes descent and Morris asked him with amusement, "You and the woman still involved?"

"Yes,"

"Serious?"

"Not really," then Romero asked, "What do you make of a woman who won't sleep over?"

"After sex?"

"Yeah."

Morris shrugged. "I'd say you should enjoy it before it burns out and know that'll burn out. A woman who won't sleep over is a woman who's not too satisfied if you ask me. Of course, I don't mean sexually, but she might not be getting her emotional needs met. So I guess this relationship is right up your alley." Morris shook his head and patted Romero's back. "Screw her and enjoy it is all I can say."

"That is my pattern," Romero admitted.

"We're private men." Morris cupped a snowflake. "Big flakes coming down."

Romero looked from his chair out the ground to floor ceiling window of his loft at the powdered landscape of the city. He had a beer in one hand and music played from the radio. He thought about the woman he had been seeing presently and then he thought about Sarah and where she was. He thought about stabbing poor Derby in the back. He hadn't liked the guy, and that was the reason they chose him to die. Derby had said yes to help him, and now Romero felt the minor sting of his betrayal. He thought on Muller whom he spared, and because of that two more men had been killed. He probably would still do the same thing. But still. Finally, he thought about Morris. His booker. The old man. The man who's brain put the plan into motion. The man who sat out there in that big lonesome house, the most dangerous codger in the city.

5

The Trojan Thief.

He was back in, and he couldn't believe it. Romero thought about how he should have stayed home to live his carefully maintained life. He was here, yet again, hiding, crouched down in a dumpster as he was being carried via garbage truck inside the fenced in lot. The garbage truck lowered him, and Romero braced himself, and when he felt the steel box make contact with the ground he peaked out. He was partially blinded by the bright glare of the truck's headlights and so he ducked back in and waited for the reed thin black man, Father Garrison, who drove, to take off with the truck. Then Romero would wait with a backpack strapped to him fully loaded and his usual duffel and make the move.

Minutes of silence passed and finally Romero peeked out the lid once more to find the coast clear. He climbed out and quietly eased the lid down. He walked looking everywhere and found the door leading to the basement and he went to picking the pad lock studiously, and when it came free he cracked the door an inch and found nothing below but a pool of darkness to which on sight he yanked the door open and climb down, flicking a pen light on ahead of him. He shut the door with care and crept down the steps.

He wanted to rest and searched for a spot. He came to a bathroom where he turned the light on replacing his own light. Romero then sat on the toilet and took the backpack off.

He retrieved from inside it the walkie-talkie and turned it on calling quietly for Father Garrison who answered in his own whispering. "You in?"

"Yes," Romero told him. "I'll brace myself up by the door leading into the store."

"I'll get my hands on the trigger. Say when and I'll give you the cover."

Romero checked his gun and put it away, stuffing it down the small of his back.

He shut off the bathroom light now knowing where to walk. He found the flight of steps up to the street level of the large shop mart where a local drug dealer kept his cash in a safe. Father Garrison, who's meat and potatoes were strictly robbing drug dealers, had rigged a car to explode across the street. In an alley, the car sat as to minimize any civilian casualties. The idea was to provide an excuse for the door's alarm at the rear of the shop to go off. It was so rigged to protect their soon to be laundered money. The safe hidden in this room was surrounded by a cage which also functioned as a stock room. It was in this room after the alarm had been reset that he would wait between the high shelf against the wall, for the store to close. He would then drill through the safe and retrieve the money. Father Garrison would get the rear rolling gate open by hook or by crook and bring in their escape vehicle.

Romero put his hand on the doorknob, and he tried turning it but found it stiff, and then he found the keyhole, sighing at having to pick it. He was hoping they weren't smart enough to do that. Hoping the turn dial of the safe was the only precaution they needed than a lock for the basement, but these guys weren't taking chances. They were using alarms after all, so he figured he shouldn't be so surprised.

Romero got out his light and flicked it on and knelt on the dusty step and began the process of working on the tines in the keyhole. He got the pick in and the tension bar and went to work and was startled momentarily by the boom of hip-hop music up above followed by laughter. When Romero finished, eased the pick and tension bar out and wiggled the knob finding it unlocked, and he extracted the talkie again giving Father Garrison the green light. "Ready?" he asked him.

"Alright," Father Garrison said. "You hear the boom—and you will—pop that door on open and hide your ass."

"Will do."

Romero listened closely. He smirked at the notion of listening closely for a bomb to go off and when it did he was stunned by the boom. He froze before jerking himself out of it and into action; Romero opened the door setting off the alarm. Out in the urban night, the alarms of several parked cars went off as well, adding cover for his bypassing the door.

He got into the storage room and shut the door locking it behind him, and he made for the nook behind the shelf, and he pushed the duffel ahead of him. He hunkered down as far back as he could against the concrete wall. He pushed a large tub of ketchup to the side to spy out from behind. It was at least a minute before the alarm stopped as well as the alarms of several cars outside. Then footsteps came and outside the cage, an intimidating black guy peered in sweeping his eyes before closing them to the locked door. He seemed satisfied it was locked, and he strutted off with a relaxed gait.

Fire engines came and then police. All the while Romero waited and waited until the shop should have been closed. Finally, the shop did close after an extra hour of business. Romero presumed it was because the men in the shop wanted to gawk at the fire engine and cop cars. The uniformed men and women marching around maintaining the crowd, Romero imagined. Bomb squad up there perhaps but he didn't think so. Father Garrison's improvisational bomb was nothing to make the police worry about another Unabomber. However, he expected bomb squad would poke around to make sure what's what and standard procedure. Write it off as more inner-city mischief.

Romero heard the grate being lowered and locked over the doors and windows.

He listened for another few minutes and then got out the talkie. "It's me. I'm doing my thing now."

"Right on," Father Garrison whispered.

Romero put the drill together and plugged it into a socket he found behind several boxes of toilet paper. He got the magnet humming fastening it to the safe. He flicked the power and the bit whirred. It cut in, and Romero turned the wheel guiding the bit in further until he was certain he was through in the wail of the drilling. He saw the familiar brass of the locking mechanism and got out the hammer and chisel and freeze gun, and he zapped the brass until it was white. The cracking sound, that was minute, came to his ears. He wedged in the chisel and struck roughly with the large hammer shattering the mechanism and the safe was his.

He loaded up the money into the backpack and the rest in the duffel, and he lugged it over by the door to the cellar. He told Father Garrison that he was ready and waiting, and he hefted the duffel breathlessly and put one hand on the knob. He made himself take one more breath, and he unlocked the door and swung it open setting off the alarm once more. Romero ran down the steps almost tripping because of the duffel, and he jumped the last few steps making a dash for the door to outside and the lot area. He climbed out huffing some, telling himself that he would use his gym membership, for real this time and he almost fainted when he saw the getaway car crash through the gate and squeal to a stop in front of him with Father Garrison behind the wheel.

They were taking off with curious glances from young men on the street who wouldn't see them well as the interior lights were off. Some were wandering to the shop, and some ran toward it. Corner boys checking on their bosses profits.

Father Garrison laughed a few minutes later as he slowed down going into some high walled and barren underpass in the night. "We did it, Romero. We did it."

"Yes," Romero just said.

"Feels good! Feels real motherfucking good!"

150, 000 dollars divided two ways left Romero and Father Garrison 75, 000 each exactly.

They did the cut while relaxing at Father Garrison's pad above a pizzeria that was closed for the night. Father Garrison was ecstatic and lit up a joint and Romero passed telling Garrison he'd better be off. That he would drive the rest of the way to Philly, and he shook Garrison's hand and took his cut along with his tools. He left the talkie as that belonged to Father Garrison along with the backpack. He had his money snug in the heavy duffel.

Romero was then back on the road in one of the cars from his lot back in the city.

He was again in the underpass where up ahead he would take a right away from where they'd come, and get himself back on the road home. He saw the distant sky-scrapers and couldn't see the appeal of Pittsburg. He had been here before, but he had a lousy time with a girlfriend, and maybe that was it.

He heard the car shudder and then in the middle of the underpass the car slowed, then it coughed and shud-dered some more, and before he knew it the car crawled to a stop dead in the street leaving Romero sitting looking up around at the high slabs of concrete around him.

Romero pushed the car along with him which was a near impossibility as he was going up an incline. He had checked under the hood, and no cause for its demise was present in his cursory examination. He figured it could have been the battery, but he wasn't sure and he cursed himself for not bringing along a spare one. He supposed he expected to be given a lucky break and that a job will go smoothly, but if a dead battery had to be his obstacle, it was sure more welcoming than finding the ROC on his back.

That and burying a body under the new exhibit in an aquarium, or pondering setting up a fellow heist man to be executed. So he pushed the car up and listened to the night sounds. Once a car came by and came to a stop, but then for some reason it took off again. He didn't get angry he just kept up pushing the car along.

When he reached out of the underpass and was free from the walls that leered over, he grabbed the wheel, and turned it to the right to guide the car toward the side of the street. Once he got it as far to the side as it would go he sat back in and threw on the emergency brake and turned the ignition. The car coughed and briefly shuddered before it died again. Romero hissed loudly and went around back to get his stuff.

He was walking away from the underpass and the useless car and passing a park soaked in the darkness that leaked from out of the trees, shrubbery and jogging paths. It was out of this shadow land that a tall black young man in a do-rag came out dressed in black. He walked out to the street ahead of Romero with his eyes firmly fixed on him, and it was as if he had been waiting for Romero the whole time. He had that lean of the head that read that he loved to cause trouble. He stopped in front of Romero a few feet ahead, his feet in a wide stance. Romero raised the duffel up by his waist slowly to cover his free hand as it reached to touch the butt of the 22. S&W in his waistband.

The thug said, "What's in the bag? Bag looks heavy, what's in it?"

"Seventy five thousand dollars and the tools I used to steal it with," Romero said.

"Okay," the thug replied, unfazed. "Hand it over."

"Or?"

"Or? Oh!" the thug laughed. "Or I'll cut you!" He produced a large boning knife from his side. He waved it up by his face. "Come on man," he told him, "give me the bag, bitch."

"No."

"Okay," the thug came toward him, locking his eyes to Romero's.

"Alright," Romero said holding the duffel out to the thug, his arm shaking at its weight.

The thug crept forward and lowered the knife, and he had a gleam in his eyes at his new victory, and as his fingers closed around the straps of the duffel Romero stepped forward still holding the bag. He pushed the muzzle of the gun up in the thug's face and told him to drop it. The thug froze, and his eyes became calculating. He yanked the duffel one more time and made as if to run off, but he then turned suddenly in his feign. Romero didn't buy the ruse, and he brought the gun up under the thug's chin and pulled the trigger twice.

He dragged the thug into the park and put him deep in a cleft under a bush and left him.

Then he returned to the car and once again tried the ignition which roared the car into life. Romero was flabbergasted. He had the crazy notion that the car wanted a sacrifice.

That Romero, by shooting dead his would be mugger had pleased the car god, and it started as a reward. Romero sat behind the wheel and revved it awhile and saw he had enough gas and drove.

It was on the interstate that he called Diane who answered sleepily from bed.

"It's me," he said.

"You done?" she asked.

"Yes, I'm coming home now."

"Wake me up," she said amorously.

"If I get there in time."

"I don't care if you get back here at five in the morning or six. I want you on top of me, do you hear?" she giggled.

"I'll do what I can," he said. "My car died, and I almost got mugged."

"Oh no," she became suddenly seriously worried. "You okay?"

"I made off with my lightening speed and I lost him. Then I circled back for my car and it thankfully started again, and I took off."

"I'm glad baby," she purred. "Get home safe."

"Go to sleep,"

"You want to talk some more? I'll stay with you until you get back?" she said, and he saw her in his mind rolling around under the sheets in her nightie with the phone to her ear.

"It's okay, babe," he said. "Go to sleep and I'll wake you when I get back."

She had been staying at his place more and more and the issue about her not being able to sleep over was settled. Diane had, in fact, been in a relationship with a boyfriend and was cheating on him and Romero to some extent. When she told she had broken it off with the boyfriend and had kicked him out, Romero shrugged and said all was forgiven.

Since then, she had been a stabile and reliable girl-friend. She was loving and sexual, and Romero never had to sit around staring at the wall wondering what to do. She was full of ideas and not intrusive about what he did professionally every now and then. Which to her was invest-ment speculation. She didn't probe too much into it, so he didn't have to lie much. To her he was just finding ways to make his wealth grow.

Romero found himself abruptly with a social circle that she had brought with her to the relationship. He didn't care for much of her friends, but he was courteous and tried to be charismatic. The dinners and bowling and mov-ies with them were becoming the norm, and it was hard to adjust to in the beginning. Before he told women almost as a rule that he had been a loner by nature, and they had to respect that. However, as time passed, he seemed to tolerate people more and more. He forced himself to get out there and connect with others. It didn't work. He didn't connect, but he made like he did and found that, sometimes faking he was invested in the relationships, was enough compared to the barren private life he had to deal with before Diane. Hell, before Sarah. Before all of the women.

At home, he crept to his trunk and unlocked the padlock. He stuffed his tools into the now spacey trunk and then the money with it. He smiled at the bills he played with momentarily, and he locked it up. He had, on a discussion with Morris, come to a plan that would settle once and for all his inability to stop working. Romero told Morris that he would accept jobs in order to reach his limit. A financial goal he would reach. Romero gave him the number 3 million, and he went to work. He was already a little over a millionaire, but he had nightmares of destitution where he was back in the hovel where he was after his mother died. Back among family and he couldn't squelch the insatiable urge that came to pad his retirement fund. Romero realized he was now obsessed with becoming rich. Becoming secure.

He said to Morris as if coming clean: "I want to be wealthy."

Morris nodded and said, "Okay. You like Pittsburgh?"

So Romero now had a healthy 75 grand to fatten his kitty. He would invest it and wait for another solid job. He would exercise at the gym and lunch out. He would eat a dinner with her friends and spend lazy afternoons and nights more often than not in his pad. Comfortable in the knowledge that his ill gotten gains were laundered and invested properly. It was Morris who taught him all the tricks and skills to handle himself in the event of his dying eventually.

Christ if that ever happened. A pit opened inside Romero's chest. He knew he would feel like the loneliest person on the planet. He thought again how wise it was to make himself try to be the better friend to Diane's group.

Romero slid into bed beside Diane, and he wanted to sleep. His hand though ran up her thigh, and suddenly he had to have her.

Romero was at the gym when he saw a familiar face wandering by outside downtown. He jumped off the treadmill and quickly wiped his face and made for the door leaving the machine running. Outside he saw her from the back with her familiar crazed hair and he shouted, and her eyes widened and she smiled putting both hands over her mouth.

Romero felt oddly naked out in the cold wearing running pants and a muscle shirt with his small white towel around his shoulders.

"I'm so glad to see you!" she said, and they awkwardly hugged.

He took her by the arm and guided them away from sidewalk traffic. "Glad to see you too," he said. "I was in the gym," he pointed over his shoulder.

"You must be so cold right now," Sarah chuckled.

"Listen, where are you going?"

"I have a job interview, and I'm trying to be punctual because I have these fears about being late," she said in her usual neurotic way. "I'm sure if it came down to it, I would show up early for my own execution. I mean I really don't like being late." Then her hands came up defensively, and she said, "Not that I'm trying to make any excuses because I'm so happy to run into you. I broke up with my boyfriend to move out here.

I've been seeing no one except my mother. I've been sitting around by myself for the *entire month* I've been here. Which isn't any different than when I was back home working that dead end job. I'm so glad to have left, so..." she nodded and, "How are you?"

"I'm cold," he said.

"Oh! I'm sorry I trapped you out here!" she put her palm to her forehead.

"No it's fine because I'm glad to run into you too. Listen why don't you go do your thing and then ring my cell number, and we'll do, I guess, brunch. Huh?"

He walked back into the gym; his machine still unoccupied and he climbed aboard to finish his run. He had to admit he was incredibly glad to see her and that she was in town. He just didn't know why. Is it because she's single? So what? He wondered if the entire time he had wanted some relationship with her, but he wasn't sure if that were it either. He had been aggravated when he found out she was seeing someone else and he didn't know why. He told himself that it was because he wouldn't have anyone to talk to on the phone. He knew there was a certain amount of escape when talking to Sarah. He didn't feel like himself. He felt like a young man with opportunities that were noble. Or at least more tolerable, morally.

They had brunch, and she was taken with how much the city had changed. She said he had meant what he said about the nightlife and the multitude of places one can go within walking distance downtown. Sarah ate gingerly and when asked about how her job interview went she exhaled and began once more with her nervousness. She said, "I was qualified so there was that. But I always feel my personality turns off people from hiring me. I'm too neurotic and jumpy." She rolled her eyes. "I might as well say it, I'm also twitchy. I get this weird thing where I twitch during interviews."

"Twitch?"

"Yes. What happens is I'll be sitting there and I can feel my left eyelid start to twitch, and I know it's not physical because I'll be in another interview. Like my last one. And I'll feel my right eyelid start up and then it becomes embarrassing by—by the *intensity* of it." Her voice took on a shakiness to it, and she seemed to gather all the sudden the nervousness as if reliving the event. "And— Oh!" she covered her eyes with both hands suddenly a wreck and then her hands did a sweep further messing her hair some more. "She asked me! Do you understand? She asked me if I needed an ambulance.

Oh my god!" she said and took in some drink from her straw.

"That's something," he said. "But I'm sure you'll get work. Like you said you're qualified."

"Oh thank you," she quietly said and smiled.

"So what are you doing now?" she asked him later.

"I made a very successful deal and so I don't have to work if I want. But I did, and it went surprisingly well. My car coming back died, and I almost got mugged, but by and large I think my luck has turned. I got a nice place; so I'm more worried about keeping my position as handsome and lazy man about town."

"But are you having fun?"

"I'm enjoying myself," he admitted. "I don't think I know what fun feels like anymore. Except sometimes after a job has passed, I feel this thrill at recollecting it.

Reliving it."

"Well good," she commented picking at her food. "You're taking satisfaction with your job. That's what I want."

"You'll get it," he assured her.

He was juicing as he usually did only at noon because of his brunch. He was a bit behind schedule and after mixing the vegetables, he stood by the sink drinking it out of a large glass. He was rerunning his conversation with Sarah. Then the phone rang, and he answered to hear Morris tell him bad news he had.

"What bad news?" Romero asked.

"Father Garrison is in a jam."

"Oh?"

"He's being followed. Or so he thinks. He says he's certain no one knows you were with him on the job."

"Good luck to him, is what I say," Romero shrugged.

"He wants your help, Romero. Said if he gets grabbed up and tortured he might rat you out. Bastard was honest at least," Morris said bitterly.

"Well I'd do the same thing," Romero commented. "So what? He wants me to drive on down there. And do what? He wants me to protect him?"

"He wants you to watch his back."

"Stupid."

"He says that this dealer is following him with some guys or has some guys following him. He says he left home and was being tailed. He saw the car trailing him on his usual rounds." Morris said, "He just wants you to have his back for his leave from town. Father Garrison says that this young mope is no threat outside the city, let alone outside the country and that he's going down eventually. So he won't have to worry forever."

Romero raised his window shades letting the sun warm him through the glass.

The temperature, frigid outside. "Father Garrison is right. These young dealers in the city don't have much of a shelf life. Although he might be around a few more years, given the money he's making." He exhaled and stood. "Okay. I'll go and watch his back until he leaves town."

"Shouldn't take long," Morris tried comforting him. "Says he'll be swapping rides and he's gone. He just wants you to be with him as he makes his collection rounds."

"Me? muscle?"

"You said you have been spending a lot of time at the gym."

"In the morning is all."

Romero packed with a gun and some spare clothes just in case. He took one fat brick of cash on the chance he couldn't use his cash cards for whatever reason. He told Diane he was leaving for maybe a day or two. He kissed her goodbye and headed out certain she was plenty baffled by his abrupt departure.

He drove through the underpass once more and only tossed the quickest of a glance out the side window at where he had dragged the thug's body. He wondered if it was still there and then pushed it from his mind.

Romero parked a block from Father Garrison's place. It was dark now but still early in the evening. He dug into his small suitcase and pulled a gun out. It was a Luger with a silencer attached by a clamping arrangement, as it was for a bigger gun. Romero stuffed it into his pea coat pocket, got out the car with a suitcase in the other hand. His free gun hand firmly gripped the butt of the weapon letting it rest in his palm inside the pocket. Up ahead he saw the neon red and green of the pizza sign where up above Father Garrison stayed in a closet of an apartment. As he got close enough to cross the street, he saw something that made him stop.

Romero was fairly certain he got back to the car without being seen, and he sat at the wheel and ran again what he saw. Romero had seen parked at the front of the pizzeria a Ford Explorer. Inside a black man was on a cell phone which was visible by a square source of light from a screen and he was listening or talking. He also had his head tilted up at Father Garrison's place, and his focus was up there alright. Romero was certain he wasn't there alone. There had to be a couple of guys up in Father Garrison's place.

"Or?" Romero said aloud.

He could work there, be waiting for his next delivery. He could have family inside ordering. So what if he looked up at the apartment? Just some guy ordering a pizza and waiting.

Romero drove off looking for a payphone, and he came to one further along by ten minutes. It sat by its lonesome outside a bank. Romero parked and dropped some ready quarters and called Father Garrison. His phone rang and rang and on the third he answered suddenly, and he sounded uncharacteristically serious somehow. It was as if the cock had lost its strut. He was either scared or in some danger at the moment. As in someone was in the room with him.

"Are you alone?" Romero asked him.

"I'm sorry what?" he answered back.

"Are you alone?" Romero repeated tensely.

"Oh! No, no. No, you got the wrong number. No, that's fine it's downstairs. Add a three after the number instead of the four. Yeah. That's the pizza place."

"How many?"

"Alright! No, I said, add a *three* at the end. No, at the end. Okay. Bye." He hung up.

Three men upstairs with him. They had Father Garrison up there for a torture kill session. Make him give up where the money was and then kill him and find and whack the accomplice.

He got back in the car and drove back toward Father Garrison's place unsure what he would do, but it had to be something and quick.

Romero knocked on the Explorer's passenger side window across the driver who jerked a look at him and frowned. Romero smiling raised a small pizza box and said, "Friends ordered this for you."

For a moment, the driver looked blankly at him and then suspicion and desire both played over his face as he eyed the pizza box. Then it happened. The driver lowered the window and stooped to grab the box and Romero shoved it in and aimed the gun at the driver's face. The driver stared at what must have looked like a large barrel a bowling ball could roll out of aimed right on him. His eyes widened, and he sniffed before putting on a mask of anger. "Open the door," Romero told him.

When Romero slid in he and the driver took a moment to gawk at each other.

Romero motioned to the wheel with his gun and said, "Grab the steering wheel. Ten and two. Then bow your head." The driver quietly did what he was told but was fuming.

Romero told him to close his eyes. The driver's eyes bugged some. He made to say something but stopped himself. "Close your eyes," Romero repeated smoothly. The driver did, and Romero raised the gun. With the butt, he whacked the back of the driver's head once, twice, and three times until the driver groaned and collapsed against his door. Romero watched the whites of his eyes as they had rolled up, lids fluttering.

He handled the driver and ignored the loud music that made for the driver's ringtone and he made sure the man was hogtied. Then with the driver's own socks he rolled them up and used them as a gag and taped it in his mouth with electrical tape. All this he did while the unconscious driver lay across the backseat.

He looked up out the window toward Garrison's and saw the light was on, but no one peered down. Romero got out on the driver's side, and he ran behind the alley between row houses and the pizzeria. He looked and found beside a dumpster a fire escape and he moved the dumpster under it and he climbed up trying not to make a commotion. He stopped outside the window that glowed orange from the dingy bulb that illuminated the dank hall that led to Father Garrison's place. He tried the window, but it wouldn't open. He cursed under his breath, then peered into the window carefully and saw standing outside Father Garrison's hall, a heavy set black man who could have been three hundred pounds easy. The man had shades and was wearing all black and Romero leaned back and sat against the brick wall with the night wind whipping around him above the streets. It was chilly. His hands were back in his pockets, and he pondered and sensing that time was running out he slinked back to the window and spied the interior.

Now the heavy set man looked down the stairs, and he whirled around, and with some intent, he made his way back to Father Garrison's door and opened it. He didn't go in.

Instead, he stopped halfway in and seemed to be talking. He was gesturing with his arms it seemed and Romero knew it had to be about the driver.

When Romero tapped loudly against the window with his finger, it was when the heavy set man was going down the stairs. Romero saw an opportunity but also a bold act that needed to be done, he reasoned, in order to stop the heavy set man from finding the body of the driver all trussed up in the back. The tapping got the attention and the heavy set man began to turn. Romero ducked away but now with the silencer he continued tapping the very bottom of the glass. He wouldn't see the long barrel of the suppressor. He would look for a branch or maybe a bird and any way here he came.

Romero could see his palms press against the glass. The man couldn't see around clearly in the night and Romero hoped—but wait. Here, he is lifting open the window. Romero heard the fat man wheezing and a hot stream of steam licked out like dragon's breath. As soon as Romero saw the round ebony head come out the window, Romero brought the gun up and down, up and down, up and down, until the fat man vomited and whined for a moment in his throat, like some little girl seeing a bug.

Romero waited just a moment for any comment or action from within the hall, and nothing came except the labored breathing of the big guy. Romero pulled him out forcefully, and he hogtied him as well with the electrical tape. He used the heavy fellow's socks as another make shift gag. He taped it in and examined his second piece of work of the night.

Romero waited by the window for another investigation from one of the men in the apartment with Father Garrison. Romero checked his tape and saw he was not going to have enough, and as if aware of the thought, another someone opened Father Garrison's door, and he could hear keys being punched. They beeped, and it came to him with sudden alarm that he needed to get the fat man's cell phone.

He was too late. It rang a tune out that was loud. Romero found it, and it was lit up and vibrating in his hand.

Huh, Romero thought. One of the men calling was nicknamed *Slippery D*. Christ!

Romero shook his head. He shut the thing off and chucked it off the fire escape where it exploded loudly, but what did it matter anymore. He wanted Slippery D to come. (That didn't sound right.) He wanted Slippery D to make his approach. When the thug thankfully stuck his head out while gripping a Berretta, Romero smiled at him and pressed the Luger against Slippery D's eye socket and shot him.

Romero climbed into the hall and walked brazen to the room. A commotion sounded, and it was coming straight to the door. Romero hugged the wall beside the door.

When the door swung open forcefully, Romero twirled and kicked a leg out, and a skinny little man with dreadlocks made a loud '*Woof*' sound, and he fell on his back. The little brother on the floor was gripping a Magnum revolver which was silver and too large for him. Romero stepped in and kicked the gun away, and he shut the door behind him and scanned around finding no one else inside. At least anyone standing because Father Garrison was shirtless and bloody. His blood was also mixed in sweat, and his chest heaved. His one open eye was leaking tears while the other was swollen shut. Romero saw the cigarette burns and knife cuts and one shoulder looked dislocated. Romero saw the baseball bat against the wall. Pliers sat on a dinner tray; two molars bloodied beside it; Romero saw the trickling of blood out the corner of Father Garrison's grimacing mouth.

Dreadlocks tried to stand, and Romero kicked him in the teeth with the toe of his shoe and the tiny man yelped loudly and cupped his mouth. Blood began seeping out from between his fingers. Romero exhaled wearily and came up close to Dreadlocks, pressed the barrel against his chest where the heart was, and he fired twice, and the gun only emitted small popping sounds.

❖

Father Garrison thanked him over and over again with sloppy sounding words. Romero saw that his jaw was broken, and he helped the broken bodied man to his feet. He helped Father Garrison with a shirt. It was a button up job and Romero put it over him carefully with it already buttoned. He got a pair of sunglasses on Father Garrison and a fedora from his closet and he halfway looked healthy.

Halfway.

They made it down the stairs and out into the street where Romero could see no commotion coming from the backseat of the explorer. Father Garrison lit a smoke against the hood of the vehicle while Romero climbed in shotgun, carefully with his gun out, and he checked and saw the eyes of the driver watching him, alert and furious.

The eyes beamed murderous hate.

Father Garrison smoked gratefully and watched beyond the glass into the sleepy but still open pizzeria. He heard the passenger door close and saw Romero put his gun hand back behind the seat in the darkened interior. He saw his savior turn his face away from what was about to happen in the backseat. The gun's report was like a paper bag popping from inside the vehicle. Father Garrison looked through the glass, and he saw no indication from the staff who ran the place that they heard anything.

The Explorer went out the underpass where he had killed that would be mugger, and it parked. Father Garrison offered to help, but Romero told him to relax, and he would get him to a hospital over the state line in no time. The three bodies joined where the mugger was still rotting under a cleft covered by a thick layer of twigs and leaves. He pushed them as far in as he possibly could and he pulled the tape off the driver as the tape had his fingerprints on them.

He crossed the state line and got Father Garrison to the hospital. As soon as Romero removed the shirt, hat and glasses off of Father Garrison, the doctor hissed and demanded to know what happened.

"He was mugged," Romero told him. "He wouldn't pay up, and they beat him with a bat and held him down and did this!" he threw an angry hand at the wounded body.

More thanks came, and Romero waved off the gratitude. He asked Father Garrison, "Where's the money?"

Answering from a pleasant land of painkiller, he told Romero his money from the job was stashed behind his radiator in a compartment in his bedroom. Romero assured him that he would get it and left a heavily sedated Father Garrison to sleep.

The pizzeria was closed, and the street was still ignorant of the violence that had been happening in it. Romero got the money which was wrapped in a heavy duty trash bag. He threw it over his shoulder and made sure to wipe any surface he touched. He didn't think it would matter, but he wanted to be careful.

Out in the hall he felt the chill as he stopped at the steps. He spun around and saw the window. Romero pulled his gun out, and he crept over.

Outside, the heavy man was watching him. Fear was in his eyes. His mouth still taped. In the chill of the early morning, the cold had made snot hang out one nostril.

Romero sat the bag of money aside and tucked the gun behind him. He said, "I'm contemplating mercy. Stand up," he twirled a finger for illustration. "Turn around. Come on. Come on. Don't be scared. I'm going to cut the tape off. Good. Good boy."

Romero broke his neck, and another nook in the park was filled.

6

Thief in the Mist.

Miami.

Romero had called Sarah before he got to the hotel where he was staying with Diane. He dialed and waited, sitting in the parking lot, and she answered with the uncertainty that was always common in her voice.

"Sounds like a drag!" she laughed.

"Well I'm not too crazy about her friends, but I have to be nice."

"Still. You don't like golf? What about swimming pools? I would imagine you don't care for either of them."

"I don't particularly enjoy either, no." He said, "I'll be spending my time down here, watching Diane and her friends trollop around laughing and such."

"Which you're not about doing?"

"No," Romero admitted. "But I'll sit and be good and not complain. I'll wait while they have their fun as long as we're out here."

"Well I'll leave you to it, Alex," she started.

"Have to get back to work?"

"Yes,"

"How's that going?"

"You know it just doesn't feel right that you keep sneaking calls to me," she said.

"Just a friendly chat."

"I'm not so sure your girlfriend would be comfortable though. I mean I know if I would've made calls to someone of the opposite sex there would have been jealousy."

"Duly noted," Romero sighed. "It's just I hate this town and that we have to spend so much time with her friends. I try and find reasons to like them, but I just can't warm up to them. The entire flight here all I thought about was my apartment, my car, my favorite bar and calling you." He thought while silence hung over the other end of the phone. "Well, also about another investment."

"You said the last one was a real nightmare, I believe?"

"I did, huh?"

Sarah, he could imagine then, shrugging from across the phone lines saying, "But if it's something you need to do."

"No," he assured her and tried assuring himself. "No I'm done with the whole thing. It's too risky. I made the mistake of believing the last investment would finally be easy, and it reverted into a bloodbath." He watched an attractive woman in white shorts pass the front of his windshield. She was wearing large aviator glasses out in the blaring sun and he could see from where he was that, in the distance, there was the haze of heat rising out of the ground in seemingly thick waves. "I have to do what we discussed before."

"What do you mean?"

"About filling the void."

"Well what about the painting? You said you got into that real well. I saw the duck you sent me, and it was incredible. I mean they say talent like that comes when you're born, but you seem to grasp it a lot quicker than I was able. So then I said, fuck it and went to abstract. Which was just a way I admitted to myself: Sarah? You can't paint worth shit," Sarah laughed then and ceased abruptly. "Oh, listen I have to go so..."

"Right. Well later then."

Silence. Then she said. "Sure. Later." She hung up.

He sat with Diane and the couple, her friends that she brought with her, Peter Donovan and Lisa Donovan. They sat under an umbrella by the pool, and Romero was grateful for the sunglasses for the dual reasons of shielding him from the glare of the sun and he felt it gave him a measure of distance from the three of them. Peter was going on about politics which was the worst thing next to religion to discuss for Romero or anybody for that matter. He had of course no opinion as he had no interest in the world at large. He knew he still should, but, the feelings weren't there. Romero then supposed it would be smart to adopt the ideology of Peter to make himself look better, and it would be a straightforward matter of bobbing the head in perpetual agreement with whatever he said.

The incredible thing would be that, in all of the silent bobbing of the head, Peter would remember it as a bonding moment with him and Romero who would get off easy without actually having to say anything.

Diane, who was now tanned, leaned over to him looking odd with the sun lotion on her nose and the large straw hat she was wearing. She asked him, "You alright? You haven't said anything all day. Pretty much been in your head. You sick?" She rubbed a bicep.

"Fine," he said nodding at her.

Peter was going on. "So this entire time it's an exercise of frustration." Lisa was hugging one of his arms, and she was wearing a large floppy straw hat. "I just feel like I've been screwed over one too many times by these people, you know?"

Romero didn't.

"You hope this guy is it, and it's back to business as usual," Peter waved a fly away. Lisa, nodding at his words, seemingly thinking distracted with her own thoughts. "I wonder if these guys know when they're running for office. Like is it—like they get to the oval office and some secret door opens, and men in black suits come out and are like,

'Hey mister president? Yeah, uh, this is the real deal. This is what's actually going down.'"

Romero rolled his eyes behind his sunglasses.

"Anyway," Peter abruptly finished, "that's why I don't vote anymore."

What a loss, Romero thought.

"What do you think, Alex?" Lisa asked him, and it grated Romero to hear her say his first name. Bad enough Diane used it. He preferred it remain used only in the private world of his conversations with Sarah and it felt like each time it was used by these clowns that the name lost its luster.

"I feel we lose sight of the fact that all government is, is legalized organized crime." He breathed in the hot air and continued. "Like the mafia. The mafia and all other criminal organizations are set up like governments. You have your soldiers or your button men. You have your captains and generals who are the capos and so on. That's all it is.

The era of idealism and the notion of fundamental goodness of American might and foreign policy never existed. Yes, it's good we helped finally with Hitler, but what other reasons brought us to war? Pearl Harbor, of course. Revenge. World War Two was about retaliation and then giving the economy a boom through war production than about saving the Jews from the furnaces." Romero just lifted his shoulders and remained silent looking off into the pool, and he asked himself how many of those little brats peed into it? He said next as if formally finishing his thought, "So we as a culture now are aware of our lie of moral superiority. We know now that it never existed, and so we are a generation trying to make peace with that."

They remained silent among the hubbub of the pool area in the leering presence of the resort until a waitress gratefully came by and asked them if they wanted a drink.

Lisa said, "Where are we going tonight?"

"Dancing," Diane said excitedly.

"Oh wonderful," Peter with little enthusiasm. Something he and Romero shared about the whole prospect of dancing.

"Now don't be like that!" Lisa scolded playfully.

Romero drank some of his beer and closed his eyes behind the glasses and just listened to the prattle back and forth, and he took flight, slowing down his breath, deep into his hall of memory, scrutinizing all of the past jobs since that armored truck job that have gone disastrously wrong. He dreamed on where it all went wrong, and he played all of his kills back, and he always circled back to Nelson. The snap of his neck sounding in his head and he listened only faintly to the pool's water rolling and the splashing, and he wondered if that body could possibly still be able to sit down there?

Diane jumped into the pool, and he admired her figure. In the old days, Romero would fly to Europe for a vacation awhile in between jobs. He hadn't done that in awhile, and he liked staying in some hotel in London or in Scotland. Being by his lonesome and walking the streets and taking in the sights and sounds and striking the odd discussion with someone he would never see again. This Donovan couple felt like dead weight.

He was bored and didn't know if it would be proper just getting up and leaving so he waited some, and when his aggravation grew he rose and went back into the hotel and up the elevator to the fourth floor. Romero went into the cool room, collapsing on the bed, grateful to be alone with his thoughts. He thought about his business investments and some money he had socked away around the U.S. in case of an emergency, and he knew that in today's economy that *stashed money* wasn't enough for him to survive on if the worst came and he had to run for the rest of his life. He knew money would have to go abroad and invested. He calculated on how it could be done, and he would inquire

Morris on the topic. Romero also stashed some guns in places around the country. He had read somewhere that spies did that, so when their cover was blown in some foreign country they knew where to dig and get weapons to protect themselves, and that they also did this with travel money. Romero, having read this thought it was ingenious, and early on whenever a job had come up out of town, he would make a point finding some secluded spot, like under an overpass, and bury a bag with a gun or two underneath. He even had a map marked in a small lockbox at home so he could remember where.

Romero had stopped that activity awhile ago, and he tried visualizing the spots, and they came to him clearly from the dark corridor of his mind.

He fell asleep.

When he awoke, he showered and redressed and was back out into the faded sun where the heat was still oppressive. He found the Donovan's at the table and Diane nowhere to be seen. He sat down at his seat and watched the still flooded pool with more children polluting it.

Diane sat across from him and asked him how his nap was, and Romero said fine, and he looked past her into the skyline beyond her shoulders and wondered when this long day would end. He had been a fool to agree to stay a week, and leaving Pennsylvania was the worst idea for a vacation. Diane with her prodding to go someplace warm for the winter and his need to distance himself from that Pittsburgh bloodbath.

From the images of Father Garrison's tortured body. Romero hoped he sealed things off by breaking that heavy fellow's neck.

They went back and forth about where to have dinner and Romero said he didn't care where unless he could eat a steak. So they decided on some place a stone's throw from the hotel where they drove the rented car. Inside they were seated in a booth.

Romero nixed another beer and got a ginger ale. He kept his sunglasses on until Diane pulled them off. "Stop hiding behind them, dear," she said.

Peter said as they dined: "Next time we should just go to Atlantic City, so we could gamble, right Alex?"

"You gamble," Romero gestured.

Lisa protested, "I hate New Jersey. Why would anyone want to vacation there?

It's bad enough we live close to that cesspool but to spend our downtime? No." She shuddered. "No chance."

"Such a snob," he teased. "Ms. 'Let's get a house in the Hampton's. Ms. Let's move to New York. Philadelphia is *so gauche.*'"

"Stop!" she slapped his arm good naturedly.

Romero examined a portion of the sirloin that was impaled on his fork. He considered what Big G did with Geiger's remains. He thought that maybe some unfortunate public got some of the Nazi in their own meat when they went to that little butcher shop Big G no longer had a piece of after having moved into the City of Brotherly Love. Romero said to himself that he would ask his butcher if Emmett Grandview owned a piece of his business or if he knew him. If he didn't, then Romero would continue to get his meat there.

"—lesbian experience in college and so I'm weird because I haven't?" Diane laughed. "Right?"

"I know!" Lisa lifted her glass of red wine which she had too many of. "Why do you guys care so much about that? It's like, yuck!"

The girls wanted to dance. Peter told Lisa that she was too drunk for dancing and sleepy, and she pouted but agreed that they would go dancing the next night.

In the room, Romero just lay on the bed and watched the spin of the ceiling fan and Diane went into the bathroom and showered. He toyed with the idea of calling Sarah or even Morris but stopped himself afraid for a brief second what he would hear. It was as if he wanted to avoid any pull toward what he had been trying to run from while down here in Florida. He didn't want to hear Morris going on about a job or take any chance that some problem had sprouted up whether Russian mob or friends of that drug crew he wiped out in Pittsburgh.

Diane climbed off of him in the dark and laid down with her breasts pressed against him.

He knew that even after the sex he wasn't going to be able to sleep. He felt alert, and he began to dress. He said he wasn't tired yet, and he would go down to the bar for a nightcap to which Diane sleepily grumbled and sighed seemingly already gone into her slumber. He thanked the red wine for that and stepped out into the hall and down the elevator.

He took his drink and sat by the glowing pool, as it was lit up for the night. The wavy shimmers of light danced around him and the entire pool side. He sat at their prior table watching the water, and in it a few adult couples swam in the now roomy pool. It was a quiet affair, and he felt that they chose to be down here at the present moment for the same reasons he did. A man with long blonde going to grey hair bobbed up and down with his eyes closed against the steel ladder. An attractive brunette and a blonde woman were in quiet discussion neck deep in the water while a man with the build of an ex football player, crew cut and all, was sitting in the shallow end with a beer, his head leaned back.

Later, he walked down to the beach and was pleased that he could see some stars glittering above, and he ruminated on how few he had seen while in the city. Now on the beach with a few other stragglers out and about, couples being romantic and such on the sand or on a towel, he felt some minor degree of enjoyment in his vacation. He felt the loosening of limbs. The pressure brought on by the company that was with him the entire trip, suddenly gone. He felt fully in himself. He allowed himself to dream some on owning seaside property here in Miami or maybe abroad. He wondered in his still young age how further into wealth he could push himself and what kind of life was possible from it. He was already feeling the gravitational pull of another job and he settled on how *The Take* must be high for him to become involved. It would have to be quite extraordinary.

He came to rocks off the side of the beach, and he climbed them in the dark illuminated by aid of the thin band of moonlight, and he came to the edge where water beat up around his feet. Whether it be a walk in the rain on a deserted street or sitting atop the roof while his original crew—now imprisoned—robbed below, the sense of another self would be near like a ghost offering to possess. Where the chance of the void inside could be filled fully, and all of the world around him could be new again.

Those who saw him from on the beach barely paid any strict attention. He was just a lone figure standing atop the rocks while the water beat around him and the mists off from the sea put him into a haze where his form became imprecise and as unreal and dreamlike as he thought of himself. The indistinct man, all haze and malformed.

7

Thief in a dead City.

Alone for miles in an overgrown grass yard with the
moon high up and a quarter full. No breeze, just the
drone of the cicadas around them. It was Romero and a
tall Texan named Baker. With them, the squat and reliable
Steinway. They roamed along the grass looking for the glint
of steel. Some indication that the access door was present.
The bomb shelter.

Morris received the call from Baker who had heard of
valuables long since abandoned inside of a bomb shelter
demolished long ago. The property all but abandoned
leaving the grass to overgrowth and stray cats to stalk rats
that scavenged around for food. Inside heirlooms of gold
and diamonds along with rare art were stored and left to
rot away by the property owner who had descended into
complete madness. He was loaded and alone, and the
prized possessions that made for his name taking up space
in the papers and the unique sections of certain high quality art and antique smug magazines made it likely for Baker

that there was the real possibility that his prized possessions were still there. But Baker didn't know where for about a year until he inquired about the property, which no longer existed in terms of livability, and he went to Records and got his hands on the plans of the house and garage. Baker had said there was still nothing and he inquired into the old plans searching for any comparison he could make. Maybe a redesign had been made, some strange, unnecessary architecture and when he saw the old plans he found it. The pool had been a new addition but what got his attention was listed in the old plans on the lower left. It was a marker identifying itself as a bomb shelter which was put in just three weeks after the Cuban Missile Crisis ended. Baker had told himself 'Bingo!' and contacted Morris.

Baker held a machete, and he swung through the darkness while the two men followed. Finally after five minutes, Baker's foot landed on top the hatch door with a typical hollow thud. He turned being careful to lower the large knife, and he raised his foot and brought it up and then down. He did this once and then twice, and they exchanged looks and knelt down pulling away the overgrowth that had covered the shelter's door entirely in green. It wasn't even much of a door. It looked more like a cellar door you would find leading under a house than belonging to a bomb shelter.

The lock was easily disabled after a few hard blows with a chisel and hammer. Romero tossed it aside. The door opened with a shriek and their flashlights cut into the ink black below revealing the cement steps.

"Shut the door," Baker whispered to Steinway. "Shut it gently."

They walked down into the vast cavern and along the walls covered in sheets were shapes of various sizes. Romero pulled the cover off of a concealed shape. He was greeted with a display case. He peered in seeing several small coins. Some were gold, and some were silver, some had faces, and some had buildings and animals on them. All of them, not American, so all of them mysterious to Romero. Steinway revealed four wide shipping containers and it was assumed that paintings were inside. Baker ogled these reveals, and he excitedly went about pulling the cover off of a six foot high glass case where statues stood atop shelves. All of the statues were as tall as an Oscar and were dark stone. Their expressions were also stone-like. Cold and distant with only the general outlines of faces. Some seemed to be in poses of contemplation or sadness. A few had wings and were wearing robes. They looked like monks and even had stone carved representations of a length of rope around their waists and the wrinkled presence of a hood at their backs.

More paintings were revealed, and silverware was what greeted them in a crate they pried open. Inside Baker gently pulled a folded fabric wrapped in plastic. He eased it out atop the lid of the crate which was on the ground and when he rose with it, it unfolded showing itself as an SS uniform. Baker pulled the cap out of the plastic cover and put it on his head.

Later, Steinway backed the truck up, and Romero went to work with the machete cutting a path in the high grass for them to carry the stuff into the back. Romero, the entire time, wondered when the shit would hit the fan, and he said as much to Baker when he got back down to the shelter.

"Yeah, you had some bad run didn't you?" he commented.

"Thought the last job would be easy, and then Father Garrison got himself in trouble."

"Yeah and you bailed him out, I heard." Baker whistled. "That was some baddassery on your part, man."

"It was more of trying to stop losing people I work with. You know what I mean? That truck job wiped out a pretty reliable couple of guys. King. Cohn. Deltoro.

Geiger to a certain extent before his craziness destroyed him."

Steinway came down the steps and said, "Is it true some pimp and drug dealer you know cut him up with a chainsaw?"

"Morris liked spreading the story down the grapevine didn't he?" Romero mildly amused, said, "But yes. There was a chainsaw involved."

They loaded up the goods and the coolness made it easy. Romero found Detroit surprisingly to his liking. Something about the abandoned spaces. It was as if society were being rebuilt after an apocalypse. A regeneration. Downtown was fascinating.

Desperation in duplicating a functional downtown, was all he saw, and he found it all appealing, and he wondered what Sarah would say about his sudden fondness for the decaying metropolis.

The truck was loaded up and now they all found themselves covered in a sheen of sweat. It was Baker who commented on the ease in which their operation would be carried out since this area of the city like some others were becoming vast, deserted places where cops only occasionally roamed. This place occupied few to no people so, it isn't an area that needed real protecting.

Down in the cellar Romero wiped his face with his sleeve and roamed around with his light checking for anything they might have missed. All he found were spider webs and pools of shadow. He climbed up and out and shut the door with care so it wouldn't bang and he walked the path to the truck where Baker was lowering the back door. He locked up and headed for the passenger seat while Romero jogged to the end of the block to his car. Once inside the car, he could see a weary, dirty figure pushing a shopping cart further up behind him. This figure was almost ghost like, and it stopped suddenly in the street and seemed to be watching him and the truck. The orange glow of the street lamp behind this ghost, gave it an almost halo effect that was eerie.

The growl of the truck taking off got Romero's attention and he started up the car and pulled to follow behind. He cast a furtive look into the windshield and this ghost began pushing the cart again across the street of this surrounding wasteland.

His hotel was perfectly suitable, and he woke to a sheet of rain coming down the window.

By noon, the sun was out sporadically being cut off by clouds moving swiftly in the current of air above the tall buildings. He paraded downtown as the wait inside his room was too much. He stepped into a used bookstore where an older woman, handsome, seemed grateful to see him. The place was pretty crowded with books and narrow walkways between high shelves. He walked in between aisles and perused not certain what he was searching for. After a careful study, he opted on a reasonably well taken care of paperback of *The Great Gatsby* and virtually new looking copy of *The Beautiful and Damned.* He paid with the woman smiling and telling him that he made great selections and that she was a fan of these works.

"I need something to amuse myself with," he told her. "I'm stuck in my hotel room. I don't exactly know anybody here, and I'm just waiting for a call to come so I can finish my deal and head home." He meant get his money from Baker after the goods were handed over to his fence.

"Where are you from if you don't mind?" she asked him and bagged his purchases.

"Philadelphia,"

"I've never been. It must be a lot better than here."

"Detroit has its charms."

She had a throaty laugh. "I've never heard that before. But instead of sounding sarcastic you sound like you mean it."

"If the occasion comes and I'm stuck here a little while longer, do you have any idea where a business man such as myself could spend an evening?"

She put the receipts in his bag and looked up toward the ceiling. "Well," she began, "you could go to the Belmont Hotel. The bar and restaurant is a night life in its own right."

"Spend time much down there?" he asked her.

She smiled a secretive smile and kept her blue eyes steady on him. He saw she was wearing pearls and he took in the almost too butch cut of her blonde hair. She seemed attracted, and he figured there would be no harm. Then as if reading his mind she said, "Only on the chance I might meet an interesting gentleman."

"I'm very much the gentleman," he told her leaning on the countertop.

A couple came in. The bell above the door jangling.

"I'll stop by at eight," Romero told her. "Come on down."

"You're too nice," she said quietly as the couple passed behind Romero.

"I'm just looking for company until I leave town. Don't see why it can't be you.

Right?"

So he had a date tonight at the Belmont Hotel. Dinner and drinks and maybe more. It didn't seriously bother him that he was cheating on Diane seeing as the relationship was winding down. She stopped sleeping over as much, and he was certain when he got back, she would tell him that they were over. It was always like that really.

With Diane, it started right after the Florida vacation.

He read enough of *The Beautiful and Damned* to wonder how much money this Anthony Patch actually had. He caught some unnerving sense of similarities with the man and it seemed to do with his general loafing about. He put the book down and wondered when Baker would call. He felt a curious excitement in the speculation of how much his cut would turn out from this wildly easy score. Then the notion of when the problem would arise? When would he have to run out into the night with his gun to fix a wrong or take revenge on a betrayal? What loose end would he have to clean up?

He read some more and then he put the book aside and took a shower. He dressed in a suit, and tie and splashed on some cologne. He wasn't sure why he found Margaret attractive. There was something, some charged sexual energy going on there. She had wide hips and full breasts. She carried herself in a prim manner, and she was awash in class.

He arrived at the hotel, and she was there at a round table. It was certainly a classy affair and she dressed well with a top that showed ample cleavage and a long skirt with flower print. They ordered and ate and exchanged the pleasantries of standard date talk with questions he deftly handled about his profession. He as usual turned it all back on her so as to limit inquires into his life. It was surprisingly easy, and he settled on how she knew just as much as he did the real reason behind this dinner. They were engaging in the play of a date, while the real intent was to get to the bedroom. She passed on dessert and Romero paid strict attention to her after she had done so. She had a glimmer in the eye and was smiling, and he took it as more urgency to leave and get to it than deem the dinner disastrous.

Later, they were in his bed after taking the walk a few blocks over. She was wild and energetic, and when he checked downstairs they told him a message came, and that he should call back. He jotted the number sitting up in bed, and he called as she slipped over and kissed up his back.

Baker answered almost at once. "Romero?"

"Yes? Well?"

"The stuff is still finding its way around. The things are being shopped. It'll take some time."

"Wonderful."

"Hey this is going to be a huge payoff, I know it. Now listen why don't you get on down here and we'll drink at the place around from my house. Come on. Steinway is with me."

"Thanks but I'm entertaining a woman at the moment."

"Lucky son of a bitch," Baker commented.

He read while Margaret slept. He loved the lifestyle of this Anthony Patch. The entire first portion with his waking and him in the bathroom and the sheer laziness. The slothful creature comforts that soaked the pages of the wealthy man were almost intoxicating. He finally put the book aside when sleep came over him. He let his head settle into his pillow. He dreamed of moving to New York. Getting one of those obscenely expensive apartments.

Going to need plenty more dough, he admitted. He wondered what his cut would be. Paintings of a rare nature. Statues. Coins. They had to generate a real profit. Three men—well four in on the split—the fourth being the fence? It could be a real kill.

Probably the best since he took down Golovin's safe in Brighton Beach. Christ! What a catastrophe it had turned into. Nearly dodged a Russian mobster's bullet on more than one occasion.

"Still awake?" she asked him.

"Just thinking," he said.

"You do seem the type to do that a lot."

"Shut up," he said lightly and rolled on her.

"That much, huh?" Romero said, and Baker nodded. "The painting and the statues and coins? Everything?"

"That's right." Baker said.

They were in his house, a large brownstone. They sat across each other in the kitchen and the paper bag stuffed with 36, 453 in dollars sat inside. Romero gave this disappointing bag of chump change a look, and he turned his focus back on Baker. On a hunch, he said, "You're kidding?"

"Kidding?" Baker laughed, and, "No. No, I'm not kidding. I'm as disappointed as you are. But I suppose we should be happy to get something. I mean it was a fairly easy job and thirty grand a piece ain't exactly chump change." He watched Romero watching him and couldn't hold the eye contact with him. Then he began rubbing his chin, and Romero took note of this self consoling act of his body language.

Romero continued his probing. "Where's Steinway?"

"Oh, he went back home. He was going to stay a few weeks, but his in-laws left back to Houston earlier than expected, so he booked the earliest flight that was possible and was off like a shot." Another gesture. This time he ran some fingers over his left brow. "You're fence must have been disappointed?" Romero asked him.

"Big time," Baker commented and made an exaggerated lifting of his eyebrows.

Later, with the bag beside him on the bed Romero called Morris and updated him and replayed the conversation with Baker.

"Your instincts are correct," Morris told him. "Though I can't understand why Baker would do such a thing as ripping off a fellow heister. Granted the whole honor among thieves thing is true, but I make a point setting us up with reliable people. Men who have proven to us that they can be honest in the work."

"You should contact Steinway for us. He should be back home tomorrow, and I want a full report from him."

"Will do. Now, in the meantime I take it you'll be staying the while in Detroit?"

"Yes," Romero smoothed his hair absently with his fingers then exhaled tiredly. "I thought this city was alright when I got here, and we were driving along it. I dug the abandoned quality to it with the empty buildings and derelict settings but now the place feels strange. Real unsettling."

"Can't compare with Philadelphia, can it?" a bemused Morris asked.

"No. No, it can't. It's like you can feel the difference in vitality in Philadelphia, as compared to Detroit. People usually refer to Detroit as a dead or dying city, and while the phrase is accurate it really makes sense when you see it because then you can feel it."

Then: "Or maybe I'm talking out my ass."

Romero read more of the book and paced his room. He stopped to look out his window at some cars in the road. He ruminated on why the thirty grand was such a disappointment. What it came down to, he figured, was that he had gotten spoiled. He had been racking up some hefty numbers and now thirty grand seemed a jump back from the momentum of the recent payoffs he'd been having. That and the damned book he was reading gave him the cravings of a life bigger than what he could currently afford. It was when he got out of the can that he went back to work with a passion and under Morris's tutelage had gotten himself a decent and comfortable life. Certainly it was far more comfortable than what he had thought possible, but now he had thoughts of blatant wealth and a vulgar lifestyle of easy living.

He had lunch in a restaurant that was partially attended and ate pasta and had red wine. It was a pleasant place with dim lighting and old money made up the sparsely populated dining floor. He drank at a bar and watched the baseball game on television and when plenty buzzed he tipped the bartender and walked the street oblivious to the sudden dropping in temperature since last night. He past the concierge muttering a goodnight and once in the room he collapsed into the bed and kicked his shoes off.

He dreamed he was back on that high grass plot where the score went down. He was on his ass sitting holding a gun, and he heard the rattling of what he knew was the shopping cart. He felt his heart beat fast until a sickening feeling bloomed in his chest as if it would explode in him. Then the moonlight glinted off the shopping cart as it came around the wall of green he was peeking through. It was Geiger pushing the cart he suddenly saw. Romero's perspective changed, and he was seeing in first person. He seemed to be standing in front of the cart while Geiger who was bleeding from the head, his hair matted down in coagulated blood smiled widely, his face white as the moon itself. Then an explosion blew out of the cart and out came a geyser of blood and limbs.

A familiar face he managed to catch, before he awoke drenched in sweat and fumbling for the lights with his pistol up staring at the blank room, was Nelson's. Nelson. His head tumbling toward him with eyes bulging out and looking right at him.

"It turns out Baker has become what we've feared," Morris told him after he returned from breakfast. "Steinway is back home with thirty grand himself, and he's as suspicious as you are. Well, maybe not as suspicious until I called him. He wants to come back up and meet with you about what to do about Baker."

"Christ," Romero whispered. "I can see what's going to happen."

"Thirty thousand." Morris seemed in thought as silence hung over the phone lines. "Whatever Baker's holding back is probably sizable if the kiss off is thirty grand."

"I'll let Steinway be the tip of the spear on this," Romero said. "I don't want to be too much of a participant in any forceful extractions that might be on the horizon."

Romero rolled around in bed with Margaret at her place and got dressed to pick up Steinway at the airport. Steinway came by carrying by his side a small suitcase, and they drove first to book a room at the hotel where he got a room on the floor below Romero and then before heading off to brace Baker they sat and had lunch on Romero's dime at a fancy eatery downtown.

"It might get real heavy," Steinway said.

"You mean strap him to a chair and threaten him with pliers kind of heavy?"

"Yup," Steinway nodded and forked food into his mouth.

"It cool with you if you take that up? I figure maybe I could search the place. And to be perfectly honest I've been seeing a lot of blood lately, and I've been looking for a respite from the stuff."

Steinway offered a shrug and said casually, "Sure. No problem man. I understand plenty, you've had yourself a bad stretch. Happens to us all."

They drove riding out into a quiet suburb, and they stopped a few blocks from Baker's house. It was as if in telepathic unity that they pulled their weapons and checked the clips for ammunition then they checked the chamber for a glimmer of brass inside, and they got out of the car and walked with as casual a gait as possible given the circumstances.

Baker answered with a beer in hand, and he seemed taken aback by seeing Steinway standing beside Romero. He made to talk but then halted and turned to flatten himself against the door to let them in, and once Romero cleared the doorway he heard Steinway grabbing Baker and turned to see Baker being spun roughly around and led by his collar away from the door which Steinway closed with a kick of a foot. Steinway slammed Baker forcibly to the wall and went to work frisking him, and he told Romero to search the place to see if they were alone. Romero went off with his gun out and up and he scoured looking around. He heard Baker begin to protest before it was cut off with a grunt.

Romero found no one anywhere downstairs, and he doubled back and ran up the stairs and it was the same. Upstairs, he took some time and tossed the place only in a cursory way before heading back down where he found

Baker tied to a chair. His arms were bound to each arm of the chair, and his feet were tied together at the ankles. It was electrical tape.

Steinway standing over him with his gun in his waistband said, "You know why we're doing this?"

"No," Baker coughed. "No. What the fuck do you think I did?"

Romero sat on the arm of the recliner and queried toying with his gun before stuffing it away in his pocket: "The rest of the money? We want to know how much you stiffed us so tell us by how much and tell us where the rest of the dough is, or Steinway is going to go to work on you until you do. So for the love god you backstabbing piece of shit tell us where the dough is, and we'll actually untie you and walk the fuck out the door to go our separate ways forever."

"But you're done!" Steinway fuming called. "You're name is blackballed by Morris. Nobody is going to want to work with your cheating ass as in ever!"

Baker pissed and moaned, and Romero didn't hear any of it. He found that he was standing and walking across to Baker who was going on about how they must be crazy and that he wouldn't cheat them and who are they? A bunch of cheapskates for saying fuck you to just thirty grand and so on and so on but Romero didn't catch the other bullshit Baker was spitting, and he reached out with his hand and flicked Baker's right eye out with his thumb.

Later, Romero and Steinway were in the bedroom pulling the carpet up at the corners, and Steinway with the large butcher knife cut furiously from one side of the bedroom to the next and Romero rolled it up and tossed it across the room. Steinway began jumping up and down, and sure enough the loose floorboards center of this carpet free section sounded plenty loose. Together they knelt and with the help of the large knife the boards one after another came up and out, and they were put aside by Romero who then extracted his penlight and shone it down where numerous fifty dollar bills looked right back at him.

"Should always look under floorboards," Romero muttered to himself.

They pulled plastic wrapped phone book sized money out of the hole, and they counted.

"665, 034 dollars each!" Steinway cried and laughed wildly and jumped to his feet. He did a jig and sat back down with a shake of his head and a smile that he tried to but couldn't make go away.

They loaded the money up in heavy duty trash bags Steinway retrieved from the kitchen and they began hefting them, throwing them over their shoulders.

"So now what?" Steinway asked. "I mean about. . ." he jerked his head out the bedroom door and Romero knew he meant what do we do about Baker?

"Shit." Romero pinched his chin and thought.

"I mean I was out of my head when you did what you did, but I don't know. The hell do we do with him? We going to leave him like that?"

They eased their way down the steps as if trying not to stir Baker who was anything but asleep. They peeked around the corner and saw him still in the chair.

Romero had improvised an eye patch, and it had been a long white length of paper towel.

Now it was dark with blood and Baker's other eye was half closed in pain.

"He lives," Romero said over his shoulder, "I've created an enemy for life."

Romero stabbed Baker to death with the butcher's knife.

And so it came to pass that another job that had seemed so sweet, and so promising had deteriorated so spectacularly. Another notch had been put on his belt. He was determined to get out of town with the dough. Romero was sick, and though there was no guilt that he was aware of, he felt the enormity of death on him.

Or maybe it was Detroit.

8

The white horse Score.

Romero woke up and stretched on his King sized bed. He let himself move his limbs out and spread himself along its comforting landscape. He began this ritual with some enjoyment after Diane ended the relationship. It was a tremendous feeling not to be burdened by her presence or that of her friends Romero promptly tossed aside despite Peter's assurance that they will still hang out.

He showered and walked to the kitchen in his terry cloth robe and began his day with a Guava shake. He dressed and headed to the gym where he did three hours and had a brunch at the Continental Diner. He then drove to peruse his business investments and walked along the car lot which was barren of any activity that would be profitable. He wasn't surprised the economy being what it was and he drove on to the Mainline Bar which he had a piece of. Romero walked in, and the man who was running it for him sat behind the bar reading the paper, and Romero knew damn well it was not anything but the sports page. He cleared his throat, and the flake saw him and jumped off the chair no doubt surprised by the rare visit.

"I know," Romero told him. "Still early."

"Sure is," Clarence answered back.

"Turn around on profit could be better Clarence," Romero scolded him lightly. "I have to replace you Clarence?"

"No," Clarence shook his ferret face of his.

Romero pointed at the bottles lining up behind the bar. "Well this here don't look too professional Clarence. Look. Look. You got the gin with vodka and the vodka with the cognac. Clarence, what the fuck!?"

After scolding Clarence and becoming determined to fire him, he drove to German Town and hung around the auto repair garage and inspected the space.

Mechanics, at least three of them, were at work, and Bud Fuchs was sitting in the office with his feet up on the desk talking to someone on the phone. Romero didn't bother to knock he just walked in and sat across from Fuchs who told the person on the other line he would call them back, and he sat up.

"How's business?" Romero asked Fuchs.

"Good. We're never hurting. As you probably saw we got ourselves three guys working full time out there— sometimes four. Our service here is excellent, and we got the spots playing on the radio for us. That certainly gave us a boost."

Romero watched the mechanics going about their work, and he said farewell to Fuchs and drove back home. He wandered around some and finally collapsed into the arm chair where his gaze fixed on out the window. A few minutes later he tried painting in one of his drawings, but he didn't have the heart for it. He couldn't concentrate, and he was uncomfortable. He was fidgeting around. So he stood and went by the window and wondered on what the hell he was going to do.

First things first, he told himself, I've got to fire that turd, Clarence. Second: I've got to throw some money on advertisements for the car lot. Third: I've got to do something to take up the time other than what my mind keeps going back too which is another job.

Later he visited Morris who greeted him with a knowing smile as he let him in. "You're bored aren't you Romero?"

"Yes I am."

They went back to the counter and took up what was becoming their usual positions with Romero on his side of the stool and Morris on his stool in the kitchen side.

He had visited Morris more than usual and even once accompanied him to his evening rendezvous with his group of friends at the bar. It was all out of having nothing to do, and it was at these times when he wished Diane was still around. When he was with her, he always had something to do. He had to admit the bitch of it which was his mastery of a criminal lifestyle contrasted with the pure, complete incompetence of running his private life. He was adrift and the only time he had any sense of direction was in the planning of the job and the execution. Then there was afterward when Romero returned home with a fatter kitty. The first few weeks after he was near on top of the world.

But here he was again feeling the hole inside with only the job to fill it—or at least distract himself from it.

"You want a job?" Morris whispered seriously to him, and Romero knew he had something for him.

"Let me hear it," Romero said with his own whisper.

"Alright. This job comes from Big G himself. He knows this fellow up in New York who runs a couple of corners. Man's name is Silly Walker."

"Christ," Romero snickered.

"Yeah well, this Silly Walker is having trouble keeping his corners because his supply is all gone and dried up. You know what they do when their supply starts to dry up?"

"Tell me."

"They cut it with sugar or flour or baking soda. They ration it until their product becomes nothing but the shit they cut it with. Diluted! That's the word. They diluted it, and now this Silly Walker's business is becoming ghost."

Romero raised a brow. "Ghost?"

"That's how Emmett referred to it," Morris shrugged. "It just means this Silly Walker's business is dying. The young Turks are starting to step up, and he won't be able to defend himself and keep his corners, and he might not have any more corners if he doesn't get his crew healthy and real soon."

"So my part in this?"

"Emmett wants you to drive with him down to New York this weekend. Saturday.

He'll introduce you to Silly Walker, and you'll be informed more fully. Now Emmett said that this Walker is going to offer you a very lucrative amount for the job."

"I think I see where this is going," Romero exhaled loudly. "He wants to hire me to jack some white horse for him."

Morris tittered. "White horse. The cure. Blow. Got to love those crazy names."

"So you and Diane are done?" Morris asked him minutes later.

"Yeah. And thank god. Her friends were lousy, and I'm glad I don't have to swim the same circles as them. That vacation in Florida was the longest exercise in frustration I can recall. Hell the whole Russian hit man thing wasn't as grueling and long."

"What about that other broad?"

"Sarah?" Romero wrinkled his brow in thought. "I called her a few times. Are relationship is weird. I like talking to her, but it's not like I want to date her or even sleep with her."

"How's that?" Morris probed carefully.

"I don't know. We went to the same high school. I was there for awhile—not long, and we weren't friends or anything. I just feel like when I'm talking to her I'm not me anymore but who I was before I became. . . me."

"Being you is a problem?" Morris laughed.

"Apparently. I can't place my finger on it exactly. . ." Suddenly Romero felt on the verge of something, some insight. "Like I stopped being me and became like this... nonperson. . ." He flicked a look showing a strange smile toward Morris. "It's like I used to be a real person and then just. . . stopped."

"Now you're making me worried."

"Sorry about that."

Morris leaned forward, "So this Sarah chick makes you feel like your old self?

Okay. How do you feel now?"

"I don't know." Romero squinted some and his mouth hung open and after a moment, he shut it and shook his head. "Yeah. I don't know. . . Bored."

"Man." Morris was befuddled. "You think maybe you should see a shrink about this? Because, this seem the sort of complex psychological mumbo jumbo that they'd have a field day with."

"Shrink? No, no way.—Listen. Call Big G and tell him I'll take the trip with him.

Better yet, tell him to call me."

Big G drove Romero in his Lexus. They chatted some about old times and by old times it was the rehashing of his bloody brand of justice he let loose on Geiger, the Neo-Nazi rapist murderer who was in on an armored truck heist that had then gone totally sour.

Geiger had murdered one of Big G's women and Big G's retribution was gruesome, to say the least, but it wasn't as if Romero gave a damn about what happened to the piece of shit Aryan.

Big G pointed out the windshield every now and then and was markedly enjoying his first ever visit to the Naked City. He smiled at famous buildings, and Romero and him agreed that the city was far more oppressive in its confinement. Walls everywhere, the big slab of buildings of grey and glass. The energy was unmistakable and Romero, not for the first time fantasized about living the rest of his life in New York. He watched the men and women marching along most rushing this way and that way in that unmistakable New York fashion and he then felt some giddiness. He mentioned to Big G how delightful it felt to be a first class thief being driven into New York with a heavy weight kingpin like himself and Big G cackled and pumped his arms in agreement at the sometimes spontaneous joy they received at their underworld lifestyles.

The Lexus fought its way through downtown traffic and eventually into Brooklyn where the car turned into an alley. Big G stopped the car by a green door beside a dumpster, and he honked in three long bursts, and when he ceased doing so the door opened and a dreadlocked brother came out wearing heavy denim. He peered into the car seeing Big G and he nodded and waved for them to follow.

The dreadlocked fellow said when they got out the car, "Don't worry about your ride. I'll keep an eye on it. Nobody going to touch it." He and Big G gave one another a fist bump and half a hug and Romero just exchanged a head bob with him. The dreadlocked man introduced himself: "My name is Kenny Keane. But you can call me Swifty because everybody else does."

He led them down a white corridor, and they turned to an open door where a black man with a receding hairline and black beard, his face screwed up in seemingly constant disgust stood. This man, Silly Walker had no such walk but had the gait of a man supremely in command. He strutted around from behind a desk that was flanked on either side by intimidating brothers. Silly Walker's face broke into a smile and he quickly walked over to give Big G a hug. He said, "Emmett! You looking good! Looking good! Dressing nice I see."

"Business has been good, Silly," Big G told Silly Walker. "I got no complaints at all." He turned to face Romero, and he said, "This here is my friend Romero. The one I been talking to you about. This is the guy you want for jacking purposes. He's the real deal."

Silly walker shook Romero's hand and had an appraising eye on him. He then circled back to his desk and sat down. He gave the man on his left a look and then a look to the man on his right and they both walked on out the room and the door shut solidly behind them leaving the three men alone in the sparsely furnished office.

"You know why they call me Silly Walker?" he asked, looking at Romero.

"No," Romero answered.

"They call me Silly Walker because my last name is Walker and I'm silly in the head. I admit that, my being silly in the head. But it don't got a goddamned thing to do with how I walk. Not even a goddamned little bit. Now my man Emmett here done recommended you for this job I got in mind. It got to do with heroin. You see I had me a steady supply coming out the docks but then the motherfucking feds done did themselves a raid and my suppliers got their ass locked away for life. Only fucking victory from that raid is one of the men who acted as muscle for the suppliers managed to shoot the face off of one fed." The face of Silly Walker screwed up further, his eyes blazing wide and intensely at Romero. "I had to have my crew cut the supply we got to *shit*. Fiends out there are snorting and shooting nothing but sugar and flour and baking soda. The problem is they now know it and they gone looking for their shit elsewhere. *Also*, I got me young blood out there trying to push me out." Silly Walker grinned. "But that shit ain't happening." Silly Walker leaned forward behind the desk. "I have knowledge that one of my competitors supply is coming in through the Canadian border. It arrives in of all things a police car. It's an impressive arrangement. This cop is dirty all day long, and the border security know him well, and they allow him through with little to zero search.

Hidden away in his car is bricks of heavy weight H. You see this cop has a girl he stays with on a regular basis on the U.S. side. He's one of them fucking township cops—not city. So he can make out the border in the cruiser." Silly Walker pointed his index finger at Romero. "You got to hit that cruiser and get me that supply. That supply being a fat one. I'm talking about enough to keep my crew healthy and give me enough room to maneuver and hook up with some new connection."

"Sounds like something I could help with," Romero told him. "Might have to bring in a helper."

"That's fine. But I'm telling you that you're going to get 2 percent off the package. You got that? So, if you bring in somebody then it's split."

"Or I could work alone." Romero gave Silly Walker a smile.

"Okay." Silly Walker continued; giving him the route of the cruiser. "There's a road called *Desmond* that ain't on the map. When this cop goes down the stretch of road after passing through the border, the next left will take him onto the swerving narrow road of Desmond. Now Desmond is tree lined and nicely hidden away from any prying eyes. So that'll be where to hit the cocksucker."

Romero thought it over. "I think I can get it done quickly. Of course, barring any other vehicles nearby."

"Any other vehicles nearby?" Silly Walker mused and groaned. "If they any stray vehicles nearby then you the most unlucky motherfucker in the world because that road is about abandoned all the goddamned time. I had my boys down there keeping an eye out and they been alone sitting out there about ninety percent. Suspect most people who live close by probably don't know that stretch of tar be there."

"Seems doable."

Silly Walker leaned back in his chair. "Remember it's a cop you going to strike at. Admittedly a Canadian, but still a cop. Feds would be all over it, especially it going down over this side of the border and all. You steal it, that H might as well have disappeared as in forever."

Silly Walker pulled a map out and there in red which was circled was what appeared to be nothing but a green, wooded area, however, Silly Walker assured Romero that there was Desmond road, which snaked along until it led into the township where this Canadian cop's squeeze lived.

"Take the map," Silly told him. "Take it and study the bitch right and proper.

Know that the road is there and do the magic that Emmett here raved about."

"Two percent?"

"Two percent of the load you going to jack is nothing to sneeze at. Trust me,"

Silly told him. "You get that blow we all going to be healthy, you hear?"

"When does the next shipment come in?"

"It comes in at the end of the month. Get a calendar and know what date that is.

He passes out the border at 12 or sometimes at 3 in the afternoon. The car is white with green and gold stripes. Inside he has a shotgun and he carries a Glock on his hip. Also, the cruiser like most cop vehicles has an onboard video camera, so watch out."

"Good," Romero said. "Plenty time to get things ready. So where do I drop off the load?"

"You can give it to Emmett, and he'll deliver it to us. When my crew start turning out a profit, your cut will be put stuffed in a manila envelope and sent through the mail."

Silly Walker raised one eyebrow. "Or do you prefer it coming in another way? I could have a brother come on up to your door—"

Romero shook his head. "No. Sounds perfectly fine. And how many envelops?"

"Until the supply you hit runs out. By then I should have my new connect up and running. We'd do it ourselves. But don't want no suspicion on us, feel me?"

"Yeah," Romero stood and offered his hand to Silly Walker who stood himself and they shook. Silly's hand felt like sandpaper.

Big G drove him back home, and during the drive, Romero wondered out loud why Silly Walker had to see him in person. "Because," Big G clarified, "Silly got to see you in person. That's just the way he is. He don't like phones and second hand meetings.

Besides, I think he was curious and all. Seeing as I talked you up and shit. That's the man, you know? He's all about sizing up and taking a read on a brother. Seems pleased enough with you. Tell you this though... Don't let him down."

First things first, Romero drove out to West Chester and found the tattoo parlor. He walked in, and Jim Henley a biker in blue jeans and leather all inked up along his arms came around the desk, where a girl in Goth makeup and a pierced nose sat. Henley seeing Romero led the way silently to the back and along the way Romero gave a look at the designs that hung on the wall in frames. He passed with him into a partition covered by a curtain and inside a man was getting a skull, and some wording cut into his arm by a woman shaped like a NFL defensive lineman. Henley took him to a door where he flicked the lights on and he stepped to the side for Romero to go down first and then he followed shutting the door behind him.

Henley pulled the tarp off of a crate, and he lifted the padlock and twisted the key and with a flourish he took the padlock off and popped the lid where several shotguns and rifles lay together. "What's your pleasure?" Henley asked.

"Give me the shotgun there with the pistol grip."

"Good choice, good choice." Henley stooped down and pulled the black short barreled police issue shotgun out. He passed it to Romero who hefted it in both hands and he pumped it twice hearing the confident clack-clack sound so familiar to the shotgun.

"I'll take it,' Romero said.

"Alright," Henley sniffed. "I'll get you the shells." Henley turned around a corner leaving Romero with the gun, and he came back with a box of shells. "Anything else?

Maybe you want to take with you a rifle? Might have to do some sniping, you never know."

Romero aimed nowhere in particular and looked through the scope of the M91 rifle affixed with a two leg stand, and the gun was camouflaged for more desert combat than wilderness. Still Romero let himself ponder on the possibility between assaulting the cruiser with the shotgun or perhaps just picking off the tires. He figured abruptly that he could do both. He could see taking out the tires with the rifle and emerging out of the woods with the shotgun which would be far more intimidating than wielding a pistol.

"I'll tell you what," Romero said, "I'll take both."

"Alright, alright!" Henley nodded.

"You wouldn't happen to have a sound suppressor for this would you?"

Henley furrowed his brow then began apologizing. "Don't got any for anything but pistols and revolvers. You want some? I got me some sweet ones too. I'm talking the jury rigged clamp silencers. Screw in ones, too. Well?"

"Give me two clamp ones and three screw ins. I had one silencer before. It came attached to the gun when I got it for a job, and I didn't want to keep it around my place."

Henley did some bobbing dance. "Alright, alright. Loving it, loving it," and once more he vanished returning with a paper bag. "I got plastic if you want or is paper good?"

"You got anything bigger for the shotgun and rifle?"

"Sure do," Henley made some drunken punching motions. "You want to talk about price?"

Romero put his new duffel with a shotgun and rifle along with the necessary ammunition in the trunk along with the paper bag filled with silencers. He got back on the road and filled up on gas outside the town and drove the speed limit back home where he ate lunch and watched some television. At six in the evening, he cruised around Center City and found *Cat's Lounge* where he sat far back in a booth with a beer and watched the undulating crowd of hipsters and other urban professional types. He fiddled with his cell and found no messages. Then he got out the map Silly Walker gave him and in his words Romero studied the motherfucker. He took out a pen and in black ink he made a zigzag where the road would be. It wasn't a necessary thing to do, but he did it anyway.

He knew he would find the road.

Desmond, that's it, he thought.

Romero feeling extremely relaxed from drinking took the drive to a park off Roosevelt Boulevard and he had the duffel with him. He walked under the moonlight along the jogging path, and when he got far enough along he went off the path and made some way deeper into the woods. He stooped down and unzipped the bag, and he pulled the rifle out and lay with his legs spread some apart and stood the rifle on its tripod legs.

He looked through the scope, and he could see the scarred tree trunk up ahead by a good length of yards. Romero slipped one brass sharply tipped live round in and he locked in and settled on moving his aim to a branch higher up. The branch was thin and curved down like a broken arm. As if twisted unusually on a body, and the leaves on what looked like warped fingers were few, at least three he could determine, but they might be more he just couldn't see from his angle. Romero locked on to the thinnest part of the branch, and he squeezed the hair trigger, and the crack blew the silence away. The branch jumped off the tree and spun wildly in the air before falling and disappearing from view.

The walk to the car was amusing as lights along the block across the street from his car were now on. Romero paid these lights no serious mind, and he calmly got into the driver's seat and took off up the road for home.

The next day, Romero visited his car lot again and could find no suitable vehicle for the job. He took with him anyway the van he had used on the baseball card fiasco, and he switched the plates with that of another van he came to on the street. He surmised that the other van's owner wouldn't notice that his license plate had been switched any time soon. Romero then returned the van to the lot and got back in his car.

He then spent the night screwing on the silencers to various handguns and dry firing the shotgun and rifle to get used to the trigger pull. He locked them up in his closet and climbed into bed and was asleep shortly later.

Sarah appeared at the diner while he was digging into his bacon and scrambled eggs, and he insisted that she sit with him.

"Been awhile," he said. "How's the job?"

"Oh, it's not paying particularly well at all."

"Sorry to hear that."

"Don't be. I'm just glad to be working is all."

"This goddamned economy," Romero said.

"I just feel stuck is all."

"I know what you mean."

Her food arrived, and for a minute or two, neither of them said anything to each other. He then felt a little lighter that she was there, and he wondered if that were love or some facsimile. He then thought...no. Then he cogitated further that if what all the Rom-

Com's say is true and that he was in love, he wouldn't know he was in love, but he would realize and tell her, and then they'd be in love. After finding out that what they wanted was in front of them the whole time. . . and all that other Hollywood trite garbage.

Bullshit, he thought, It's just what I told Morris. That's all it is.

Romero broke the silence and told Sarah he missed their calls to each other and then he found trying to explain why he liked talking to her so much. For a moment, he wondered if she would be offended somehow that his intentions weren't one out of seeking some romance but then she seemed to grasp something. She looked as if she had solved some complex problem but then was embarrassed at how obvious it all was, and she told him: "You know I think maybe what you're experiencing is some sort of identity crises."

"Identity crises?" he said.

"Yes," she nodded seriously. "Maybe you see yourself as this one person and then all the sudden here comes somebody out of the past that reminds you of who you really are. I mean I sense that you're unhappy with your professional life—"

"Unhappy? I don't know—"

"Well maybe not unhappy but unfulfilled. You never really described your work as a business owner, and investor as anything but a dangerous exercise one after another.

But you do it because you keep getting bored. So you've become addicted to the only aspect of it that excites: The danger."

"The danger?"

"The money you might lose, for example."

Or my life, he almost said out loud.

"Christ," he muttered.

"I don't have much of a life," he explained as the dishes were being collected. "I do work, and I go out. My relationship with Diane gave my life some distractions, but I was never really a part of the life. It was like being outside looking in. Actually my entire life is like that. I can't seem to be invested in any of it. I enjoy the creature comforts. I got a much better place and I like making money, but it seems like I just need more but I don't know what it is."

"We're not that different Alex," she explained, "I work, and I've found some pleasure in painting, but that void inside can't seem to be filled. So I work some more, and I come home and have red wine with vicodin, and that seems to do the trick."

"I need my senses sharp because I'm going up north for a brief trip." Romero got the check and insisted on paying, and he left a tip. As they went out to the street, he said, "When I get back though I think I'll give that possibly addictive relaxation method a try."

She asked him where up north, he was going.

"Canada," he said.

"What are you doing up there?"

"Business owner's conference," he replied making it up on the spot. "Just a lot of hobnobbing and guys in suits networking."

"In Canada?"

"Yup."

He said they should keep in touch, and she agreed. He felt much lighter after their talk and he drove on over to his bar and fired his lazy bar manager and gave the pretty blonde with the large bust the job. She giggled and gave him a hug and a kiss, and he drove to the auto garage and observed the busy grease monkeys and without going in and then he was back home where he put an X on the 23rd which was the day's date. On the 27th or 28th, he would make his trip.

He drove the van to New York on the 27th, and he only slept two hours when he got too tired. He would pull into a motor motel and then eat at a nearby place before getting back on the road. He sometimes thought he was lost, but then he would confirm his directions were correct, and he would listen to the radio at nothing in particular. At some point snow fell and it began to accumulate across the windshield. Romero turned on the wipers and made sure to keep under the speed limit but still rode right on under it as he wanted not to be late for the cruiser's 30th arrival date. He stopped for gas for the third time, and the sky was peppering the dark land with fat snowflakes. The cold was abrasive, and it hurt after a while holding the gas pump and once he would be done he would climb into the van feeling the warmth from the radiator and he would sit still letting the chill release its grip from him before he hit the gas.

Romero saw two glowing yellow eyes watching from the dark, and he hit the brakes. The eyes blinked, and he saw the form of the beast appear. It was a cow by its lonesome and its legs were shaking in the chill. Romero observed this cow for some time and then when it made off away from the road to make its way through the white landscape he pushed on up north with the voices coming from the radio that acted as a reminder that he wasn't the last man on earth.

He came into town, and it was as if he had crossed a portal that took him back in time. So many cars and trucks were of a classic variety, this town was seemingly the town time forgot. The road leading into it was a narrow two lane that then curved to the right and down a tree lined corridor where the dead winter branches almost curved into one another creating a tunnel effect, and he was driving suddenly into a sleepy town with a general store right on Main St. But it was the vehicles that kept his attention. So many classics. Romero could hotwire a car, but they had to be old. Newer cars were damn near impossible to hotwire, but here he was in carjacker heaven. In this town, he also saw plenty of old people. That would make it hard to fit in too well.

He got to the four story red brick building with the awning in earth green that read *Lawson Arms*. He went in and rented a room from an old lady with white hair who was stooped, and she showed him his room on the fourth floor overlooking Main St. It was a small affair but neat and cozy. Warm too. The old woman didn't seem too suspicious, and he supposed the suit he was wearing had something to do with it. When she asked him if he needed anything, he asked her where he could eat, and she pointed to the wall on the left and told him with a wavering voice that there was a place right on across the street, called *Lillian's*. Romero thanked her and then she handed him the key and left. He locked the door and took a hot shower. He shaved and changed into a more outdoorsy outfit of flannel and blue jeans and rubber hiking boots. He sat on the bed and got out a S&W 45. and he checked the clip and chamber and stuffed it into his waistband and the duffel he closed up and crammed under the bed. The small suitcase for his clothes he put atop the dresser and he went out locking up.

Lillian's was sparsely populated, and he was almost certain no young people at all resided in the town until a busboy came out from the swinging double doors in a white apron. He was a redhead and freckled and Romero wanted to call him Opie.

"I'll have the bacon and eggs with some sausage and glass of OJ and water.

Thank you," he told the waitress who could have passed for a younger Meryl Streep.

Romero ate and kept watch out the window. He listened to the low music and could feel the kind of slowness that was unnerving for a city boy in a small town.

Everyone seemed to take their time out here. There was no bustle that needed hustling and Romero felt his nerves jangling some because of it. He watched kids outside. They were small and real young. They wore heavy jackets and mittens, and they threw snowballs at each other. Across the way was an electronics store that sold TV's and radio's and computers. Romero finished his breakfast and left behind a healthy tip. He made sure to pull the bills out his wallet with a napkin as not to leave fingerprints. He even went as far as to wipe the fork and any part of the plate he had touched. Then he realized how ridiculous he was being, and he stopped and walked back out onto the sidewalk.

Romero when he arrived outside the *Lawson Arms* heard the revving of a motor and he turned seeing an ATV with a figure riding on it. The figure was wearing black slacks and a pea coat, his face covered by the tinted visor of the black helmet. His hands were covered in leather driving gloves. Romero noticed the rider was watching him or so he supposed as he couldn't see his face. This rider revved the motor one more time, and the ATV raced forward and turned onto the street tearing its way passed him. He kept watch, but the ATV rider didn't look back.

"I'm in town," he told Big G.

"How's the place?"

"Dead quiet. A real weird place."

"How weird?"

"Right out of the 50's."

"You going to check out the spot? What was it? Desmond street?"

"I'll check it out come nightfall. I don't want to be seen anywhere down there during daylight. This is a very small town and people tend to remember a strange face easily." Romero was sitting on the bed with phone pressed to his ear, and he asked Big G to let Walker know he was ready to strike.

"Will do," Big G replied.

Romero hung up and got off the bed and he began pulling the shotgun and rifle out of the bag. He loaded them both and made sure the safety was on. Romero then stuffed the large weapons under the mattress of the bed and he locked up to walk some.

Romero stopped outside a sporting goods store and he went in and eyed the fishing reels. He examined the various floatation devices and checked out the bates and hooks. He then came to a case assorted with some things he figured he might need.

Romero got the attention of the burly bearded man behind the counter who was dressed almost exactly like him. Romero told him what he wanted, and he paid in cash.

In his room again he played with his new purchases. He had binoculars. They were small, but the distance they covered was impressive when he peered out the window. They were also expensive, so there was that. His next purchase was a hunting knife with a pearl handle—also a heavy penny—and just so he didn't look too suspicious he bought a compass and a book on expert deer hunting.

Romero cut the receipt neatly in half with the blade, and he took the two halves to the bathroom and flushed them down the toilet.

Darkness fell across the land, and Romero drove the van out to find Desmond, that barren swerve miles off of the main street. He stopped into a gravel rest area where no other cars were parked, his headlights strafing the front of the rest area building with their varied toilets and sinks laying within. He took out the map and poured over it and found himself near. According to the map all he had to do was walk across the rest area present on the map and then through the thick green area and within a fair amount of ambling he should find himself out of the tree line where Desmond would be located.

Romero cut off the headlights, and he made sure he had the knife as well as the gun. He pulled the flashlight from the glove box and tested it, and it came on bright. He climbed out and locked behind him. Romero then circled the restrooms and a waist high wooden fence of the cattle rancher era greeted him. He climbed over with ease and made his way through the thickly wooded snow covered wilderness.

He took some time getting used to the feel of the terrain and had frequent debates with himself on when would be the time to use the flashlight, but he was reticent to turn it on. Walking wasn't too much of an issue, and he seemed to have no trouble finding where he was going. The cold bit at him and sooner than he would have wanted the chill was becoming intolerable and snot began to creep out of his nose in an annoying amount. He made a filth out of the back of each of his wool gloves while attempting to wipe his nose when he just couldn't take it anymore. Then a passing flicker of light beyond made him increase his pace. Suddenly he was at the edge of the woods watching the back of a lone pickup go around a curve in the road. Its shape fading from view, its lights trailing along the snow after it, leaving him in the dark, his eyes scanning the moist road in front of him.

Romero nodded to himself and buried both hands in his pockets. He tread up back the way he came and by the time he got to the fence he was a wreck. He shook, and all his mind could go to was the shower in his room and imagining the hot torrent battering his ice block of a body. The thoughts pained, but he couldn't push them away.

He stopped dead with both hands on the fence. He didn't know why, but all thoughts of a hot shower and even the torment of the cold were no longer an issue. He watched out to the backside of the rest area and he waited some more. Then it came. It was a light. A flashlight beam and it seemed amplified somehow on the gravel ground, and Romero understood what he saw. Someone with a flashlight was shining the light into his van.

The light was coming out the other side through the glass, and that was what he was seeing on the ground in front of him, that distorted spectral radiance.

Romero went back into the woods as silently as he could trekking along, and he made an arc along the trees to where he could hunker down and from a safe distance hug against a tree, and peer out at the visitor. He did, and the thought of it as being a cop fled when he saw from his vantage point. It was the rider of the ATV who was walking around the van, flashing a light in. Romero spied on this figure who circled to the back and tried the door and found it locked. The figure was thin and medium height. There was a movement that was odd and he couldn't quite place it. Stilted somehow. The helmet was still on, and the visor was up a smidge, but from this distance, he couldn't get a clear look of the face.

Romero began to panic some when he saw the rider return from the ATV with a Slimjim. If the van got stolen he was all but dead out here in the cold, and his gear, even if he did survive, could pose a problem. All of the identifiable things inside that could lead back to him.—No he couldn't let the rider get into the van. Romero pulled his gun out, and he checked the chamber finding it loaded, and he flicked off the safety, and he swiftly made his way back around behind the rest area hidden in the full dark of the building. He straddled the fence and turned bodily over it and came over on his feet, and he jogged over and hugged the brick face. He slid his back along and sped up when he heard the sounds of the Slimjim going into the door. He came around the side and hunched some and holding the gun two fisted, the cold all forgotten, and he raced without care of making a sound and he twirled the gun up aiming exactly right on the rider who froze seeing him and the gun. The rider's hand then jerked the steel out from the driver's side window of the van and he flung himself to the ground where Romero heard the sound of him scuttling back presumably for his ATV.

Romero heard the engine of the vehicle rev up, and he ran forward. As he came around the back of the van, the glare of the lights blinded him, and he knew the rider was trying to run him down. Romero as the headlights grew coming right at him fired his gun once, and the loud report echoed, and one of the lights died. Romero threw himself away and rolled back to the cover of the van. He got up on a knee and aimed, and the ATV was gone, the sound of its engine roaring along at high speed after it into the darkness.

Romero walked to the shards of the light he shot out. He kept an eye out for blood, but it seemed he must have been uninjured, the rider, and then of course, he patted himself over and over looking for any possible wound that he had gotten during the brief but tense encounter.

Romero drove back to *Lawson Arms* after stowing the van behind a hobby shop in a small alley. He warmed himself up in a hot shower and then to equalize he briefly let cold water hit him, and he dressed trying to solve why the ATV rider was trying to break into his van and what if any part of this score did he, or she, fit in. Was it a she? He wondered, and he thought with some surprise that it might be. Or maybe an extremely feminine man.

This is getting weird, he thought.

He was hungry, and he returned to *Lillian's* and ate until he was stuffed and he went to bed.

Romero had breakfast and then checked up on the guns. He carried his belongings down the stairs, but didn't check out on the off chance he might need to stay some longer. The van had a ticket and Romero ripped it up and drove off back toward the rest area where last night's encounter happened. He kept the motor running and thought some and then backed out. He went back and found a spot which was beside a high chain link fence where there was a parking lot and beyond that, a primary school. Romero was with a lot of his gear trying not to look to inconspicuous, walked steadily and once back at the rest area, he went around and got over the fence and lugged his gear through the woods.

The exercise was intense and when he got to the edge of the tree line, he huffed and allowed himself to collapse to his knees. He felt the blood rushing through him, and he shook his arms. The cold was somehow more tolerable, and overhead the sky was dead pale. He went around a tree and propped himself up. He pulled the shotgun out and laid it across his lap. He removed from the duffel his ski mask and put it on. He then checked the time on a watch he held in his hand and tossed it back in the bag and waited.

The wind sighed, and when the sound of a car whirred in the distance Romero shook himself out of his cold hibernation. He stood and shook each limb and then he ran ahead toward the tree closest to the road. He hid behind the lifeless wood, and he saw the cruiser coming at a moderate pace on its usual run on this dead road.

The cop in the cruiser was petrified from Romero's viewpoint because his eyes widened, and his mouth was open, and the car braked a few feet in front of the man in flannel and jeans wearing a black ski mask and black wool gloves while holding an even blacker shotgun with its barrel seemingly large enough to fit a football.

Romero rushed around to the driver's side and smashed out the window. Romero shouted at him. Told him to get out the fucking car. The cop was frozen. He was a middle aged guy with jowls coming on with a faint blonde mustache and his eyes brown were stunned. But there was a defiance in the stare and Romero knew this guy was waiting for Romero to show some weakness so the cop could then feel more safely about either giving him the 'Don't do this, or you'll regret it speech,' or probably just reach for his gun. Romero asserted himself and shot out the headlight, the shotgun roared deafeningly loud, and the cop did then as Romero told him. Romero instructed him to, with only two fingers to pull the gun out his holster slowly and too kick it to him. This dumb cop tried reasoning with him telling him that he couldn't do it because it was police property and so Romero brought down the gun barrel aiming at the knee of the policeman which put him into some hysterics. When he calmed down, he did as Romero told him and kicked the gun over. Romero then pulled out a pen knife and dropped it to the tar and kicked it out sending it to the cop.

"The radio," Romero said. "Cut the cord to the radio on your coat there and kick back the knife and then lean against the car facing away from me."

The road was still free of traffic, and Romero hoped it would stay that way. He watched as the cop cut off the hand mike. Romero told him to drop it and the knife and kick them toward him. Romero picked up the knife and folded it away, and he swiped his foot out sending the hand mike off some feet away. Romero told him to take out his cuffs and then he had him put his hands behind his back, and he handcuffed him. Romero feeling safer took the cop's key ring and then systematically checked the cop for anything. Romero found a pen and pad and latex gloves. He emptied the cop's pocket of wallet and personal keys and then he unbuckled the utility belt and tossed that into the woods.

The radio squawked and Romero shot it out sending the cop into a rage. Romero hit him in the kidney with the butt of the shotgun and then when he fell he struck him twice at the side of the head, and dumped the cop in the back seat.

Romero drove the cruiser up along the road and tried finding the most desolate spot. He didn't want it too far as he had to get his van back, but he came to another gravel rest stop where a beaten old call box was hooked to a pole and behind it another wood fence.

He saw buried in snow a picnic table. Romero checked the cops pulse, and it was steady.

Romero popped the trunk and saw boxes of electronics. He pulled one out and knew immediately that there wasn't anything electronic in it. He opened it up and sure enough black plastic greeted him. He pulled it out. A phone book shape and sized mass greeted him that was wrapped in heavy duty trash bags, and inside he saw heroin as white as the wind driven snow that lay all around.

He took the cruiser back where they had come, and he left the cop in the car figuring he'd find his way out. He had to make three trips but eventually he got the boxes of white horse in the electronics boxes in a small alcove he found in the woods beside a tree. It wasn't deep enough, so he just settled on covering the others in snow. Then he made a quick sprint for the van, and whenever a car came by Romero would slow to a walk, his ski mask riding just an inch above his eyebrows. The van to his relief was unmolested, and he came back to uncover and load the H in the van.

Romero changed into his suit and paid the elderly woman off and wiped the surfaces of his room of any prints. He surveyed the block for any ATV or cops, but it was the same dull self the town always seemed. He took off in the van and didn't look back until he was on the interstate and then alone with nothing but the unrolling highway out the windshield.

He was sleeping peacefully in the motel room on the first floor. He wasn't sure what broke the peace, but when he opened his eyes he saw the light under the door that led outside. The light was steady and then it bobbed some, and he knew instantly that it was a flashlight. The doorknob began to jiggle, and Romero eased himself out of bed by sliding along on his stomach. He slipped to the floor and got his gun from the duffel. He screwed in the fat barrel of the silencer onto the small 25. He flicked the safety off and aimed for the door bracing himself against the mattress with arms stretched ahead of him.

Then he had an idea.

Romero went out the window in the bathroom. It was a tight squeeze, but he made it and landed in only his shorts and tee shirt behind the building with the gun in the waistband of his boxers. Romero's feet were bitten by the cold pavement, and he raced once more around a building with his gun ready to face whoever his night visitor was.

The figure in black was bending down to work the lock. Romero knew whoever this visitor was he wasn't a real pro. The flashlight running on along the door so anyone coming in from the street could see or anyone who couldn't sleep could call the police when they looked out their window. Suspicious of the fellow in black hunched over the knob with a flashlight.

"Don't move!" Romero spat and the figure froze. "Carefully turn around and let's see your mug."

The visitor turned around, and the hard, cold stare of a man, or actually more of a boy glared back at him. The boy was thin, and his face was soft aside from the dark drowned underwater dead eyes, and he was wearing the riding uniform that was familiar.

It was the ATV rider himself.

Romero pushed the boy into the motel room, and he flicked on the lights and shut the door behind him all the while the silencer stayed on the back of the boy.

"I take it you're here for the dope?" Romero said.

No answer.

"You can turn around," Romero instructed. "Turn around and sit down on the bed. There you go...Good. Now what do you want? It is the heroin isn't it?"

"Yeah it's the H," the soft but cold voice said.

"How'd you find out about the score?"

Silence. A longer stretch of it this time.

The flat eyes of the boy roamed around the room. He didn't seem the slightest bothered to be sitting across from a man who had a gun on him. He seemed bored if anything.

"Can't have it. The heroin's mine. It's mine to give to him," Romero finally said.

Finally, the reptilian eyes stared into and through Romero. The boy said flatly, "You won't make the run. You have a long drive ahead of you and you'll be dead before you get back home. How many motels and rest stops and gas stations can you go to before I roll up behind you and kill you and take the drugs? And if not me, one of us."

"Us?" Romero said. "Who's us? What kingpin piece of shit do you work for?"

"I don't work for a drug man, Romero."

Romero was stunned. The kid knew his name. Christ this was turning sour and in epic proportions.

The boy had his hands on his knees, and he leaned forward tilting his head in an odd insect-like movement. The boy said, "I'm with SHAPE."

"SHAPE?"

"It stands for Specialists of Heisting, Assassination, Plagiarism and Extortion."

"Christ. You're kidding right?"

The dead eyes said nothing along with the mouth.

"So if I let you go you'll keep coming after me?" Romero waited for the answer, but the silence was too heavy and long, and Romero took it as answer enough.

Romero emptied the gun into the boy's face.

Romero stole the blood soaked sheets and carried the body out the window and into the van. The mattress was dry as he had been quick to stop the spread of the blood.

Succeeding in stopping the gore from soaking through the sheets. Romero fixed things up once more wiping off any prints and was glad that as always he used an alternate ID to get the room. He drove and found a ditch. He unrolled the boy's body and drove further for miles until he came to a closed restaurant, and he tossed the sheets into the dumpster.

Romero was paranoid, and he drove feeling as if the trip would not end. He only slept once more, but it was in a hotel as he felt more secure in it. Then three hours later still groggy he made himself eat, and he took off.

He was driving along when the sound that was familiar greeted him. It was day out and Romero checked out the rearview seeing the black thing zoom abruptly out of view to the other side. He could discern no real clear shape of it against the death pall of the sky. Then there it was. It was a rice-burner and its driver attired like the dead and faceless ATV boy.

Christ Jesus almighty! Romero grimaced to himself. SHAPE is real it seems. A gun came up and thinking quickly Romero jerked the van toward the bike, and the hand holding the small Uzi with the fat silencer let it go. The gun skipped farther off into the traffic and the rider tried to right himself but could not and the bike went on its side.

Romero smiled watching as the rider rolled farther back going one way and his bike going the other, the bike sliding directly under the wheels of a semi.

Big G listened to all of this. Romero went to Big G's club where he lounged in his office.

Big G sat across from him amazed. He inspected the goods and lifted the phone to call Silly Walker. Then after giving him the update that his stuff arrived intact he nodded and handed the phone over to Romero.

"You did good kid," Walker told him, pleased. "I ain't never heard of no SHAPE. Damndest thing I ever heard, if I say so myself. Tell me how you handled them—and don't be worried about bugs because I sweep my phone every goddamned day and I know Big G does too, so go ahead."

Romero told him, and Silly Walker laughed which sounded like sandpaper. "You handled it right, Romero!

My god," he said wowed some. "Big G was right! You are a man who can get things done! As for our deal, expect the envelopes to be coming in. And again...thanks brother."

Romero was finally back home, and he kept close watch for any suspicious persons as he went back into his routine. A month later he got a manila envelope in the mail with no return address. He thought it was a book by its feel but then he opened it, and he then remembered. Inside was money. His first cut of the white horse he scored, hitting the streets. Silly Walker was a man of his word.

Romero got something else in the mail a day later. It was a white envelope with no return address just his and a stamp. Inside Romero pulled out a letter. He unfolded it, and something brass colored ran into his hand. It was a bullet. The letter read in cutout letters from a magazine: **SHAPE ALWAYS REMEMBERS!**

9

Of car chases and friendships.

Romero was doing bench presses while Strauss Buck moon, a flamboyant man, who was new to town, insisted he help him get into shape. He began with assuring Romero of no ulterior motive then Buck moon went on about the lack of desire he had toward most types of foods. He said he seemed only to eat for the utilitarian reason that if he stopped he knew naturally that he would die. He just didn't care for food. He found the whole exercise boring. Romero listened politely, and as was his routine he didn't count his reps, he just kept going until he felt he was at the limit.

At the limit, Romero's arms shook and a sheen of sweat was on him, and he could feel a bead growing fat on his forehead. Finally, he stopped, and Strauss clicked the timer off. "You timed me?" Romero asked.

"Beats counting yourself doesn't it? And you can do that now instead of counting which I know you must hate doing. I can understand why though because I find it makes workout incredibly tedious."

"You want to listen to music not count," Romero added sitting up on the bench drying himself with his hand towel.

"Yes," Strauss answered with vigor. "You want to be listening to techno or dance to get you feeling loose and feeling like you're having some fun.—If you then count the whole damn thing turns into another mechanized routine in a lifetime of mechanized sterile, cold routines."

At the treadmill running along beside him, Strauss said quietly leaning across "There's a woman here, and she's been checking you out."

"I know," Romero huffed, "I've noticed her too."

Romero was noticing many things lately. During the worst of winter Romero took a job for a drug dealer in New York named Silly Walker, a man who, in fact, didn't walk silly at all, and he found himself on a mission to steal heroin from a corrupt cop.

Unfortunately for Romero, there had been someone else who wanted the heroin. This person was an ATV riding young man with cold, dead eyes who said he was with a certain organization called SHAPE which stood for Strategists of Heisting, Assassination,

Plagiarism, Extortion. On his return home, he stopped thinking on the so called SHAPE organization until he received a letter with a live bullet. The letter was a threat, and now Romero kept his senses sharp and his gun with him at all times, and to work most of the stress off, he hit the gym harder than he ever had before. Once, about a shower not three weeks ago, he finally saw the difference as he had undressed. He had caught a look of himself in the mirror. He had become well muscled, his body with real definition.

"Are you going to talk to her?" Strauss asked teasingly.

"No."

"No? Why?"

"I just don't feel like any of that right now," Romero said dully.

"You're so shut down, Romero."

"More private. Besides I've never been in a real, loving relationship, or even really felt love, so it's not like I'm miserable. I'd be miserable if I knew what love felt like and were deprived of it. So ignorance is bliss for me, I suppose."

"Christ," Strauss said.

The watchful woman with crow black hair in a ponytail and pink top; black running shorts came up beside Strauss as he huffed on the machine. She introduced herself while her focus was settling longer on Romero than Strauss. She went about inviting both of them to a party at a friend's penthouse this coming Friday. Strauss decided to operate as a spokesman for Romero, and he assured her, Michelle, that they would be there with bells and whistles. Strauss repeated the address and took a moment to think and then smartly he said he knew where it was.

"Well great then," she said. "See you both then," and she left toward the women's lockers.

"See us both?" Strauss commented, "I don't think she even registered me at all.

And I doubt she even cares if I go or not considering the doe eyes she was giving you."

Strauss tilted his head toward Romero and gave him his own doe eyes and a flicker of eyelashes.

"Attraction bothers me more than excites me."

"How's that?"

"I guess I really just don't like any intense focus on me," Romero whipped the towel across his face while his legs began to burn wonderfully.

Romero showered at the gym wondering why he didn't feel bizarre and some insecurity at doing it next to Strauss. Strauss who had once reached the showers with Romero began to morph back into his act of heterosexuality as to stop any problems he might face while inside. Romero was momentarily struck at how thrilling it would be to be able to disguise oneself so that showering with the preferred sex was common and a private delight to the queer in the straight flock. He then turned over the woman. What was her name? Michelle? Oh yes, he thought. Michelle. However, the excitement wasn't there, and once again he thought about SHAPE and the fact that he would have to go to a party this Friday.

Romero rode his Beetle up the state road trying to think. It had become the bit of enjoyable pastime lately. The road unwinding before him and the various stops for gas and food which he would eat in the car while listening not so intently to the radio.

Various programs of conservative radio to NPR to the Jazz station. Jazz being the only type of music he could tolerate while in the car. He was enjoying the old world feel that, for him, the road brought. The feel of vast distance to travel and the old standard of technology. The radio. The wheels propelled forward by the combustible engine which moved him along Amish territory where the past was plenty alive. Nourished more to the point. He caught glimpses of the men in the field under the blaring sun, but they must be securely dressed in warm clothing as the winter hadn't yet released its chilly grip on the encroaching days of Spring.

He was driving just under the speed limit back toward the city with pictures, silent and tantalizing in his head of living the life of an Amish. Romero wondered if such a thing could be possible. He wondered what he could say to get his way in and even if there would be a chance. Maybe it was by birth for all he knew. Or maybe some pledge had to be made. However, another fantasy had at him, and it was the fantasy of escape.

Escape, as it occurred to Romero, was the greatest and most alluring of fantasies for him because the new dream, following the prior was one of the swift desire to flee the Amish life. In the new fantasy, Romero saw that he could wait until dark where he could climb out a window. He had in this dream a gun he hid on him. It was a Police Positive 38. He made off into the rows of corn for cover and then found the road where he forcefully got a vehicle and lead footed back to his loft where he would collapse gratefully. Thankful that he could sleep late into the next day and eat a pizza and drink beer again.

Romero smiled at the workings of his sick mind and was checking his speed once more when he took notice of a sound coming from behind him. He seemed to have confused it some for his own car, but this engine was growling in a way that was sinister as it gripped Romero, creating tension. The car in the rearview was silver, the sun playing along the bullet-like body and two men were in the front. They both were wearing sunglasses and by the look on their faces, they were paying him strict attention.

His door side mirror then exploded seemingly before he registered the gunfire.

Romero hit the gas and knew he had to either immediately U turn or ditch the car and make out on foot in some nearby residential area. He lowered himself into his seat and just up ahead he made out a roadhouse where the head of a pirate was winking down and in a dialogue bubble was promising the best roadside eating experience money could buy.

The gun fired again, and the sound of a large, aggressive bee droned painfully beside his ear and the windshield starred. A new draft gave him notice of the shattered back windshield. Romero gunned the car taking it dangerously too fast for the parking lot.

He twisted the steering wheel and the car righted and flew into the sparsely attended lot, and he circled out the other exit seeing the silver bullet blur passed him, and the driver seemed startled by the change of position as he braked violently in the street sending white smoke out the back. Then the wheel spun again, and the silver bullet attempted a U turn while Romero fishtailed behind it and then righted himself, and he reached under the dash and pushed the button that dropped the hidden compartment open by his side, and he took out the S&W 45. pistol. Knowing the clip was loaded he fired once out the windshield shattering it and saw the devastating slug do the same to the back windshield by blowing a hole the size of a football in the back of the silver car. The passenger leaned to the side of his door, and Romero was sure he had been hit.

Romero angered was now the one following as the silver bullet attempted to outpace him and it almost crashed head on into a semi which blasted its horn. The silver bullet took the opportunity to try and surprise Romero by swerving the opposite lane and hitting the brake and Romero wasn't fooled, and he fired out the hole in front of him, and the bullet audibly struck the body of the car. Romero came dangerously close before the silver bullet zoomed back in reverse. Romero swerved away speeding up the road and was determined to end this encounter. But how? His mind jumbled unable to think as it all happening too fast for him. The silver bullet was smoking from its radiator grill and Romero's gas pedal touched the bottom fully, and he threw his eyes to the left and right looking desperate. A bullet droned by again, and he felt a burn along the side of his head and the warm unwelcome trickling of what he knew was blood. He heard the next shot in the chaos and his radio exploded.

There! Up ahead! Romero turned the car allowing himself to slow down, and he went into the trail off the road, and he was in a tunnel of green racing along hearing the braches sigh around his vehicle. Romero blasted the horn for anyone who might be hiking or just lounging about. The silver bullet was too close for comfort, and he focused on maneuvering carefully through the green tunnel until he was spitted out into a clearing where up in the distance was a tree line. He jerked the wheel to the left and the car fishtailed while the silver bullet whipped passed.

Romero turned the wheel and followed behind the silver car. He discerned that it was of some vintage roadster type. Romero marveled at the idiocy of using such a vehicle for a job. The driver was obviously vain— some kind of showboat. Romero didn't allow the car to turn and when it tried he ran head on into it from behind where the silver machine swerved left some and then right. He wanted to push it into the trees and farther into the thick nature where Romero hoped it would be trapped. However, it fought loose. His car's nose was at the rear side of the other car and he stayed in that dominate position as the circling began.

All he heard was the roar of the engine and all he saw besides the car was the floating dust and debris the tires kicked up. The silver car's driver fired toward him, and he missed passing him. The two cars circled each other like dogs after each other's tail and Romero broke the cycle and made off back where he came, and he ignored the whine and cough of his car. He raced ahead determined to break out free. He could see in the rearview that the other car was slowing considerably. He could also see that the passenger was alive and seemed perfectly healthy. He was yelling something to the driver. Romero focused ahead and knew he needed the distance to survive this.

The silver car was gaining speed, but it was severely crippled. The beetle turned to the left and seconds later the loudly dying but fighting for speed silver bullet came after with smoke pouring out of its front. The silver car was racing now for nothing as abruptly Romero's car was gone. The roadster continued on ahead—THEN WHAM!!!—

Romero drove out of the woods ramming the passenger side of the enemy car. He pushed it forward and the silver bullet was incapable of moving further. Smoke obscured him from them, and he could make nothing of their forms. The enemy's car groaned as if in pain and then he had to hit the break swiftly as the resistance of the silver car was gone, and the smoke dissipated quickly, the sound of crashing and the rolling of the car and shattering glass greeted his ears and finally a loud splash followed by bubbling. Romero ran out the car feeling what he knew was blood leaking down his chest from his head wound.

The car was tail up in the watering hole, and the broiling water was white, large bubbles bursting at the surface and a wail from the car rose as the tail tilted forward and it sank rapidly down the water. Soon the green surface returned where bubbles broke the surface. A few seconds later all was still. Only minor bubbles rose as other areas of the car were finally breached.

Romero drove the wounded beetle back toward home. He stopped at the garage in German Town and Fuchs, the guy who ran the place for him, whistled at the car and then hissed, "Shit," at the sight of it.

He took a cab back and once in his apartment he examined the bandage deciding that Fuchs knew a little something after all about cleaning and dressing a wound. Then he rechecked to make sure the big sliding steel door was locked. Romero kicked off his shoes and swallowed a Vicodin and soon he slept.

"SHAPE," Morris said. "So you think they made their move?"

"Don't see who else it could be. Don't believe it was the Russians."

Morris was on the kitchen side of the partition sitting on a stool while across from him Romero sat on his. The evening was plenty dark when he awakened feeling the pleasantness of the pill. He took a cab over to Morris's house and filled him in on the encounter he had and its result. Morris then admired the bandaged side of Romero's head.

"No I suppose not," Morris commented. "So this SHAPE organization is real and has some teeth?"

"So it would seem."

"And the two clowns behind the wheel are dead?"

"Don't know."

"I would imagine you're going crazy?"

"Not really," Romero told him. "Actually I feel better after having showed some of their men up. Maybe it'll teach them a thing or two."

"Or maybe it'll make them even more desperate to knock you out using more advanced techniques," Morris warned.

"I think I'll be ready for them. In the meantime, what stroke of genius do you have in your head that would take them off my trail, like you did with the Red Mafia?"

Morris seemed to think on it.

"There must be something," Romero said.

"Sorry," Morris said regretfully, "at the moment I have nothing in the way of ideas. Trust me though kid, I been thinking on it since you told me about this shit after you came back from that job knocking off the cop. Just can't seem to conjure any of my mental magic."

"I'll tell you this though," Romero said, "I got this party I'm going to this Friday.

I don't know why I couldn't say no. Maybe it's because this new friend of mine wanted to go, but either way I'm stuck and probably like I always do I'm going to have a lousy time. A very lousy time."

"You really are not a party guy?" Morris asked.

"You kidding? Whatever made you think I was?"

"I don't know. You're young still! A party should make you *excited!*"

"It doesn't. I'll go and drink and mind my business and then I'll get the hell out and meditate in my comfortable apartment about what to do about these SHAPE bitches."

Morris inquired saying, "How's your car?"

"Took it to my garage in German Town. Fuchs is going to get the guys to fix it up."

"Hell of a love bug you got," Morris smiled.

"It's souped up alright. Has more horse power than when I bought it. Might be dead if I hadn't gotten those modifications."

"And they might be alive."

"Yup," Romero nodded. "The whole thing is fucked up, Morris. They came at me after most likely following me from out the city. Which means they were either hitters from out of town that had opted on killing me somewhere private like the open road or I had a chance encounter with them while they were driving toward the city."

"*Or?* Don't allow yourself to think about that." Morris said and waved a scolding finger in front of his face. "You're alive and they are most likely dead. So is the bitch they sent to your motel room that night. You already showed them you are a fierce piece of business. Now go to that party and have some drinks and get yourself laid!" Morris raised his hands up to the heavens. "Live damn you. You hear me? *Live*!"

"I'm not too pleased about what I have to wear though."

Morris rolled his eyes and muttered a swear in exasperation.

Romero was far down in the backseat of the cab as the driver took him back home and he would every so often rise to spy out the back for any tails, but he could discern no one following behind.

Romero watched TV and then after awhile he shut it off and paced wondering what to do. He went back and forth on the expansive floor and entertained the idea that his encounter was nothing but a severe case of carjacking gone wrong. However, he couldn't understand why they would want of all things a VW Beetle. He wondered then on the choice they made to come after him in a silver road-ster type vehicle. Was some mockery at play? A message? He couldn't tell.

Later, Romero continued his pacing. His mind went around and around and finally he stopped and realized he had no choice as nothing useful would come and that he was just wasting time. He went into bed and tried to sleep. Then he rose after some time and checked the locks to make sure he was safe and secured in his windowless bedroom. After more minutes of being fully awake, he reached under the bed to grip the butt of the revolver he had stashed there and then he sighed in frustration and lay in the dark on his back watching blackness.

Three hours later he was asleep.

The penthouse party atop of the of the Frasier Condos was bumping along with a crowd that seemed intentionally multiethnic. The place was large, and the crowd going on seemingly in endless discussions with one another and Romero let his eyes settle on one group before they settled again on another. The people seemed as if they had plenty to say to one another. Romero wondered how many topics could one person pull out their ass to go over with group after groups of people. For Romero, who was not in the least a party animal, the notion of such attention to others and their topics of discussion along with his lack of interest in most things was a death for him when at such parties, so he sat at the armchair beside the fire place with a beer bottle set on his knee, hand firmly clasped around it. Then he considered the thought that most things didn't interest him, and he supposed it was that the things that did hold an interest were things he was uncomfortable talking about. Such as heisting and the thrill that can be addictive during and after. After, when you're home back in comfortable surroundings, and you can entertain yourself with the dance with the danger of either getting killed or worse. Getting caught and sent upstate.

Strauss Buck moon, he observed, was maneuvering deftly through the crowd to some unknown encounter, probably to add to the gaggle of conversation that was battering Romero's ears. Romero drank and saw beyond the glass sliding door that led outside. Beyond the panes of glass, the balcony was occupied by couples in their coats.

Some smoking and some talking or tasting drinks out of champagne flutes. He rose and cut through the throng, hoping Michelle wasn't out there and wouldn't spot him as the last thing he wanted was a probing mind asking him questions.

It was a breezy night, and Romero took a spot on the far corner from the penthouse where he hoped he wouldn't be seen, and he looked at the startling view of the glimmering night around him. This landscape of lights that made up his city. He felt the momentary pull of joy at being where he was, but it fled quickly as most feelings and was replaced with a minor flutter of satisfaction at how high a station he had climbed in life.

Where he was no longer the just barely getting by thief living in some basement. Today, a man now with several businesses and a spacious expensive loft downtown. He wished then his mother was there to see how he had turned out and whatever deaths had taken place and there had been many, he would admit he felt okay about them as they seemed worth it. No guilt harassed him for such a thought, and he felt the serenity and satisfaction in his chest grow.

A few minutes into a blank reverie he heard Strauss cheerfully beckon, and he turned stunned some away from the glittering landscape below and saw Strauss coming toward him with of all people Sarah Medlow.

"I can't believe it!" Sarah laughed. "We run into one another yet again!"

"I *love* it!!!" Strauss shouted to the sky, visibly intoxicated.

"Hello Sarah," Romero greeted calmly.

"So the Chair of African studies," Sarah continued, "wanted to know why don't you come on over. You should network, and boy did I roll my eyes at that.—I mean inner rolling my eyes not doing it, so she could see—of course!" she laughed.

"And then I came along!" Strauss twirled spilling the top of his drink, "Came along and much like with you Romero, I pulled her forcefully kicking and screaming out of her shell and here you both are with me—*my children!*" Strauss embraced them both and pretended to cry.

"Well I was having a hell of a time circulating in the party," Romero admitted.

"Trouble?" Strauss leaned back examining him with his eyes. "You were crippled with the inability to socialize, and it was painful to watch." He turned to Sarah. "At least with Sarah she was awkwardly trying, which is very endearing, but you!" Romero's arm was hit lightly. "You were sitting staring, and you were so startling inanimate it was scaring the guests."

"Really?" Romero pulled from his bottle.

Strauss tilted his head at him. "You looked as lifeless as a dummy someone dressed up and put a beer bottle in its hand. Your eyes were all sleepy and watchful. Not moving. You're like a turtle I had growing up. It was real small, and my being young at the time I would think it was dead and so I would poke it with my finger and it would start to move. I swear every day I had that turtle was a day where I would wonder is this it? And of course I would poke my turtle, and I would feel relief as it went running off of its rock and go swimming."

Sarah laughing asked, "What was your turtle's name?"

"Sean Connery," Strauss said remembering bliss-fully. "Sometimes 007. Had a crush on him when a Bond marathon came on the TV. Unfortunately, poor Bond succumbed to the dangers of being cared for by a child and was buried at toilet."

A minute later Michelle came out and joined them. She gestured out to the city.

"Amazing right? Can't believe that asshole gets all the best in life. Kills my belief in karma I can tell you that." Then: "But he is my friend, so I am of course happy for him."

"What does he do?" Sarah asked.

"He runs his own advertisement firm, it's new. *Adhoc.* You ever hear of it?

Stands for Adam Hockney who of course is your host whose view you're admiring and who is hoping beyond hope that you are eating your hearts out."

"*I am,*" Strauss said.

Michelle looked back. "Oh," she said and then while circling over to Romero's side pressing her warm body seemingly innocently against him whispered, "He's coming now," and they looked over as the sliding door was being closed by a dashing looking man dressed in expensive casual clothing. His haircut even looked expensive, and his face was finely boned. His eyes were feminine, but there was the caddishness mannerism in the motion of his gait, that blew away any notion of shyness his eyes hinted at. He immediately rubbed Romero the wrong way. Romero could tell this encounter was going to be a treat, and Adam Hockney stopped in front of them. Hockney's critical look at them Romero noticed put Strauss and Sarah in visible discomfort while Michelle who was used to his behavior threw her eyes up as if in prayer and said, "Adam this is

Romero and Strauss. What is it? Buck moon. And this is Sarah. Sarah? Oh. Sarah Medlow."

"What about you, Romero?" Hockney sounding sullenly bored asked. "You got a first name too?"

"Alex," Romero replied.

"Alex? Well then Alex and Sarah and Strauss welcome to my party, which celebrates me of course and the ever strengthening evidence of my genius. Adhoc is the cock on the block and so am I. So enjoy the expensive champagne and the even more expensive view. Know that I earned all this and am not ashamed about my wealth like most of the assholes in there right now partying." Adam rolled his eyes. "Christ, if I hear more goddamned self righteous bullshit about the poor and the environment and how they should all do something and know that they won't do anything, I'm going to jump off this building but first I'll hose them down with the fire hose."

"What's wrong with them having that kind of discussion?" Michelle challenged.

"Because," Hockney strained with a temper, "they, like everyone else who has money, think they are going to change everything, and of course they never do and then they seem disappointed. How many organizations can these clowns be part of and realize that there is no better country to be fought for? All America is, like every other country, is a legal, criminal organization disguising itself as doing god's work and being about the people." He leaned close to Michelle as if to kiss her, and he whispered, eyes hooded "It's bullshit. They're all full of shit."

Romero found himself suddenly fond of Adam Hockney.

He made careful note to observe Adam having decided to use him as a muse on how he would live his life. Romero admired his self starter status and his wealth at his young age. He was two years younger than Romero, and Romero was newly entranced by his surroundings unexpectedly. He wanted to pick Adam's mind. He wanted to ask him what gym he belonged to and who did he know and what car did he drive.

"It's a great gym Alex," Adam said after Romero got up the nerve to ask. "Top notch clientele. The women are incredible. They have a pool and sauna that is to die for."

Adam motioned to him with his rocks glass. "I can get you a membership. No, don't argue. Let me do this. I'll vouch for you."

The party eventually started to dwindle, and Adam was saying more and more goodnights to the exiting guests. Eventually, the last remaining survivors were seated around the ebony glass coffee table. Sarah and Michelle seem to become the closest of friends and Adam would direct his attention with considerable ease to the Asian man to his left and to Strauss and the two women who were obviously smitten with him. He didn't seem to care about the two women, and he even answered them in a quick and dismissive manner seemingly hating to give them any attention for too long and of course, naturally, they ate it up.

"Do you golf?" Adam asked Romero out of the blue.

"Actually no."

"Good. It's a dreadful sport. I have to say I'm more of a bowling man. What about you, Alex? Do you like to hit the lanes on occasion?"

"I've bowled a long time ago, and I recall that I had some enjoyment."

"Good. You're on the team."

"Team?"

The Asian said, "We play this Thursday at seven thirty so be there."

"We'll give you your shirt when you show up. Don't worry about size," Adam said sounding bored, "we'll have a couple for you to try on."

"So what do you do?" the Asian asked and squinted at Romero.

"I own some businesses and basically collect checks." Romero puffed his cheeks and nodded waiting for a response. Whatever it might be.

"Shit," the Asian replied, "I would love to live like that. What? Your parents were rich?"

Adam looked then at Romero interested apparently in the answer as if it would be a pivotal factor in his view of him.

Romero shook his head. "No. I just got my foot in the door with a friend of mine. He showed me the ropes and then after some time he got himself out and left our business to me alone and then I got a piece of another place. A garage in German Town and then a bar. Currently I'm speculating on land or maybe getting a piece of a restaurant."

The Asian, whose name was Leo, patted Adam's arm and asked, "Aren't you looking for somebody to put some up for that dance club downtown?"

Adam not appreciating being put on the spot gave Leo a chilly smile and said, "Yes. Yes I am." He then warmed up looking toward Romero and it appeared he became more convinced with the idea of having him onboard. He became a man making a sales pitch. "It's a great place. Very large. Very popular. Now I need to move on this place fast. The club is called *Upside Hang*. You ever hear of it?"

"I have."

"Well I need to find someone who could put up a figure high up on the five digit side. I'll be putting up the same. This would of course mean that I'll be owning the place along with this partner. I've been in enough times over the last few months to get the hang of the place, see how it runs, and I'm itching to grab it." Adam then acted as if he then didn't know who this partner could be. Romero knew that if he accepted he would see Adam feign surprise and then demand that he didn't have to do that.

Romero then said, "Well show me the place."

Adam froze as he slouched in the chair and then he cast Romero a skeptical look, and he sat up straight and smiled, and his eyes twinkled. "Alright. How about tomorrow night at seven. I'll meet you at the bar, and you can just have a look.—No pressure of course."

"I had a good time," Sarah said to Romero as they walked out the building. "So are you and Adam actually going to own a club together?"

Romero jutted his chin, nodding. "Sure. I'll take a careful look around and decide.

I got some more money I'd like to invest and owning a dance club sounds great.

Wouldn't want to be there every night but it generates good profit. Or at least that better be the case."

"Are you going to call Michelle?" Sarah teased him.

So she had seen it, Romero thought. As they were leaving, Michelle had slipped Romero her card and Romero awkwardly pocketed it and gave her a quick smile before thankfully stepping out the door.

"Maybe."

"Yeah, maybe," Sarah chuckled.

A horn honked, and Strauss halted his car and shouted to them from across the passenger seat. "Sarah! Alex! Call me! We'll do something! Get seriously *fucked* up!"

The two of them waved and Strauss drove off laughing a maniacal laugh.

"Strange night," Romero commented.

"It's a diamond heist." Morris blew on his coffee sitting at the counter "Diamonds?"

"Straight out of the dark continent. Coming by courier who's arriving on a yacht which is to dock at the Harborage Marina in St. Petersburg."

"Hate Florida," Romero muttered.

"So turn it down."

"Who's the finger?"

"Some guy in the can who knows about the whole damn set up. Steinway says he has a history with the guy."

"He wants just me?" Romero pointed at himself.

"Said you and him worked together real well back in Detroit."

"Thought he would have run off after what happened."

"Oh. You mean the whole taking Baker's eye out and then stabbing him thing?"

Morris pursed his lips to drink and said, "That could have been an issue. But it seems he thinks it makes you a tough but reliable partner. You doing what you had to. Making things right. Not letting you and him get ripped off by that jackass Baker."

"Apparently."

"It's a million in diamonds, give or take."

"Bodyguards?" Romero inquired.

"Two. Steinway says they're easy to spot. They'll be the guys in the sunglasses with the stereotypical look of tough, but sturdy dullness. Steinway said he'll cover the plan in more detail after he picks you up at the airport."

"If," Romero stated.

"*If.*"

Romero told him about his possible investment in a dance club. "Think it might be a great turnover place. Could generate a real profit."

"Didn't know you'd been cruising the dance clubs. Thought you hated those places?"

"I do. But I plan on being silent. As silent a partner as possible. This guy I met at a party named Hockney is looking for someone to get on it with him. And I am looking for another investment."

Morris slurped his coffee and said, "Party boy Romero."

"Sure. Right."

"Seeing as you're doing well, you're still entertaining the idea of a score?"

"It's this guy at the party," Romero told him. "Adam Hockney. The way this guy lives is incredible. I was taking notes on how he lived. The man is incredible. I'll tell you Morris after meeting this guy I'm seeing a potential for myself."

"Meaning?"

"*High society.*"

Morris rolled his eyes. "Oh boy," he said. "You going to start wearing ascots? A house in the Hamptons? And besides, you're plenty set now anyway. 3 million and done remember? Though I think it's safe to say you've passed that mark *very* nicely."

"You ever read *The Beautiful and Damned?* F. Scott Fitzgerald?"

"In the joint, sure," Morris retorted and then, "No! I never read *The Beautiful and Damned!* Christ almighty."

"You were alive and conscious in the 20's right?"

"Asshole."

"Anyway," Romero pushed on, "let's just say much like my new possible business partner that book was a source of inspiration on how I'd like my lifestyle to be."

"So, you're going to pack your swim trunks?" Morris shot an eyebrow up.

"Yeah and my sunscreen."

10

The diamonds, the wife, and the Shape.

In St. Petersburg, Florida Romero grunted in disapproval of the muggy weather and once more told himself how much he hated the place. If only, it felt as enjoyable as it looked.

Dry heat. Anything but the feel of clammy skin.

Romero out the airport signaled for a cab but then Steinway gave a honk of his horn and Romero walked miserably to his car. A jaguar, silver with the top thankfully up, and inside the air conditioner on full blast. They exchanged a polite greeting, and fifteen minutes into the drive Steinway pointed out Romero's window showing him the Harborage harbor where in the mesmerizingly blue green water white yachts and other vessels were anchored with idyllic seagulls completing the picture of beauty the harbor was. That and the wealth it projected was what got to Romero who only entertained the idea of owning a yacht before realizing he wanted nothing to do with being out in the open water.

Steinway's house was behind a cast iron gate that swung open by a remote over the dash and he hit another button that opened one of the double garage doors. The place was a three story villa with a sparkling blue, green filled pool. Inside the house, Steinway showed Romero his room where Romero dumped his suitcase on the bed and followed him into the expansive living room. Inside it was cool, and he was given a beer and directed to the couch where he gratefully collapsed and took several gulps of the ice cold drink.

"The yacht hasn't arrived yet," Steinway told him.

"When?"

"Seven in the morning tomorrow is the estimated time."

"What's your plan?"

Steinway scrunched forward. "Okay. We get up early and get our asses down to the dock. We'll take a stolen car I got in my garage. We watch for them to get into their ride, and we follow them. Now, my finger says they'll be going to the Deluxe Hotel to make the deal. One of us follows them up to the room and using walkie-talkie tells whichever of us is in the car the room number. We'll both wear disguises. I'm talking wigs and mustaches and glasses."

"I'll follow," Romero said.

"Good. Okay. You'll have a gun on you as well with a silencer. You'll make yourself look none too suspicious while you wait for me to show up. I'll come on up, and we'll knock on the door or kick it in—however it goes— and we'll get them. Tell the jerkoffs to get their hands up, or we'll give them a new navel!" Steinway wiped the air with both hands and continued. "One million in diamonds and another million in cash."

"For the exchange?" Romero sat up.

"Yeah. Split three ways of course. I got to pay my finger something for giving me the info. He'll be out of the can soon, and he wants a nice cushion to land on."

"I got no problem with that," Romero said. "Why not hit them at the harbor?"

"You seen the place? It's got cameras and armed security and a lot of witnesses."

"We could hit them on the road," Romero swilled some more beer and put it aside. "Jack them on the road. Then again we wouldn't get the cash million waiting for them at the hotel." He rubbed his chin thoughtfully. "Unless we hit them on the way back from the hotel but still we'll be doing it on the road and a cop might—so who knows?"

"Exactly."

"I just don't like hitting them while they're behind closed doors. Two armed bodyguards plus the smuggler and the cash man who probably has his own security. So what's that? Six armed men against the two of us? Steinway, this can't be done."

Steinway nodded trying to put a thought together seemingly trying to salvage the job. Finally, he snapped his fingers. "Unless!" he shouted energetically.

"Unless?" Romero watched the man carefully.

"Why else would you come all the way down here, Romero? Just for some fun in the sun? Because you miss me? Want to rehash old times like when you took Baker's eye out and stabbed him to death? No. No, you got some other idea fluttering around in that reptile brain of yours, you sociopathic criminal genius." He was stabbing the air toward Romero with a glint in his eye.

"Don't use big words you don't fully understand, Steinway. You're right though."

"Ha!" Steinway slapped his knee.

"Listen," said Romero scrunching over the edge of the couch across from Steinway who leaned forward. "The costume thing is perfect. But here's where we do it my way. We wait until the yacht docks. When the smuggler and the two guards make their way to the parking lot, we produce fake badges. Where we get them, we'll figure that out. We'll whip them out and up fast and then back in our pockets, so they don't get a clear view. We'll have handcuffs, and we'll take their weapons and cuff them. We have the diamonds after searching the smuggler, and now all we got to do is keep these three clowns on ice and squeeze the smuggler about where the meet is going to be. We let them figure out we aren't cops and we keep the appointment. We use the cop ruse again and disarm the money men, this time taking the money. We need the rest of today to plan this and god, I wish we had more time, but we don't have any. We need to move now. We got to get those badges and cuffs and make it more airtight. We still got two of us against three." Romero raised a finger. "Steinway, I'm telling you if there are more than three guys we got to deal with I'm on the next flight home. I'm not taking any fool chances.

Got it?"

Steinway nodded wildly. "Yeah, yeah, yeah. Okay."

Steinway hit the road looking for cuffs and badges and even said he would head on to a costume shop and check out some police uniforms but only if they were realistic.

Romero then told him maintenance man uniforms would do also and to get them if no genuine looking police uniforms could be found. When Steinway inquired as to why Romero told him that subliminally they would associate the overalls as typical undercover cop wear and that it would it add more realism to the dummy arrest.

Romero showered and changed into a khaki pants and tropical cotton shirt. He treated himself to another beer and paced around the big house with his feet echoing along on the wood floor. Wood? No, it was marble! Romero was impressed. He was also somewhat in a black mood. He wished Steinway hadn't talked about Baker. He didn't want to hear that shit. And sociopathic!? Really? Like Steinway knew what that word even meant. Romero had read the works of Robert Hare PhD. Knew about Psychopathy and its characteristics. He knew he wasn't one. He didn't wet himself late into his teens or set fires or mutilate animals. He was emotionally shallow, but if he saw a hell of a movie he could feel moved and if liquor were involved he even had to stifle tears. He never enjoyed killing the times he had to do it, and in his mind, it was because he had to do it. The cops, Nelson, Freemont, the others? They were a problem that had to be solved and so he did. He wasn't a sociopath either because it was the same as psychopathy except it was more environmentally made than a damaged or not underdeveloped amygdala. And who cares why I am the way I am? I don't, he thought.

Steinway returned, and he had two maintenance men overalls. They were dark blue with tags on the upper right of the chest, white background with white cursive that read ACME on it. Romero told him to get his or buy two tool boxes or lunch pails, but Steinway said he already had them in the garage, and he was smiling with glee. Next came the wigs and mustaches, and Romero told him to forget the wig and instead they would wear ball caps and the mustaches and sunglasses. The guns were on the table.

Romero unscrewed the silencer off the Glock 17, and he pulled the slide back seeing the glimmer of brass then letting the slide ease back gently he stuffed it into one of the zipper pockets of his overall.

Romero examined the stolen car. It was a blue Chevy. The door opened with a squeal and started roughly. He checked the lights, and they all seemed fine. He saw they had half a tank of gas, and he told Steinway that they weren't leaving unless the car was on Full. Steinway retrieved a gas can and slipped the long black snout of the can into the back and the dial slowly made its way up where it tolerably settled two spaces below FULL. Romero nodded with satisfaction and patted the dashboard.

They ate that evening behind Steinway's house with the glowing pool casting a blue, watery shimmer on everything. Steinway made grilled steak and potatoes, and they ate on lawn chairs. High green plant walls that surrounded the both of them. He marveled then at his partners home and had to admit it made his loft seem modest in comparison.

Romero, however, missed his home and wanted to get this over and done with. Before he left he had sealed the deal with Adam Hockney, and he was now in partnership to own half a dance club. The two of them spent time talking about giving the place there own flavor but then they had decided not to change anything too drastically as the place was already turning over a solid profit. Personally? Strauss Buck moon he enjoyed some.

Sarah had become the best of friends with Strauss, and now he saw more of her as well as Romero who found himself with a fragile new network of friends—and friends that he could tolerate. It was something to behold for him. It seemed it was all there now in his reach. He had done it. He had built a real, workable life. An empire he had fantasized on all the while in the roach ridden basement of his youth and then in the ice cold tiled prison where he spent six years. All the jobs and murders, all of it built what he now had.

He was not even remotely sorry for any of it as he looked fixedly into the pool.

The yacht came in with bow spreading the radiant blue, green sea. Romero sat in the front with Steinway behind the wheel. They were in the parking lot watching and waiting for the boat to dock and when the anchor went crashing below the waves it was the signal that got them out of the car. They got to the trunk and retrieved the toolboxes. Both of them in the dark blue overalls with baseball caps pulled down on their foreheads. Both of them with a thick black mustache held to them by adhesive.

The pilot of the boat waved as the men made off across the gangplank which led them down to the wood of the dock walkway. A seagull cried, and the man center of the two beefy men in dark suits looked skyward watching the bird make a lazy arc in the sky.

The man center was in a white suit with pale blue shirt. His sunglasses were aviator—the best kind—and his hair slicked back, and his gate was of a pompous kind that Romero told himself that he would enjoy correcting.

The captain of the yacht seemed to disappear, and Romero and Steinway walked toward the men with their eyes shooting everywhere keeping an eye out for cops and security. They could see none, and in unison, they increased their steps and Romero put his hand in his pocket seeing Steinway do the same. The men now off the gangway didn't pay them any real mind and Romero dropped the toolbox and pulled the gun out and aimed. He shouted, "Police! Hands up! Do it now! Hands up! Police!"

Steinway was calling along with Romero for the same. Both of them training their weapons back and forth along the three stunned men who stood dead still in front of them. The two bodyguards had raised their hands palms out toward them while the smuggler in the middle only had a minor mask of irritation on his face.

"Come on!" Romero called to them. "Lay down on the ground and cross your knees behind your ankles! DO IT!"

The men did, and Steinway gave him a Cheshire cat grin.

Sirens came. Steinway swore, and Romero told him to get the diamonds.

The smuggler said, "You guys aren't cops." He seemed to realize his own words as Steinway pulled the paper book sized packet out of his pocket in the jacket. "You guys are fucking takedown artists!" He looked at his guards and demanded, "Get them! Stop them you pieces of shit! Come on!"

"They don't want to get shot, you stupid fuck!" Steinway told him and kicked the smuggler across the face. The smuggler cupped his mouth and began spitting blood on the dry wood below him. Romero forced himself to search for and collect the guns, pulling them out of the holsters of the two guards while Steinway held his gun rigid in front of him while tossing the occasional look behind him as the sirens grew closer blocks away. Romero dropped the two guns into his and Steinway's toolbox, said, "Fuck it!" and they ran for the car.

Romero pulled them out of the dock at high speed and took them up the way they came, away from the freeway that led to the dock. The car purred and then coughed up the road, and he found them in the wrong lane as a van honked angrily. Romero twisted the car away to the right and he shot the car passed a legal speed obeying gold Saturn, and suddenly they were on the right lane. Romero took the angry honk and tossed a glance to the dock and watched a fire engine roar by and the three men still down there standing in some discussion. When the fire engine passed the sirens faded and before he could react Steinway was laughing himself hoarse.

"These are the diamonds?" Steinway asked and pinched one between thumb and forefinger. "Look too small to be worth anywhere near a million."

"Quality not quantity," Romero said.

They were parked in the parking lot of a pharmacy going over their score. The packet opened spilling diamonds atop the pillow Steinway took from the back seat. On the square throw pillow, it couldn't hold all of the diamonds, but it still didn't seem an impressive lot. Steinway wondered if they had been jibbed and Romero didn't think so.

Although, the numbers were not that unique or the size he saw the quality for what it was.

It was plenty for at least two hundred, even three hundred grand under 1 million. These diamonds, Romero smirked, it was as if they glowed from within. Even from the shadowy cool interior of the car.

"The plan backfired," Romero said. "Well at least we got something out of it. Not 2 million but something."

"What are you talking about?" Steinway asked.

"We were supposed to abduct them remember? Now the three of them are on their way to go and notify the cash man what happened. Probably going to kill him to make sure they get the money."

Steinway hissed, and his face screwed up, and he had the look of a gargoyle.

Romero tried to hide his smile, as it was comical to him for some reason. Seeing this man practically blow his gasket. Steinway seemed strung out about the loss of profit. It was highly unusual of him. It was quite a change from Detroit. The man then had been a go along with as even a temper as Romero. So what's was the deal? Romero asked himself and then asked Steinway.

"It's just hard to adjust," Steinway tried explaining. "You expect two million. I mean that would have been one million apiece. Now?" He tried laughing, but it died on the vine. He rubbed his forehead and his mouth involuntarily turned downward. "I'm getting a divorce," Steinway said and then closed his eyes. "The bitch is going to take me for everything Romero. Everything."

Romero watched him. Steinway trying to control his breathing and sweat accumulating on his brow and at the cleft of his chin. His chest rising and falling quickly.

Romero said, "You got any money stashed away? Any at all?"

"Not enough," Steinway replied, hating even hearing the question it seemed. "All my dough I made went into the club and restaurant." He looked mournfully at Romero and began shaking his head and damned if he didn't look as if he were going to cry. "I don't know what to do!" he sobbed uncontrollably out. "She fucked me good! Romero! She fucked me good!" Big fat tears rolled down his cheeks, and his face was red and shame of his crying had increased his torment. "I can't be poor like I was! My house! She's going to take my house, Romero! I can't! I can't!" He wailed and punched himself in the knee with a ham fist.

"What?" Romero queried, "You cheat or something?"

"No," he sobbed in answer. "I just made a bad mistake! I thought the bitch loved me man! She'd been cheating on me all the damn time! I don't know what I'm going to do! Romero!? Romero!? It was always about my money with her! Oh Christ! Oh Christ!"

Romero reached over and yanked off Steinway's mustache, and the crying dimmed down some as the blubbering mess calmed massaging below his nose. Romero took off his with as much strength, but he didn't even wince.

A minute went and passed. Steinway lit a cigarette, and he seemed under some control. Romero felt pretty lousy for the guy.

Because of the guy, Romero realized correcting himself.

Romero asked, "You got a good lawyer?"

Steinway stopped his head in mid-shake. "He says I got to expect a lot of losses.

A lot. She's good." Steinway was staring out his window a sour turn of the lower lip. "She's got it all in order. Probably her lawyer preparing her. All the expensive clothes she got. Suddenly she's walking around like she can barely rub two cents together. All of it an act so she can stand before the judge and rape me."

"That sucks," Romero said flatly.

"It does."

Steinway sniffed. After a moment, of silence Romero started the car. He told his wet cheeked partner, "Half a million is a good beginning."

"She'll get that too," Steinway said confidently.

Romero shut the car off and his mouth hung open. He cast a look at Steinway and then back through the windshield. He turned the thought over in his mind and grinned but then a flash of horror stopped him. Then holy shit if it didn't come rising on back out of the depths of him, and here came the justifications Romero began making.

Steinway coughed and put out the cigarette. He then apologized to Romero for making a fool of himself and Romero just nodded along assuring him that it was perfectly acceptable.

Romero said almost in a trance, "I understand." Romero was tasting his words as he spoke. He speculated again on his lack of psychopathy, and that maybe he was wrong.

That he had it, or maybe he was half one. If there were such a thing as being a half of a psychopath. Romero continued, "After my mother died I had to live in the base-ment of relatives. Full of roaches and lousy cooking. It would get noisy. . .they were loud. They were lousy people I couldn't care about. I felt utterly alone after my mother died. Felt like an alien. But then I began ripping and jacking and then joined a crew and made enough money to move out. Man was I free! Then I got sent to the can for six years. Promised myself that I would never go back. Never. I guess that's why I keep working. No matter how much money I make I get worried it's not enough. So here I am even though I don't have to rob anymore." He turned bodily to Steinway who was watching him, beaten down look on his face. It was like a shadow Romero thought. "Now you listen to me Steinway. Listen to me and listen good. I'm about to make you an offer you can live with.

Okay? Listening?"

Silence and Steinway broke it by saying, "Okay. Sure." He offered a nod almost frightened about what was going to be said, as if he knew what was going to be said.

Romero sighed. He checked the time on the dash and went for it. "I want all of the diamonds. All the one million for myself." He bore his stare into Steinway. "Give me that. Give me that, Steinway... and I'll kill your wife."

She was a bottle blonde with breasts large and fake. Romero watched her climb out of her Ferrari and she had this unusual gait that was odd, until he looked at the four inch heels she was tottering on. Everything about her read trouble yet somehow Steinway missed it.

Or maybe he wanted to miss it. Romero marveled at the stupidity of other men when it came to women. Sure he was fixated on the occasional female, but he was never crazy about any of them either. Relationships and sex were just never that big a deal. The whole stupid show of going crazy over some chick was something he couldn't understand. But he thought he possibly could. He often equated a sizeable score as being sexual.

He followed her on a run to the gym and then after she got some groceries and all out of the blue he wasn't sure he was going to go through with it. He waited for some sign that she was the ruthless operator that Steinway made her out to be, but he never saw it. Just some trashy broad going about her business. He missed openings to get to her because of his analyzing. He wasn't, however, ready to make a move just yet.

He wanted the diamonds. He did also want to help Steinway, god help him. So he continued his tailing of her. Hoping beyond hope, he would have the moment that would tell him that it was all peachy. Here, is the time. Rub her out for once and for all and you'd be doing the world a favor, more importantly, yourself.

He pictured the light radiating out of the unblemished diamonds. Live little things that were calling out. Captured light in them. Florida sunshine. Tropical light winking at him. All of them. For him if he did this deed. This was the test. The time. Would he take some trailer trash down for them?

The woman parked her Ferrari and instead of the sloppy rags Steinway said she would wear she was decked out in a miniskirt and red top. She swung a handbag. He

couldn't determine the price, and he wondered what con-
stituted rags to Steinway. For all he knew, she had a closet
of pants suits that Steinway had gotten her under mistaken
impression that they were signs of wealth. Then again
Romero was never adept at reading the clothes of a woman
let alone clothes in general. Everyone dancing seemed
dressed casually for the night weather. He could make no
determination about her income by her skirt length. She
seemed to be clothed in something he had seen girls back
home where when hitting the town in the evening heat of
summer. Nothing too unusual. Flashy.

He sneakily gained access to the party. It was a large
outdoor affair with too loud music–and the worst kind,
Merengue. Romero burrowed through the crowd and
finally came up to the bar and ordered a bottle of beer.
He sipped his drink while scanning the crowd, and only let
his eyes settle on her momentarily before examining the
throng. She danced and was nothing too special it seemed,
with most of the men, as the place was loaded for bear with
women in her range or more. But still she had a dance with
more than one man and Romero still found after taking
in the final gulp of beer that he wasn't sure he would do
it. So he watched her dance and then turn down a drink.
Romero got another beer and left the bar to take up a spot
off to where white circular tables were arranged under a
green canopy with tiki torches burning above.

The night played itself out with her dancing and yam-
mering away. She took a cigarette out and then seemingly
catching herself, she plucked it out of her mouth and
stuffed it back in her handbag. She waved off another beer
moments later and then exchanged words with another

guy trying to pick her up which he didn't do as she danced another dance with the same guy.

Romero, goaded by the heat and oppressive beat of music and distasteful environment, got to the Ferrari, and he shone the penlight in. He could find nothing. The interior was impeccable, and he estimated on where she lived and how long it would take for her to get there from the party. He looked at his watch and saw it had not even been two hours. Christ it felt longer. A lot longer and he got into his ride and took off for her home.

It was a motel room on the second tier. He bypassed the lock easily and shone his penlight around. The place was a lot more of a mess than the Ferrari, and he was careful not to disrupt her trail of debris. He found the trash bin in the bathroom, and he dug. He found what he was searching for. The whole turning down drinks and smokes. That thin thread that got him to go through her car. The hunch had been right.

She was pregnant.

"It's a hustle!" Steinway called. "A scam!"

"I saw the strip," Romero said. "I found it, and I found the box and read the instructions and it said pregnant. Also, I found another test and another. Apparently she desperately wants to make sure."

"It's not mine! I can tell you that!"

They sat across from each other as they did when discussing the job. Steinway twisted his hands. Wringing them and tapping his fingers against each other invariably throughout their talk. His eyes failing to fix steadily for too long on Romero. Romero broke the quiet telling him that if the case turned out he wasn't the father the court may look favorably on him. Then Steinway just tossed him a look of contempt and said, "I am the father! Christ! Happy!?"

"Don't know what to tell you, Steinway. You got money and so while you have it get yourself two good attorneys and fight this. Make her an offer."

"So you're not going to do it!" Steinway asked.

"Do it?" Romero slit his eyes toward Steinway. "Do what!? Whack her!? What are you out of your fucking mind!? *She's preggers*!?"

Steinway rose and paced. He jammed both hands down his pockets, and Romero stood himself. He went over and watched the pool out in the sun and again thought that if it weren't for the oppressive weather he could imagine living in Florida.

"You want all the diamonds, right?" Steinway asked.

"Of course." Romero kept his back to Steinway. "Not enough to whack a pregnant woman. No way."

"Okay. Okay I'll find someone who will then. I'll get my cut of the diamonds to a fence and pay him off in cold, hard cash." Steinway must have slapped a palm on a pant leg. So it sounded.

Romero passed Steinway, and he went behind the bar and dug around for a beer in the cooler. He found the bottle opener and took a pull feeling the cold go down his throat and backtrack where it chilled his face. Welcoming it. Romero saw what he wanted, and he lifted it and turned it this way, and that and he hefted it. Steinway suddenly was in a mollifying mood. He put on a hangdog expression and gave a tilt of the head and a flicker of a friendly smile, that died from nervousness. Steinway told him: "After what happened with Baker, I just thought that if anyone could do this for me it would be you, Romero."

"I thought that too Steinway. I thought I could too. But even before I found she was knocked up I was losing my will. So, I want my cut of the diamonds, and you'll get yourself that lawyer or lawyers and keep your head up. You'll make out." Romero raised the bottle in a one sided toast, and he drank.

Steinway had a gun when he came back down the stairs. It wasn't out, but Romero could see it. He could see it as the way the back of his shirt jutted out just the tad. Steinway came on with the too-cool-for-school walk. A walk that said I got you, you son of a bitch. You're dead, but you don't know it. He had with him in one hand a bandana. It was rolled up, and it was dark red. Steinway set it on the bar and unrolled it, and diamonds glittered their magic light again. Tropical light. Romero could feel the pulse of them in his veins. Romero didn't think he ever felt this way about a person let alone a woman. But then again this was magic he was seeing. These glittering beauties were everything he worked for, and they were a balm on all the pained years.

For the six years spent in that correctional facility, and the ones in the basement.

"Every time I see them," Romero leaned closer, "I can see the appeal. Why women are crazy for them. You're going to find someone to kill her. Aren't you Steinway?"

"Or do it myself," Steinway's eyes glittered themselves with their own light. He even smirked. "I thought you were the king shit, Romero. You're just a pussy. Thought you could get

this done for me. For a brother hoister. No, just a sob sister."
Steinway's hand moved behind him, his eyes locked over the
bar, his expression set in faux thought as he tried to pull a fast
one and surprise Romero with the gun. Romero sensing his
intent just set the bottle down and he threw a rough hand on
the back of Steinway's neck bringing him closer, and he raised
the other hand from behind the bar.

Romero drove the four inch paring knife into Steinway's
heart.

The fence went over the diamonds. He brought along
his eyeglass, which he screwed into an eye. He lifted one
and then another and another with tweezers and set them
down on the large square spread of the bandana. The
fence, Seth, a wiry large nosed man with straw hair in a
Hawaiian shirt unscrewed the eyeglass and said, "I can get
you 123, 000 dollars."

"What?" Romero said wincing at the man. "That's it?
For all of them?"

"How much diamonds did you think you needed?"
When he saw he was getting no answer from Romero he
sighed. "You jack diamonds before, right?"

"Yes. Although, I would admit I was never the one to fix
the value on them. I have my own man who moves things
for me. I'm not really a jewel thief though as I've said I have
dabbled."

"Perhaps your partner screwed you then?"

"I was there on the takedown," Romero shook his
head. "He either inflated the number to get me down here
because of another matter or he was in the dark about diamonds as I am."

"Still the amount you could accrue is nothing to sneeze at."

"Right," was all Romero said.

"But I understand the disappointment. It is a letdown from one million to just a little over a hundred grand."

Romero stood looking down into the deep end of the pool. Down at the bundle which sat because of two dumbbells from Steinway's gym. He got in the car next and stopped off at Harborage and found the yacht still there. He drove around and then finding another perspective he pulled the binoculars out and peered downward from off the freeway, his hood up and emergency lights going as a precaution from any marauding cop looking to nose into his business.

The loss of just a hundred grand was no sweat for the man on the yacht. He sat on a lawn chair wearing only swimming trunks. His body gold and he was in some good shape. The smuggler was also wearing sunglasses and lotion covered his nose. For the brief moment, Romero thought he was spotted spying as the smuggler tilted his head up as if looking directly at Romero but then he said something and apparently heard an answer from somewhere. The person who the smuggler heard was coming into view by emerging from steps leading down into the boat. It was one of the beefy guards in all white. The two of them exchanged words, and the smuggler nodded and rose. He stretched and quickly made off down the stairs.

Romero read the paper while he ate his early lunch. He had been right. The smuggler hadn't let being robbed of the diamonds stop him from collecting the million.

The headline read: **TRIPLE MURDER! OAKWOOD HOTEL BECOMES GANGLAND SHOOTING GALLERY!**

Romero read that no one heard the shooting, in fact and the police statement indicated the weapons were of low caliber and were used with a sound suppressor. Romero knew enough that a low caliber round with a silencer was the best kind of silenced weapon because that's what it would exactly do. Silence it.

Large calibers like 38.'s and 45.'s? It didn't truly matter. They were just as loud, and unless you made one as large as a paint can, the silencer would still be noisy.

Three men. No mention of money. Romero congratulated himself on his foresight despite how unremarkable it was, and he ate determined to put some plan together.

Night.

Romero could hardly swim, but he could float. Romero bobbed along on the stolen floatation device he was wearing. He had stolen it from a fishing vessel being loaded up by a smiling and happy looking family, and back at Steinway's he wrapped it and taped it with a heavy duty trash bag. He wanted the orange brightness gone. He wanted stealth. Camouflage. His face was blackened by oil he found in the garage. Taped to his stomach was another bundle. Two guns wrapped in more trash bags sealed by adhesive and utterly airtight. Romero was naked except for dark blue trunks and the extent of his camouflage included smearing his upper body and legs. The oil wouldn't stay on forever, and he was watching it fade on his arms as he guided himself through the dark water. He was close though.

A guard stood sentry on the gangplank and Romero could see him continuing his scanning forward and as long as that was where his eyes were fixed then Romero could see this coming off the way he wanted it to.

Romero found the anchor chain and began his ascent. The days hammering at himself in the gym paid off. He was advancing out the water slowly. First getting hisfeel but also not to make a commotion in the water. Before he knew it, Romero was throwing one arm up and then another and another until he had his eyes level through the circular hole the chain originated from. He could see the deck. The light on below the stairs. Footsteps and the other guard with gun visible tucked into the front of his waistband came into view. He had one hand on a beer bottle, and he would occasionally pull from it seemingly enjoying these rare moments his job afforded him.

Romero pulled the knife taped to his thigh. It was a black combat dagger. Another of Steinway's treasure trove. The tape he eased off slowly, and it sighed softly as it came free from his skin. He dropped the dead snake skin of tape to the water and set the blade between his teeth. Romero held onto the chain with one arm and tested how it felt. He could hold himself real soundly that way if he had to. He took the dagger out his mouth and gripped the handle firmly. He watched the guard stand with his back to Romero watching out into the water. The dock surely, as well. The guard drank and sighed in audible satisfaction with his drink and station. He brought the bottle up to his mouth, but he couldn't drink all the sudden as a hand was clasped over his mouth and Romero rammed the blade up between the ribs where he knew the heart was and the beer bottle fell silently landing on the guard's shoes before rolling away too loudly for Romero's comfort. The guard was then lowered noiselessly to the deck.

The smuggler was stroking the top a Doberman's head while sitting on an armchair. He was watching soccer, and with his other hand, he was throwing some cheese snacks into his mouth. Romero advanced and before the dog could even send up its alert bark he pressed the silenced Berretta 25. against the back of the smuggler's head. "Don't move," he said coolly. "Just tell the dog to be quiet."

The smuggler hissed sharply at the now wildly barking dog, and it flinched going quiet, and it settled down on its stomach observing closely but silently. Romero told himthat he could get up but to do it slow. Then they walked.

He had the smuggler use the rope to tie himself to the opening where the anchor chain went through. Romero checked it for tightness, and it was solid. The smuggler was unarmed, and he didn't say a word just watched Romero with a faint impatience.

"Alright," Romero said squatting down beside the smuggler. "Where are the rest of the diamonds?"

The eyes of the smuggler looked like fish eyes and were calm. He decided it seemed that he would on some principal just not talk. Romero took a handful of hair and yanked the head back hard and pressed the suppressor up under the chin. He said, "Look.

I had to kill two people already. I've killed before. You're a piece of shit to me. Huh?

You could tell me, and the cops can get you or I can kill you and that guard down there and trash the place until I find it. So what's it going to be?"

The eyes rose meeting Romero's. The smuggler said excepting his fate, "SHAPE is going to kill me when they found out you jacked me so what's the difference? Shit.

You'd be putting me out of my misery. So go ahead. Right in the skull."

"SHAPE? What's their stake in this?"

"I'm going to tell you right?" the smuggler smiled some. "Yeah well why not huh? Okay. What's their stake? We're just here to take out competitors is all."

"You mean the men in the hotel room?"

"Yeah! Them."

"So SHAPE didn't wanted you to sell them diamonds but instead whack them?"

"That's about it." The smuggler sniffed, and he smiled again with disbelief.

"Where are the other diamonds?"

"I told you, you took them all," he said louder.

"So they were for what? *Show?*"

The smuggler's smile died. "Yeah. Just show. SHAPE wanted the clowns gone, and I owed them a favor is all."

Romero nuzzled the silencer into the smuggler's stomach. "I'm no fool. So stop ever subtly raising your voice to warn the guard. Okay?"

Then the smuggler twisted his head sharply and began to open his mouth to call out, and Romero stood and acted swiftly. Romero brought the gun barrel up and down on the top of the man's skull until the smuggler's eyes rolled back white and the mouth wired to blow slackened staying finally in a useless gap.

The Berretta coughed a second time in the cabin and the lock blew off the cabinet door. Romero pulled the leather suitcase out. He knelt down and cracked it open.

Beautiful greenbacks looked up at Romero and ruining the reverie the smuggler croaked loudly and then screamed shrilly for help and Romero knew the guard was on the way, and just as the thought came, he could hear him now. The guard's shoes beating up the gangway and Romero jumped over the dog who lay dead and he flew up the steps barely feeling the weight of the money.

He watched the guard who had his gun out. The guard looked sharply into the dark. He was tense and his eyes bugging. He was trying to breathe, and he had undoubtedly put it together that his coworker was dead.

Romero waited for the perfect opportunity. The Berretta at the current range was unreliable. He needed him close for the kill. Then, as he leveled to shoot the sirens cried out, and Romero stuffed the gun into the ripped open plastic sack taped to his stomach.

He tugged the floatation device firmly down hard, and he gripped the case of money and gently he swung over the edge, and he hit the water in a splash.

Romero wasn't worried about floating to the surface. The suitcase with its weight acted against the buoyancy. So he guided himself along by hand and foot at the bottom and thanked his favor that he was close to a rise that would take him out from underneath the waves.

He used his one arm to push himself along the silt bottom and occasionally he would glance up at the wooden walkways of the dock. His lungs were holding air steady, and he pushed along soon feeling the sloping upward, and he craned his head forward to see the curvature of the underwater landscape sloping up where lights flickered by, and he could swear he could see a brief strip of green plant life up above. He pushed closer, and he made out the head-lights of cars flashing by. This was perfect as he parked the vehicle somewhere up there along the road strip.

He squeezed himself out from between ground and the wood dock and pulled the suitcase up which was even heavier with water. His arm in his socket felt languid. The weight of one million dollars plus water equaled an enor-mous strain during the crawl as the suitcase fought every step of the way against movement. Romero hugged the suitcase to him smelling the delicious leather still coming from it and he ran with his poor man's black lamp all but washed off of his body. Now, if anyone paid close attention, he was just some crazy man running holding a suitcase like a child with a plastic trash bag taped to his torso.

He got to the car, and he circled around. He was smil-ing, and he even cackled some. He found the yacht gone. Romero adjusting his view and he saw the boat cruising fast with its lights on for wherever it came from.

He wiped his prints off the guns. He would ditch the car after wiping it and he would take a rental and take the long way back up. Romero wondered on finding himself back in SHAPE's orbit. He tried figuring on what they would think when the smuggler got back to them.

Would they kill him? Would they put it together that Romero played a role in the affair? Affair! This whole job! Steinway and his personal predicament and SHAPE again!

But Romero opened the case and saw the money.

Balm for the pained years, he thought. Balm for this whole fucking trip.

11

The Aryan Massacre.

Relieved to be outside the deafening thump of the club and the intense light show and the crowds, Romero limply walked to his VW Beetle and drove intent to keep his radio off and just listen to the gentle hum that comes with a smooth quiet late evening drive. Once in his apartment, he took a shower and shirtless and barefoot wearing only blue cotton boxer shorts, he walked into the living room and lay on the couch. His eyes became heavy, and he allowed them to close and reran the day through his mind. The celebration with Adam Hockney and Michelle and Susan along with Strauss Buck moon. Also in attendance were other riff-raff that made up his friends. All of them chortling and drinking and even dancing. Romero of course sitting or standing but strictly as usual in his observer mode. He had no desire to be there, but one needed friends and one needed to keep up appearances especially as a wealthy business owner. The whole thing though became too much, and he began to miss his life of solitary living.

Romero felt himself beginning to drift down into sleep. He affirmed that he would take a stance against the demands of time his new friends were making.

I mean how many times, he thought, can a man have breakfast or lunch with a group of people? How many calls about hanging out and so on and so forth? It was tasking, and he was beginning to loathe picking up the phone. He had lied last week about going to New York for a few days to be able to keep to himself for awhile. Susan was now property of the gang and her time was monopolized by the others, especially Strauss, who was her new best friend. These relationship aspects that never interested Romero before were becoming an obsession, and he wondered if this is what a teenager had to deal with, and if so he supposed he was an extremely late bloomer. The whole damn thing was too much.

Romero woke, and the sun was just starting to come through the windows in orange bands of light that gave his floor a ghostly glow. He dressed and made breakfast and ate at his counter. He turned over last night's thoughts and when the phone rang he put the fork down and answered. It was Morris, and he listened. Romero nodded some and said he would be there around 1, and he hung up. Morris's voice was absent of any lightness. He seemed incredibly worried about something, and he wouldn't budge on what it was on the phone.

Romero looked around his large loft, and a shadow fell across his mind. He thought back on the diamond job which went down two months ago. He wondered if he screwed something up. If Morris's call was about SHAPE, or even the Red Mafia which might want pay back. Though it was less with the Russians. His worrying was focused on SHAPE whom he had encountered yet again on a diamond score in Florida.

Romero drove to his bar and eyeballed the new fixed up exterior with the new employees. The business, which was dire before, had picked up, and it was getting a steady upper income crowd. He figured that when the nearby gentrification finished his bar would be doing quite well. Next, he drove to German Town and watched his garage and then the car lot and then he took off for the gym.

Strauss came in at his usual time which was ten minutes after Romero got in, and Strauss went into a topic as if Romero knew what he was talking about, and all Romero made out were some macabre details and he stopped bench pressing and said, "What?"

"I said," Strauss began doing curls, "the city is becoming suddenly this shit hole of violence. You read the paper, Alex?"

"No."

"In the past two weeks there have been racially motivated attacks and gay bashing along with two rapes on unsuspecting women." Strauss groaned and sighed. "Now according to the paper and of course channel 3 news, which I've taken to watching religiously, ever since the crime wave began all of the victims have indicated that the men were either bald or were in some form wearing or saying things that revealed them to be white supremacist."

"Aryans, huh?" Romero looked thoughtful.

"There must be a gang of them that just popped up here in our fair city." Strauss looked forward and out the window seeing beyond it. "I think I should get a gun."

"Everyone should have one," Romero said bench pressing again.

"I might be killed." Strauss said with real anxiety. "I might get an aluminum bat across the face. Or thrown off a bridge. God."

"Carry a gun. Get a permit."

"I'm against guns," he protested.

"Can't be against anything if you get your brains bashed out."

"Christ," Strauss moaned and increased the speed of his curls.

"Actually," Romero sat up again, "I found a swastika spray painted on the side of one of my businesses."

"It's like they're invading the city!" Strauss blared dramatically.

Romero was driving to Morris's and going pass the usual street, and he hit his breaks at what he spotted up ahead. Romero registered what he saw and sped up. He felt a pit opening in the bottom of his stomach. A black spray paint of an arrow was pointed back toward Romero's building. The words below read: **Thief? Try that way!**

Morris let him in and Big G was sitting at the counter at Romero's usual spot, and he gave a nod with one large hand around a glass of some amber liquid.

"Now that you're here," Morris said, "let's get started. Romero pull that stool over, there's room. There you go. Sit on down. Now, if any of you have been seeing the news, you know there's been a rash of hate crimes going around.

Now before it even started I got an anonymous phone call telling me that somebody you both know has friends who are going to pay the three of us a visit. This voice said that these guys were a little more than upset when they found out that one of their guys got taken apart by a chainsaw."

"Shit!" Big G snarled and bang a fist down on the tile counter.

"Christ," Romero whispered.

"This voice," Morris pushed on, "then hung up. I have no idea who called. I have no idea why. The voice didn't seem threatening and if anything he seemed to be doing us a favor by warning us to watch our asses. As in watch them because somebody is coming for you, and he and his crew are going to kick it in. Now we know what the city doesn't know. That these Aryan bastards have set up shop here and are gunning for us."

"Crazy to come after me," Big G said. "I got too much muscle for a bunch of rednecks."

"Still," said Morris, "the Aryan brotherhood isn't known for rationality. These people are like Vikings. All they know is rape and pillage. So be careful. Arm yourself."

He came over to Big G and put a fatherly arm on a shoulder and pointed a finger at him. "Now I know you're going to put some guys on Romero." He then jabbed his own chest with a thumb. "I could use somebody watching my ass too."

"Of course!" Big G laughed lowly. "I'll take care of this fo' real."

Morris nodded and was in thought. He rubbed his chin. "If these Aryans are pals with Geiger then they're from out of town. If I know how these psychos work, then they're holed up somewhere together. Aryans from out of town would want to hide out with other pieces of shit like them."

"So we find them." Big G rubbed his palms. "How many we talking about?"

"Honestly I think these guys are probably out somewhere close by in the townships," Morris said. "They would want to be close by to drive in and scope us out.

Do their nightly havoc that the news is reporting. Christ these guys are depraved. The damn news is talking about another beating, and a teenage girl is missing."

Romero's cell chimed. He answered and listened some, said, "Christ," and then he said, "Yes. Alright I'll be there." Romero hung up and gave Morris and Big G a look. "That beating you were just talking about? Looks like it's a friend of mine."

"Where you going?" Big G asked, getting off the stool.

"Making appearances," Romero said.

"We got to discuss what we going to do!" Big G called.

Morris interjected saying with a weary sigh,

"Nothing we can do really. Not yet.

Anyway we covered the essentials. Big G you supply Romero and me with a security detail. Until we think of something, or the cops do their goddamned jobs for a change and lock these animals up, we stay alert." Morris pointed to Romero. "Tell your friend I hope he pulls through."

Strauss was beaten with a lead pipe instead of an aluminum bat. His face was swollen and bandaged. One arm was broken in three places, and a knee was busted. He was in a twilight place where the pain couldn't get to him.

Adam, Sarah and Michelle, were sitting around. The women naturally were teary eyed and Adam was mumbling indiscernible threats of some kind. Romero listened to Adam trying to make out the words more clearly and Adam rushed over, and they stood side by side watching the battered man in the bed.

Adam said, "He might lose his right eye. The doctors are optimistic but still."

"Christ," Romero said flatly.

Sarah shrilly asked, "Where the hell did these skinheads come from?"

"Hell," Michelle answered. "Hopefully they'll get back there soon."

Romero knew he was responsible, and Big G as well but he was calm in the face of this event. He felt empty of everything but the irritation at being unable to strike at the Aryans. How many and where? Who ratted out what Big G and him did to Geiger?

Romero surmised that it had to have been SHAPE. Had to be. But how did they know?

Romero sat with the others for awhile waiting for the appropriate time when he could say they should leave. Maybe get some sleep or some such thing. But the time never arrived. It got darker and finally it was Sarah who stood and smoothed down the front of her skirt. "We should really try and get some sleep."

"I know you and him are tight," Romero told her walking to her car. "Probably talk to him on the phone as much as we used too."

"Well," she said her voice watery. "You could call too, you know?"

"I suppose, but I have trouble finding what to talk about seeing as how we now cover it when we're all together. We sort of lost our own thing."

"Well that doesn't have to stay true." She put a hand on his forearm as they walked. "Maybe we should start a book club between the two of us. That way we have something to discuss with each other. Or we could paint again. You know because I've been thinking about starting again."

Romero watched her drive out the lot and walking back Adam and Michelle were already in the lot. They exchanged goodbyes, and Romero lingered some after they drove off in their respective cars. He scanned the lot looking for the bald head and camouflage that the Aryans tend to sport, and he saw nothing. No shadow moved in the lot and finally he started the engine and drove home.

Big G's men were in an Explorer parked across the street. Romero wasn't sure how many through the tinted glass, though he knew they were armed and mean, and he felt a tad comfortable knowing their presence was there and also knowing Morris was being as closely watched.

Paranoid he gave a once over of his apartment and found nothing out of place. His sleep was fitful and twice he got up to make sure the bedroom door was locked. He would also slide his hand under the bed feeling the S&W 1911. He drifted in and out of sleep wondering how Strauss was doing and where a certain teen girl was.

Morris said to both Big G and Romero, "I know who the head honcho is. I made a call upstate at our old stomping grounds. This old friend asked around the block and came up with the name *Roy Stokes*. According to my man inside, it was one of your homeboys Emmett that bragged to this Aryan about Geiger. Not only did he brag, he mentioned Romero's name."

"Shit!" Big G hissed.

"Yeah well, we can't get to this Roy as he's inside—"

"Wanna bet!" Big G told Morris.

"How so?" Morris's brow wrinkled.

"I got a man up in that bitch for life! He'll do it. May take time, but he could work something out. The brother is straight crazy enough." Big G laughed. "But we take out this mother fuck a, what we do about the rest going wild out here?"

"Listen to this," Morris told them, "By my keen intellect and the use of a computer at the library, I have dug up brief articles from our city's paper on this white trash. Arrested for possession of stolen firearms. A repeat offence twenty-five to life. He lives up in West Chester! I have the address through some phone sleight of hand. A little trick from the good old days. Just needed a phone book for West Chester and a gimmick for when I found his number."

"Who answered?" Romero queried.

"His not-so-lovely-wife, that's who." Morris laughed some at the memory. "Now get this. I'm jabbering away at this woman who sounds as if she was born eating." Morris rubbed his chin with a thumb. "So I ask her in my probing manner to fill in some questions for me, so I can send her,

her free pizza certificate. Now, if this woman is as obese as she sounds then she was game, and thank god she was."

"She answered your question?" Big G grinned.

"Boy did she! The most important question being... Are you ready for this? How much family you got staying with you? I asked her that. I said, 'You must have a full house, right?' 'Or is my psychic powers telling me that a lovely woman like yourself is all by her lonesome?'" Morris snickered away. "So she goes all girly of course, and she mentions that I should be careful because her husband is in jail. Now I want to get back on track, and I say, 'Well do you have a full house at the moment because I can process your card and because I'm loving your voice I could have a couple of pizzas sent over.'

How about that?'"

"Well done," Romero clapped.

"And so she goes on about how her house is packed some with her husband's friends. I pretend I'm psychic again and start guessing numbers. I guess wrong three times until laughing she gives me the magic number of *ten*."

Big G moaned in reflection. "Ten is work," he said. "I got more than ten. But still it could be rough."

"If they got that teen girl," Romero started, "we got to be careful how we go in."

Morris exchanged a look with Big G, and he rubbed his palms together and looked down at the floor before leaning his back against the wall. "The girl is at the hospital."

"Damn," said Romero.

"Found her rouged up pretty bad in Fairmont Park." Morris made a sign of the cross and Romero couldn't remember the last time he'd seen him do that. "So gentleman, what is the battle plan?"

The three men were silent for many minutes with only the sound of a wall clock breaking the quiet.

Michelle was wound up and fidgeting and pacing some. Strauss lay with one eye open and was surprisingly cheerful. He was glad he said to have that experience over with. The doctor came in and was vocal about the real, likelihood that his whole eye and its vision would be perfectly acceptable. There was talk of rehab and the use of a cane for some time, and when all was said and done Strauss took it on the chin and smiled some.

Romero alone in the corridor asked Michelle why she was so on edge.

"I didn't want to say anything because I didn't want to ruin the positivity in the room," she said, "but last night when I got home? I was unlocking my door and I heard footsteps rushing toward me from out of the alley across from my place. I didn't even look I just unlocked as fast as I could and I *jumped* in." She made a sweeping motion with her hand. "I mean I practically flew in. Then I tried shutting the door, but this guy got his *fingers* in and started *pulling*." Her face paled some in memory, and her eyes were wide. "Finally I start stabbing the fingers with my keys of all things, and I hear him hiss and the fingers are gone. I slam the door and lock it and call the police." She said hushed, "I'm not sure but whoever it was had a bald head. I'm thinking it was one of those crazy neo-Nazis that bashed Strauss and have been causing problems."

"Wait a minute!" Romero looked into the ICU room where Adam and Strauss were in some discussion. He looked back at Michelle, and he asked her, "Where's Sarah?"

Michelle sat beside him as he hovered a hair over the speed limit. The drive felt too long, and Romero fought the urge to gun it. Finally, they came to Sarah's apartment building. It was not guarded, and the foyer door leading to the steps was unlocked. The corridor was vacant as well as the stairs. Romero without thinking pulled his Luger out, and he heard Michelle gasp. They went up the steps, and Susan's door appeared okay. No damage was present. No lock knocked out or pry marks. Nothing indicating a scuffle.

Romero lowered the gun, and he simply pressed the buzzer.

A muffled sound came to them, and Romero backed up and kicked the door open sending it slamming into the wall behind it. Sarah ran to them, and she screamed for them to stop or she would shoot. She had a Magnum 44. in both of her hands, or Dirty Harry's gun and she was shaking. Romero and Michelle kept still until she then saw who they were. She lowered the gun slowly and sighed and fell flat on her ass with relief.

"Maybe you should try carrying a gun you could..." Romero shrugged. "You know... carry?"

"I really like this one," Sarah answered running a thumbnail on the sandalwood grip. "Yours is nice too. A Luger right?"

"Didn't know you were gun crazy," Michelle said chuckling.

They were at her table. Romero and Sarah with their guns exposed in front of them. The good thing about this

Romero deduced was that it would lend credibility to it being a gun he just legally purchased for protection. Sarah was so badly frightened by the story on the news about what had happened to those two women and now, unfortunately, teen girl that she guiltily walked into a gun shop and forced herself to buy one.

"Hell of a gun to buy," Romero said.

"I wanted something to look mean," she nodded at her process. "I have to say though. Since I bought it. I just can't stop lifting it now and then. It really is a *sexy* weapon."

"Size queen," Michelle teased.

"*Maybe*," Sarah replied semi-seriously. "Maybe that's it."

They drove with Sarah in tow, to see Strauss, and before leaving Romero pulled Michelle to him. "You file a police report?"

"I did. I'm not enthusiastic."

"If you need a weapon maybe I could help until you get one.—Legally that is."

"Uh, no that's alright. I got pepper spray." She pulled the black little can out of her purse and shook it some. "I'm going to be holding this tight for the foreseeable future."

Romero and Adam were drinking at a booth. Romero made sure to grab the seat facing the door.

"Alex?" Adam wanted to know, his eyes hooded from too many shots. "How come you don't knock boots with Michelle? Are you and Sarah a thing or what?"

"Didn't know she was interested," Romero lied.

"Just put her out of her misery and bang her, huh?"

Thankfully Adam's phone bleeped a tune out. He answered with a bored yes, which was typical of him, and Romero watched him sober up quickly. "Fuck!!!" He ended the call and roughly jammed the cell phone into his jacket pocket and stood. It was as if he forgot Romero as he did a double take seeing him, and he said not being able to believe the words coming out his mouth, he said, "Two psychos just fired machine guns into the crowd at our club!"

When they arrived bodies were being pulled out on stretchers. Some were hooked to respirators and others, the many others were coming out in plastic body bags. Romero had never seen so many ambulances in one place before. The streets outside the club with its own neon pulse of lights.

"I'm sorry," Morris said to him.

"Only good thing that came out of it was that are security is off duty cops off the clock. So one of the officers killed one shooter on the spot, and the other rather be arrested than go down like his friend."

"Skinheads?"

"Both of them right out of the Aryan Life & Times catalogue." Romero stood off the stool. "No more of this shit! I'm going up to West Chester! Call Big G and tell him we go tonight, and if he can't I'm going alone."

The doorbell chimed. Morris said with a smile playing at the corners of his mouth "Guess who?"

Two vans from Romero's lot. Six men a van loaded for bear with MP5's with sound suppressors and subsonic rounds. Laser sights. Grenades. All of them dressed in black with a knit cap cut to ski mask on their heads. Many of the brothers had gold chains but then in mid drive they took them off placing them gently in a toolbox that was being passed around. The men knew enough that the chain rattling could be death for them. Big G called these hardened killers his 'Ghost Unit.' Big G brought a chainsaw, and he laughed with mirth, his lunatic eyes shining when he showed it to Romero.

The drive would take them eventually to a shit poor house in the middle of nowhere. Perfect. They would wait until 3, maybe 4 in the morning to strike as most of them were out partying most likely. Empty bottles of cognac stood in three milk crates.

Romero had no clue what they were for until a Ghost named Roland Garland began stuffing white handkerchiefs into each one. Romero could see the quicksilver of what had to be gasoline swaying as the van rocketed up the darkening road toward battle.

A hole was dug for them to piss in. It would be filled before they left. Romero marveled at the quiet efficiency of Ghost Unit. They seem to know what to do. The sun was dying in the sky. The orange rays pulled back and down. The cicadas had started up.

The vans were hidden in the tree line, and Romero's mouth actually dropped open when the Ghost Unit begins covering the vans with a camouflage sheet.

They marched through the woods as the point man with the map took them toward the house. The temperature was down and the men began seeing their breath. Big G signaled that it was time to lower the ski masks, and they did. Romero and the unit continued on. He watched Big G lugging the chainsaw easily as if he were carrying a lunchbox to school.

The house looked like one large long container you see a semi pulling. With windows and a door naturally. Lights inside were on and through the binoculars the men saw some movement. It was quiet. A dog was seen inside wagging its tail, and soon there she was all three hundred pounds at least waddling by. A recon team returned with no sightings of a vehicle of any kind. The men, still out causing trouble.

The unit actually ate rations and Romero gave Big G a look of disbelief at what he was seeing. Big G just shrugged and laughed quietly to himself, and as time passed Romero found himself eating the things and thinking they're not that awful.

Three in the morning on the dot they arrived in two pickup trucks. Probably at a nearby bar having a ball. They all had bald heads. They have the jungle fatigue thing going, and they have that drawl only white trash rednecks sustain despite being so close to the city limits. One of them is wearing a tee shirt with the confederate flag on it. All of the Ghost Unit, including Big G and Romero, began counting.

Eight men. The two down is one shot dead at the club, and the other was on his way to jail for his participation in the shootout. Eight and the fat broad. Big G and Romero pondered on what to do with the woman. Romero tried figuring a plan, but Big G told him that he had the veto, and they discuss some more until Romero said, fuck it, and the woman was now to die with the men.

Another hour and the lights went out. Fifteen minutes Ghost Unit rushed in, and the other three men circle around the house. Windows broke, and arms flung grenades in, the men dropped almost in perfect synchronization. A yellow flash with a loud CRACK! followed by windows blowing out and smoke pouring into the night air. Small fires were burning. The unit retreated some yards and then they dropped to their stomachs with MP5's aimed. Behind the house, the other team did the same.

Shapes. Shadows in the smoke. A gun was fired. Some hollering could be heard, and a bald, fat bellied man charged out the door on unsteady feet, and he was riddled with subsonic bullets. The guns firing sounding like hundreds of tiny fists punching a pillow and the man, perforated, dropped straight down. Behind the house, the MP5's fired as well. A door slammed, and there was a scream from one man followed by various shapes dancing inside. Roland lit the fuses and took two of the lighted Molotov Cocktails, and he threw both in, and he charged off where he began lighting two more, and he chucked them both inside.

He was smiling.

The fire raged and Big G revved up the chainsaw. He waved and his men ceased their sporadic firing and he braced himself against the door. The fire engulfed; a red and blistering Aryan bolted out the window coughing brutally. Big G raised the chainsaw and the Aryan's eyes popped out in horror like eggs they're so big, and Ghost Unit watches unfazed as the skinhead is cut down screaming. Still alive when his torso goes each their own way.

The door ripped open, and two naked men fired guns blindly and before they can be cut down they make it to the woods where Big G is after them. The screams are the only indicator that Big G had reached them, and the Ghost Unit stood and advanced on the house emptying their guns.

Then they reloaded and watched as Roland tossed more cocktails. From behind the house came the rest of Ghost Unit, which reunites, with their other three.

The screaming stopped. Big G's laughter came out of the woods, and one and then the second head was flung out in a beautiful high arc where they landed with a dead thud.

The piss hole was being buried. The unit had developed an appetite and were eating quickly, sitting or laying sprawled out on the ground. Romero ate too. He watched Big G have a one-sided conversation with one of the heads.

Romero told himself that he kind of liked killing now.

12

The SHAPE Agent.

Romero took the flight to Dallas and was greeted by a sign with his name written in bold black magic marker held by a bald block of a man, and he nodded a greeting and followed his driver out the terminal into the broiling heat of a Texas summer. Before Romero got in the car, the door being held open by the stoic valet, he cast a glance over his shoulder seeing a van familiar to him, and he stooped into the cool interior of the car.

The black town car wound its way through traffic, and no words were exchanged with the driver, and Romero was plenty glad that he wasn't stuck with some talkative fellow. Romero in a funk for the last month since a series of unfortunate events caused a gang of Aryans to hunt for him. People close to him got hurt because of it.

He hadn't taken a job since, and he was undoubtedly done with the whole dangerous affair. His routine was the same. He would get up and have a drink from the juicer and then breakfast followed by a drive to his businesses and then a stop at the gym where he would remain for two mostly three hours now. He would sometimes go see a movie and get together occasionally with his friends and even pay his booker, Morris, a visit. He was single and looking to stay that way awhile as he was already getting enough socializing with his friends and the intimacy of a woman would be like a vulture on his shoulder pecking at him as he tried focusing on his thoughts while alone in his expansive loft.

The driver turned, and they were out of the traffic and abruptly in an area of warehouses and plants of a sort. There was a soda bottling company and then a fence where many trucks for the obvious purpose of driving them to and fro on routes around the city were parked. The driver turned into an incline leading up between a large factory and office building all brick high up around them. This parking area was large, and a truck sat with its rear in a garage. No one seemed about. Two other cars were parked with stairs leading up to a blue door in between them. The driver pulled beside another door, and Romero listened as the car engine died. He watched the driver exit and Romero followed along.

Three days previously.

Morris called Romero and told him to stop by as he had some urgent business to discuss with him. Romero said sure and hung up and was on the road firmly in the mode of turning down whatever job Morris might wave in front of him. Although, the old man had stopped doing that as the months passed.

Romero knocked and rang the bell and Morris let him in and they resumed their usual space at the counter with Morris across on his stool and Romero on his.

Morris said, "Got a call, Romero. Voice sounded very familiar. It was him."

"Him?"

"The guy who called us to warn us about the Aryans? It was him."

"What did he want?" Romero asked not liking where this was going.

Morris rubbed his palms together and looked away for a moment then back. "He wants to meet you. Said he was with SHAPE."

"Fuck," Romero hisses, shook his head looking down at the tile countertop.

"Where?"

"Dallas, Texas. Three days. He'll have a man meet you at the airport to greet you. You know? One of them valets. He'll have a sign with your name on it. This guy says it's for one day and you'll be set up in a nice hotel."

"So they can kill me."

"He said his employer would be willing to let things slide if you do a job for them. One job to get you even and make up for the money you cost them."

"Don't believe that," Romero said, ran his hands down his face. "Bullshit set up, and it's plain and clear."

"Now this guy says they would use their own guys, but this job required your mind. That it's a tricky gambit, is I believe what this voice said to me."

"How?"

Morris sighed and threw up his hands. "Don't know, he won't say. Not on the phone. He wants to go over it with you in Dallas and talk about payment options." Morris leaned forward across the countertop, and he whispered, "Romero, he's talking about 5 million dollars for this one job."

"So I should go on down there?" Romero said.

"No!" Morris waved. "Don't trust this bastard!"

"But?"

"But?" Morris seemed contemplative and sad even. "Do you want to spend the rest of your days looking over your shoulder? I just think you should figure out if this is what you want to do. Might be the score of a lifetime. The last big one." Morris tilted his head, a shadow seemed to fall across his face. "Then again this could be you walking into certain death."

"Then I should stay away," Romero got off the stool and stretched. "They haven't gotten me yet. Haven't sent anyone else since I sent two of their boys into the drink. I got nothing to worry about than I usually do. And to be perfectly honest Morris? I haven't given them much of an obsessive thought since I stopped working. And!" Romero held up his finger. "I've got to say I'm enjoying my retirement. So, if SHAPE comes? I'll be damned good and ready. You know why, Morris? Because, I've killed three of their guys, and I whacked at least over a dozen people, so I'm not worried in the slightest." Romero paced. "Months and they know where I live, and they haven't planted a bomb or set up a sniper or anything. Tells me they are nothing but showboat guns is all they are. Just some crew trying to build a name for themselves. I waste three of their guys, and they were this slow to retaliate? No, it had to be because I whacked most of their guys. I sent them reeling, and they've been trying to recover." Romero nodded at his own thoughts. "That is what I think, Morris."

"Then good!" Morris slapped the countertop. "Stay the fuck away from Dallas!"

"Not an issue."

"One last piece of business then." Morris raised the newspaper. "Just in case you haven't heard—"

"Stokes is dead."

Morris chucked the paper smiling. "Emmett is good."

Romero hardly heard as he was toying with Dallas against his better judgment.

Romero followed the valet down a well lit corridor where the thump and hum of machinery assaulted him. At the end stood a set of blue double doors. The valet punched the keypad on the side of the door and Romero could hear a whining suddenly.

He looked up and saw a security camera whirring, red light blinking. It stopped and watched Romero and he could see it zoom, the iris closing in scrutiny.

The valet opened the door and stood aside, and Romero walked in to the comfortably furnished and spacious room. The floors were burnished wood and they glowed in the powerful overhead lamps. The walls were wood paneled and there was a jukebox against the wall, and off to the left a pool table where a man in a white suit looking the part of a young, handsome Colonel Sanders. His hair black and slicked back. He was tall and he only threw Romero a cursory look before resuming his lone game of billiards. Romero saw a bar and he went for it not waiting for an invitation. He found the cooler and took a bottle of beer out and drank on the stool waiting for whatever to happen to happen. Feeling the nakedness of not having a weapon on him.

"You play?" the man in white asked.

"No," Romero said.

The man in white dropped the pool cue on the green baize and walked over and offered his hand. His smile seemed genuine, and there was no trace of coldness in the eyes Romero could discern. He shook the hand and noticed the blaring white teeth. The man sat next to him and said as if talking to a patient of his in a clinic, "So you're the man. The heister that has been a headache to us. The thief who stole are heroin. You know we had a guy on that?" The man in white laughed. "Of course you do! You killed him!" He rose and circled the bar, dug into the cooler and got himself a drink. He twisted the cap and stopped as if in sudden revelation. "Shot his face off, right?" He looked disapproving. "Injured another of are men. Drowned two others." He drank and bobbed his head seemingly in visible surprise at the quality of the brew. "However Romero there is a way to tilt the scale back to balance."

"Oh?" Romero droned and kept drinking.

"Yes. We have a job in California. Very dangerous. You're going to have to do it alone." The man in white put a hand up expecting some vocal opposition that never came and he plundered on. "I know, I know! But hear me out on this. Heroin and cocaine. Heavy pounds of it coming via two trucks. Semis. They'll be unloaded under Red Mafia guard. I'm talking machine guns, shotgun, the works."

"No," Romero said and kept drinking feeling pleasant all the sudden.

"5 million dollars," the man in white grinned like some shyster lawyer.

"No," Romero said again. "I'm retired."

The man in white came around from behind the bar and tried putting a hand on Romero's shoulder. "Do you realize that we'll have to keep coming after you. To make up for what you did... right?"

"You can try." Romero gave him a faint smile.

The man in white seemed genuinely flummoxed, and he put the beer bottle down roughly on top of the bar. He spun some and ran a hand through his hair. He whirled back around and raised and then dropped a finger, his mouth working and shutting working and shutting. Finally, he managed to speak. "I'm trying to do you a favor, Romero. Don't you realize this is a huge opportunity? If you pull this off we're talking about 5 million and a permanent position within our organization. Now if that isn't a hell of a deal then..."

"No." Romero put down the beer and got up to leave.

He made it to the door when the man in white spoke up. "Wait a second! Wait a second *dammit*! Will you wait a second!?"

Romero stopped.

"Thank you," the man said. He put up both hands accentuating as he spoke. "Now I don't want to make threats, but if you care about not just your life but the life of your friends then—"

Romero rabbit punched him in the throat, and the man in white fell on his back.

Romero kicked him in the stomach as the man coughed violently. Suddenly the glint of light coming off the gun came into view as the man pulled it from behind him. Romero tried to act, but he seemed to slow and then gun cocked, and there was a blast.

Romero had lunch with his friends and listened to them go on about their day. It wasn't too out of the ordinary as the lounge was where they met up on occasion. Sarah was contemplating a move into a safer building, and Michelle was alluding to some guy from work who wanted to go out with her, and that she thought she might take him up on it.

Romero guessed she was trying to make him jealous, but all it did was make him uncomfortable and he thought back on his meet up with Morris. Strauss then went into how well he felt. He said his therapy went great, and his stiffness was going away, and he was proud to say that he would be saying goodbye to the cane within the next few months which earned an applause from everyone. Adam went on about the dance club, and Romero forced himself to add in his two cents.

These friends of his talked and talked and even more glaring than usual was the realization that it never mattered. He was never one of them and never going to be. He observed Sarah closely and he was glad that she had the group of friends she needed. He could see he was wrong that they were alike. She was connected to them. Close.

She was alive in ways he had no understanding of. Except on those minor spiritual type moments where he did feel connected. He thought about that walk in the rain up that dark road. It was coming down heavy, but it was warm, so he didn't mind. He had a gun in the backpack filled with the takedown of a pawn shop where the crooked owner kept dirty money from selling marijuana. It was a sweet 15, 675 dollars. He felt wonderfully alive after, and the rain was magical along with the sensation. That long walk up to his stolen car and then back to the hovel where he would stuff the money in the beaten mattress. All the cash accumulating into a nice some. He could finally move and be free. On his own.

He watched Sarah and realized he no longer had a monopoly on her once again.

And it was fine. He was pleased she was going to be alright with her friends and functional life.

Romero understood suddenly, as if the decision had been made for him, that he was going to Dallas. That he would keep his appointment with this SHAPE agent. That he would hear him out.

Romero stood and said goodbye. He waved on his way out from the booth, and he squeezed a lingering hand on Sarah's shoulder, and he gave her, her own goodbye, and he left hearing their voices fade back, away. Goodbye. . . as in forever.

The blast stunned the man in white who swayed from the explosion. The tiny nickel plated gun he carried bobbed away from Romero who got his hand on it as the large window behind them was nothing more but a smoking crater. Romero fought the man who was stronger than he looked and Romero saw the red dot climb toward the man in white's face stopping at his forehead. Romero dropped while still holding onto the gun, and clap of gunfire came, and the man in white's head erupted like a volcano from the top tarnishing his suit in crimson. He fell to his knees, and Romero rolled away from the ruined figure.

Romero tossed a thumbs up out what used to be the window and stopped down to retrieve the tiny gun.

The valet eventually ran in holding some black, bulky weapon, and he wildly searched the room. Romero came from behind the door. Pressed the gun against the valet's head and fired once, and he got the car keys and ran.

The corridor felt like a long walk, and the thump and whine of machinery felt louder and more inside of him than out. He got to the door and threw it open and aimed, but no one was outside. Romero ran for the car and pulled out and took off down the incline and pulled into traffic.

It was a few seconds away from the building that he heard the muffled blast behind him as Ghost Unit fired several RPG's into the window pulverizing the furnished billiard room, and the valet, and SHAPE agent's corpse along with it.

13

Meditation on impending doom.

Romero was on the road. California was much better than he remembered. It was hot and he cruised along with the window down feeling the wind against his face. Father Garrison was asleep behind him after they had fed on a massive chicken lunch before hitting the road. Behind trailing along was Glimmer Dan, a native American. He had the guns with him and beside him rode the short and weeble shaped Clifton O' Day.

The four of them off to disaster. Or at least they thought. But the amount of the coin they could net was too tempting. So they were on the road to hit the Red Mob's dope connection.

Romero was watching the road unwinding in front of him, and he felt some anticipation. It was going to be dangerous. Too many armed Russians. Many things could happen and from his experience over the course of the year they probably would.

Then he thought that when it did go wrong, and he survived how fucking sweet that would be.

Romero had an incredible place lined up for him in New York. A real topnotch pad. A real obscene show of his wealth. He decided to invest around New York as well as in Philadelphia. He had gotten the call before he arraigned this job with Morris from the realtor and she told him that he was going to get the place. His lonely cool, comfortable place atop the city.

He kept below the speed limit and heard Father Garrison mumble in his sleep. He seemed to be having some horribly unpleasant dream.

A portent of things to come? Romero thought. He smiled grimly to himself and hit the gas oblivious of the speed limit. He cut a swath in the hot desert air, and closer to an impending doom he knew in his gut had to be coming.

The End.

ROMERO'S CREW.

www.ingramcontent.com/pod-product-compliance
Lightning Source LLC
Chambersburg PA
CBHW051411170626
46809CB00006B/2112